MURDER
at
THE DRISKILL

by
Kathleen Kaska

A Sydney Lockhart Mystery

Murder at The Driskill

A Sydney Lockhart Mystery

ISBN: 978-0-9905655-9-8
Paperback version
© 2014 by Kathleen Kaska

Published by LL-Publications 2014
www.ll-publications.com
P. O. Box 542
Bedford, Texas 76095

Edited by Billye Johnson
Proofreading by Zetta Brown
Book layout and typesetting by jimandzetta.com
Cover art and design by Amanda Kelsey razzdazzdesign.com © 2014

Printed in the UK and the USA

To Ruth

Other books by Kathleen Kaska

The Classic Mystery Triviography™ Series
The Agatha Christie Triviography and Quiz Book
The Alfred Hitchcock Triviography and Quiz Book
The Sherlock Holmes Triviography and Quiz Book

The Sydney Lockhart Mysteries
Murder at The Arlington
Murder at The Luther
Murder at The Galvez
Murder at The Driskill

The Man Who Saved the Whooping Crane:
The Robert Porter Allen Story

MURDER
at
THE DRISKILL

Chapter One

I HEARD JELLY BLUESTEEN laughing his fool head off as I darted out the door in pursuit of the slime ball I was assigned to watch. If the guy had only swiped the till, I would have turned around and told Jelly to catch his own thief. But the guy snatched my overcoat on his way out the door. Inside was my new PI license and fifty bucks from our agency's petty cash, making the thievery a personal issue.

The man I was after was the bartender at The Blue Mist, a popular sleaze joint on Sabine, a few blocks from The Next to Nothing Live Theatre. Jelly, the owner of The Blue Mist, came to our detective agency for help. He was certain one of his bartenders had been stuffing his pockets rather than replenishing the cash drawer.

My partner and boyfriend, Ralph Dixon, advised against taking the case since he suspected Jelly of being as crooked as his employees, but I was eager to get our new agency off the ground. Being a novice investigator, I could use the practice. Besides, the nighttime work would not interfere with my day job. Dixon reluctantly agreed.

It was my third night at the bar. My sleuthing required that I dress in male disguise and smoke and drink while trying to keep a low profile, which was easy since most folks came to The Blue Mist to do just that, except for the dressing in disguise part. But, hey, I might be wrong. After all, it was 1953, and weird things happened in downtown Austin, Texas.

I suspected this particular bartender the first night. He had a pattern to his pilfering. Once the joint became busy, he'd move to the far end of the bar where the overhead lights failed to reach. When someone paid for the drink, the guy pretended to stuff the money into the register, but instead he executed a quick flicking motion with his fingers, and the bills slid up his cuff.

Tonight had been busier than normal and I watched as a small fortune filled the bartender's sleeve. At closing time, Jelly came out from the back room and caught my eye. I nodded toward the guilty party. The bartender noticed our sly communication and he suddenly became twitchy. Jelly hurriedly ushered the last drunk out the door, flipped off the neon OPEN sign, and reached for his billy club. In one swift motion, the bartender snatched a wad of cash from the register *and* my coat off the rack and made a beeline for the door. Since Jelly was too fat to run, I took up the chase, alone.

I pursued the guy down Sixth Street all the way to The Driskill Hotel when suddenly he darted down the alley and became swallowed up in the steam rising off the pavement. I thought I'd lost him until I heard a pile of rags bundled near the dumpster say, "He turned right at the end of the alley, Miss Sydney."

I thanked the man whom I'd come to know as Backyard Benny, a bum who earned his moniker by sleeping in backyards and alleys in the downtown area. I took off in that direction as a tower of empty food crates tumbled in my path. Thanks to my long legs, I hurdled the debris, sending an annoyed family of raccoons scattering. In dodging the scavengers, I slipped on their food refuse, regained my footing, and within seconds I had the guy in sight again. Turning down Seventh toward Red River Street, he headed away from the downtown area and the streetlights illuminating the path to the State Capitol. My youth and athletic ability gave me the only hope of catching him before he vanished into the crevices of broken down warehouses, or worse yet, into the darkness of Waterloo Park. The guy was at least twenty years my senior and had obviously not graced the inside of a gymnasium since high school. But he did have the advantage of being prey, driven by survival and escape.

I was about forty yards behind him when I caught sight of a slow moving mass on the opposite side of the street—a collection of stumbling drunks, or so I thought. When I saw the glint of a switchblade, I realized the drunks were malcontents intent on relieving late-nighters of whatever cash remained in their pockets.

The guy paid no notice to the thugs following him. He leapt over a low wooden fence and disappeared behind a vacant house. I pulled my gun from my shoulder holster and fired a couple of shots into the air. Someone shouted, "Cops!" and the hoodlums fled. I wasn't often mistaken for one of Austin's finest. It must have been my man clothes. I prayed my long red hair would stay put under my fedora as I scaled the fence after him.

I should have listened to my wise and experienced partner and not gotten involved in this case. I should have also listened to him when he told me to meet him at the office as soon as the bar closed. That was almost an hour ago. But I couldn't let this guy escape. My pride was at stake.

If I were lucky, Dixon would head down to The Blue Mist and Jelly would put him on my trail. If not, I might end up like so many other women who found themselves alone after dark on the bad side of town, looking for trouble and finding it. My gun would do me little good if a thug's switchblade found its way between my ribs.

As I rounded the corner of a three-story warehouse, the side door flew opened and caught me in the right shoulder, knocking me to the ground. From the crashing noise, I knew the bartender had dashed inside. I followed, but pulled up short when the door behind me slammed shut and I was clothed in darkness. I stopped and listened. Nothing. No running footsteps. No tumbling boxes. No heavy breathing. Okay, I knew when to quit. I backed toward the door when I heard it. Music. Suddenly, the room lit up like Times Square. I now stood between a headless man and a rabbit whose nose twitched to the beat of my pounding heart. Dracula's image reflected off the blade of the guillotine.

I jerked around to confront the Transylvania bloodsucker and came face-to-face with a girl dressed in organdy and lace; a blue sash wrapped around an empire waist and tied into a bow in back. This I could see from the reflection in the mirror behind her. On her feet were patent leather Mary Janes in the brightest shade of lavender I'd ever seen. She held a Bible to her chest. When she spoke in a clear, calm voice, I knew it was beyond hope that the smell of brewing coffee would wake me from the nightmare. I blinked twice. She was still there. So, I did the only sensible thing; I placed my gun back into its holster and asked her where she bought her shoes.

"I found them. Who are you?"

"I could ask you the same question. Did you see an old chubby guy running through here?"

"No one's been here all night except me."

"Why aren't you at home?"

"I am."

"You live here?"

She raised her eyes upward. "On top. Our apartment. I come down here when my dad snores."

"Do you always dress as if you're going to your First Communion?"

"I'm considering a new persona. Dad doesn't like me coming down here at night. But I find the time alone in the prop room, playing dress-up, generates my creative side. Do you play dress-up too?"

The tone of her question was not that of an innocent child. It dripped of sarcasm spoken by a well-seasoned cynic. I looked down at my grubby suit and cowboy boots and sighed. "I do play dress-up, evidently. Listen, I got to go, and you'd better get back upstairs before your father wakes up."

"After he comes home from work, he hits the bed and doesn't wake up until late. He runs the theater next door."

"The Next to Nothing Theater?"

"Uh-huh."

"Where's the front door to this building?"

"This way."

I followed her through the warehouse, going in one door and out another, up a half flight of stairs, and down a long narrow hallway when she reached a door and pushed it open. Until now, I hadn't realized that in chasing the guy, we'd doubled back. I was back out on Sixth Street and Sabine. The Blue Mist was across the street two blocks away. Then I noticed the marquee for the theatre. I stepped back and scanned the structures. The warehouse and theatre, and apparently this girl's apartment, were all part of one huge building. We went back inside and returned to the prop room.

"I'm sure the guy came in that backdoor," I said.

"He could have. To the left of the door are stairs that lead to the roof. He could have gone up there and down the fire escape. Why were you after him?"

"Let's just say it's business. Show me the roof."

"Sure. What's your name?" she asked, leading me to the stairs.

"Sydney."

"No, your real name. I know you're not a man."

"Thank you. Sydney with a *y* and you are?"

"Florence, but you can all me Lydia, with a *y* too."

"Is that a phonograph you're playing?"

"My favorite record. It's a special night."

I listened. Billie Holiday singing "Blue Moon." "Great song. Why is it so special to a young girl like you?"

"Not the song, the night," she scoffed and pushed opened the door. "Tonight is a Blue Moon. Only comes around once every twenty-two months. I was a mere child the last time it happened. I wouldn't miss it this time for anything in the world."

"I wish it would show itself. It's damn dark out there."

"It was out earlier just for a moment when the clouds parted. It was magical."

"Sorry I missed it." We stepped out onto the roof and I found the fire escape, which led down into the alley. No use looking for the guy now. He could be halfway to San Antonio.

"Sorry I bothered your fantasy world, Lydia. Do me a favor and lock up after I leave. There are some dangerous people hanging around this neighborhood at night."

"Oh, I'm not worried. If the bums around here know you, they pretty much leave you alone."

"Maybe you should walk me back to my office."

"Hey, come by tomorrow and I'll get you a ticket to the show. It's great entertainment."

"I'll do that. Gotta go."

"Unless you're known around here like me, I'd stay out of these alleys. Life is too wondrous and beautiful to squander in the cesspools of the devil."

I jerked around, but Lydia had disappeared. When I shut the door behind me, I heard the lock click. I pulled out my gun for the eight-block stroll back to the office. All of a sudden, the hair on my arms stood up. I spun around, giving him the opportunity to grab my shoulders and push my back against the wall.

"You never listen, do you?" he said.

"Get used to it, buddy," I replied.

His eyes narrowed. I replaced my gun in its holster and flung my arms around his neck as the wail of sirens drifted off in the distance.

"We'll never get any work done this way," Dixon said.

"It's the Blue Moon."

"It's *not* the Blue Moon, believe me."

He kissed me again, this time softer and gentler. My knees buckled.

Chapter Two

BACK AT THE OFFICE, Dixon listened to my excuse for chasing the bartender while I attempted to comb the tangles from my hair.

"I doubt Jelly will ever see that guy again," Dixon said. "I say tomorrow we report our findings, collect our fee, and consider the case closed."

"But the slime ball took my coat, my PI license, and our cash." I turned to face Dixon.

"All replaceable. You're not. Downtown Austin at one in the morning is not the safest place for a woman alone."

"I wasn't actually alone. Backyard Benny was lounging in the alley behind The Driskill."

"Thanks for setting me straight. I feel much better now. Come on. I'll walk you to your car." He placed his coat around my shoulders. "You need to get some sleep. You have an early morning ahead of you and I'm ready to hit the sack myself."

"How long are you and Billy planning on living at that hotel?"

"Billy likes the Alamo Hotel."

"He's young and doesn't know better."

"We'll comb the rental ads for apartments this weekend."

BY THE TIME I GOT BACK to my apartment, I was too keyed up to sleep. Besides detective work, I'm a reporter for the *Austin American*. I pulled the cover off my Smith and Corona and poured myself a glass of gin. Since I had neglected to refill the ice trays, I took my ice pick and chipped off a chunk of ice that had formed on the outside of the freezer and plunked it in my glass. I wanted to put the finishing touches on two stories I'd been working on. If I was lucky, I could knock off early at the newspaper tomorrow and get a head start on a nice, quiet weekend.

GRATEFUL THE CROWD at The Driskill's Victorian Bar was minding its own business, I made my way to an empty stool. It still felt odd to me to be a member of one of the hotel's private clubs. In order to serve and sell cocktails to the public in Texas, establishments had to offer club memberships, which they did for a nominal fee. There were other, more *private* clubs at the hotel, but Dixon insisted we join the hotel's primary bar, claiming a place this popular most certainly had its pulse on what was *really* happening in the city.

I sipped my martini, allowing the gin to sooth my frayed nerves. The day didn't go as smoothly as I had planned. Come to think of it, it rarely does. Recently, my life had me on an emotional roller coaster. Two weeks ago, the Dixon, Lockhart, and Ludlow Detective Agency opened its doors for the first time. My boss at the *American* doesn't know I'm moonlighting as a PI. I hadn't yet handed over my press card. I wasn't sure I wanted to. I enjoyed being a reporter, but sooner or later, I had to level with Ernest, my editor. I'd only been with the newspaper for a few months. He had given me a chance to prove myself as a reporter, moving me from the travel section of the *Sunday American Statesman* to the *Austin American*, the city's daily. I could not let him down. He deserved to hear about my partnership in the agency from me rather than through the grapevine. Living in a state of limbo was fast weighing on my nerves. I had to make a decision soon and I was eager to talk it over with Dixon. We'd agreed to meet here at The Driskill after work. He was late. My eagerness turned to impatience, and I began pacing the lobby. When I noticed Joey, the bartender, start to remove my martini glass, I rushed over to assure him I was still around and asked to use the phone. Billy Ludlow, our young partner, answered on the first ring, "Detective Agency."

"Billy, has Dixon left the office yet?"

"Miss Lockhart—"

"Sydney." I've almost given up trying to convince the boy to use my first name. Politeness and manners were bred into Southern men so long ago, any hope of changing that, not that I necessarily wanted to, disappeared with Lee's surrender at

Appomattox. I think it's kind of cute, but I was not in the mood for sweet and innocent.

"Oh, sorry, Sydney. I just came in and Boss was gone. He left a note on the desk saying something came up at the last minute and he went to meet some guy. That's probably why he's late."

Billy also had a difficult time referring to Dixon by any name other than Boss, even though young Billy was a full partner in the agency.

"Who was the guy?"

"I don't know, but it might have been the one who called shortly after lunch. He insisted he meet with Dixon as soon as possible, today in fact. He needed someone investigated, but he wouldn't say anymore over the phone. The appointment book was full and Dixon told him to come by on Monday. The guy hung up. Don't worry, Miss, I mean Sydney. I'm sure there's a good reason he's late."

"You're right. What are your plans tonight?"

"I wish I could say I had a hot date, but I don't. I'm still working on setting up the case files. Office work is not my long suit. Just when I think I have a system worked out that we can all use, I realize it would make sense only to me. I've been at it most of the day, and all I've accomplished was a bigger mess."

"Leave it for now. It'll get done. Lock up the office and join us."

The sixty-seven year-old Driskill Hotel stands in the heart of downtown Austin just a few blocks south of the state capitol building. Built by cattle baron Jesse Driskill, this hotel has a past as colorful as the state's history. It opened in 1886 to a rocky start and closed a year later when Driskill lost his fortune and eventually lost the hotel when he gambled it away playing poker. Since then, the hotel has had several owners and renovations, the latest resulted in a grand expansion and the addition of private baths in every room. During its earlier years, it was home to several prominent people. A railroad pioneer named Peter Lawless lived here for thirty-one years. He stayed on even after his death in 1916. Lawless is just one of the many resident ghosts rumored to inhabit the hotel, if you believe in that sort of thing.

I ordered another martini and listened to lounge singer Lola

Love's sultry rendition of "Echo of Your Last Goodbye." Slowly, my insane day at the newspaper office rolled off my back, and I relaxed for the first time since I opened my eyes at five this morning, or at least I thought I had. Funny how the brain plays tricks on one's mood. I glanced toward the revolving doors, the anxiety returned. I'm not the most patient person in the world, but for some reason, I didn't have a good feeling about Dixon being late. I drummed my nails on the bar, folded my cocktail napkin into a square small enough to stuff up my nose, and glanced at Lola who had three men drooling in their highballs. I turned back toward the door. I took my olive toothpick and jabbed it into my dead cigarette. If Dixon didn't arrive in the next ten seconds, I was going to bang my head against the wall. A bellboy saved me from a self-induced concussion.

"Miss Lockhart?"

"That's me." He handed me a slip of paper.

"Front desk said to deliver it to a Sydney Lockhart sitting in the bar. The caller described you as the tall, gorgeous redhead who could give a man a heart attack with one simple look. Since that describes you to a T, and you're the only dame sitting at the bar without a companion, I figured it was you. We got the note about twenty minutes ago, but the front desk was busy. Sorry."

I unfolded the note. It was from Dixon: *Running a bit late, hon. Order another drink on me, and ask Joey for another bowl of peanuts. Be there soon. Love, Dixon.*

While I waited for my two partners, I pulled a fresh bar napkin over and began to jot down some ideas about a case that had recently come our way. A Mrs. Paul Noonie called about her husband's missing will. Mr. Noonie had kicked the bucket, and all that remained in his safe deposit box was a codicil to his original will leaving everything to the New Light Church. According to the wife, her husband didn't have a religious bone in his body. Leaving his money to the church was more evidence of his insane behavior over the past six months. What was even more bizarre was when her seventy-five year-old hubby enrolled in tennis lessons. Before he retired, he made his living as a shrimper on the Texas coast. Tennis and religion didn't fit the profile. Something must have happened to cause the old guy to trade in his fishing duds for a tennis sweater. That something most likely led to his surprising behavior and the changing of the will. He and his wife had been married for fifty-one years. Just when you think you know someone, they surprise you. I thought of Dixon. I couldn't picture him ever pulling that stunt on me, even after half a century of marriage. But then, again, I was only twenty-nine and single.

I'd just made a note to ask the wife the name of the lawyer who drew up the original will when Billy walked in. He pulled out his wallet before he sat down. Billy was only a couple of years younger than me, but with that baby face, bartenders will card him until he's forty. Even though we were members here, Joey asks to see Billy's license every time. I often wondered if it was jealously. Billy was tall, lean, and walked with a slight slouch that took nothing away from his looks. In fact, it added to his innocence, which drew women to him like bears to honey. Without being asked, he showed Joey his ID, and ordered a bottle of Schlitz.

"Hey, Miss, Sydney. Boss isn't here yet?"

"Nope, but I got a message. He's on his way. What went on at the office today?"

"Jelly Bluestein called first thing this morning. He said he was still laughing at the sight of you rushing out of the bar after his thieving bartender. The wife of the old fart who changed his will called and said she thought it important to share with us that she found a book of matches in his suit pocket from the West Side Country Club."

"Tennis and now an expensive country club. I smell a rat."

"So, do I. I'll keep checking." Billy said.

The telephone behind the bar rang. Joey answered. "Yeah, she's here. Hold on. Miss Lockhart." He stretched the phone cord and handed me the receiver.

"Hey, hon, did you get my note?"

"The front desk was busy. I didn't get the note until about five minutes ago. "

"Sorry you had to wait. What are you wearing?"

"Kind of early for that, don't you think?" Dixon's voice brought to mind a stream of lava, viscous, rich, and hot.

"Never too early for that. Is Billy with you? What's he wearing?"

"I hope you're not suggesting anything funny."

Dixon laughed. "Slight change of plans. I'm on my way to a swanky cocktail party going on in the hotel's Yellow Rose Suite up on the fifth floor, and you two need to join me. I'll explain later."

"How swanky?"

"Let's just say I could not have gotten in wearing my work suit unless I had a personal invitation."

"Billy's dressed like usual, no suit jacket and his tie needs straightening."

At hearing my comment, Billy ran his fingers through his hair and brushed some dust off his pants.

"He'll at least need a coat. Tell him to ask the front desk for a courtesy jacket. How about you?"

"My usual, too, slacks, jacket, and saddle shoes."

"No fedora?"

"Didn't need one today. I was at my desk pounding out a couple of stories."

"Fluff your hair, unbutton the top button of your blouse, that and your attitude should do the trick."

"Where are you now?"

"I'm right above you on the second floor in the Citadel Club with our host."

"I'll meet you up there."

"No! We're on our way to the fifth floor to the Yellow Rose Suite. Meet me there instead."

Dixon hung up rather abruptly.

"Everything okay?" Billy asked.

"Uh...sure. You heard. Dixon's upstairs. We're invited to a highbrow party. This must have something to do with a case. Let's find you a jacket."

BILLY AND I STEPPED OFF THE ELEVATOR, and the sound of a jazzy piano pulled us in the direction of the party. The door to the Yellow Rose Suite was opened and a guy held out his hand. He eyed my wardrobe with apparent disapproval. "Invitation, please."

"It came by telephone," I responded.

"Sorry, ma'am. I can't let you in without an invitation."

Several more people came up behind us. I took the opportunity, grabbed Billy's arm and pushed our way in.

This was the first time I'd ventured above the mezzanine, and I was not prepared for the luxury spread before me. The décor spoke of rustic elegance. A rack of polished deer antlers hung over a lit fireplace, a baby grand sat in the corner, and books filled the built-in shelves that stretched from floor to the top of the twelve-foot ceiling. A bartender mixed drinks at the counter that divided the living room from the kitchenette. Gold brocade drapes floated down the sides of two floor-to-ceiling windows that looked out over Brazos Street.

I scanned the room, expecting to see elegant women donned in the latest fashion and men dressed in Texas formal attire: suits, boots, cowboy hats, and string ties. The four people who mingled at the bar could best be described as classy bohemia meets artsy avant-garde. One woman wore a red-and-gold silk wrap and clearly very little underneath. A stuffed chickadee perched on her head; no hat, just the bird. The young man standing next to her wore stage make-up. His black coat covered a pair of faded yellow slacks. He wore sandals and no socks. Another woman, probably in her mid-forties and heavy-set in a voluptuous sort of way, wore a full-length fur and gorgeous veiled cap. She winked at Dixon. Suddenly I realized that the veil was an illusion. Cross marks had been painted over her face. A guy whom I assumed was her escort, judging by the way he attended to her, must have been trying for the Picasso look. A beret slouched over his left eye and a black-and-white horizontal striped sweater hung loose over his slim frame. Their celebratory mood struck me as being somewhat mutinous, considering their I-dare-you-to-throw-us-out glances.

A completely different crowd had gathered on the other side of the room as if an invisible boundary line divided the avant-garde hip from the high-class swanky. But it wasn't only the form of dress that separated the two groups, these properly attired folks appeared tense as if expecting the beatniks to bring out the bongos any minute now. A tall, middle-aged woman caught my attention. She stood by the fireplace, martini glass held in one hand and a cigarette in the other. Her satin burgundy dress hugged her slim frame and caught the glow of firelight. Short, stylish auburn hair swept up into a ducktail in back, accentuating her high cheekbones. Blue eyes blazed with a sinister quality that struck like lightning. Several guests had gathered around and seemed to hang on her every word. Another woman, clearly distressed, sat slumped in a lounge chair. Her face was drawn, and the dark circles under her eyes looked as if they were a permanent fixture. She said something, and the woman holding court threw back her head and chortled. "Oh, Eleanor, honey, cheer up." She handed Eleanor the martini and motioned for the waiter to bring another. "My little sister has been off her stride lately."

Eleanor sat the drink down. "'Off my stride.' That's a great way to put it, Fiona. Excuse me." As she rose to leave, she tottered. Fiona reached out to steady her, but Eleanor jerked her arm away. "I'm fine," she said and walked away. Fiona shrugged and turned back to the other guests.

The invitation despot came up behind us. "Without an invitation, you're going to have to leave, ma'am."

At that tense moment, Dixon arrived carrying two glasses of champagne. "They're with me," he said. The guy hesitated. "Mr. Maynard invited us." Dixon gave me a light kiss and handed Billy and me each a glass.

"What's this all about?" I asked.

"A potential client. Come on. I'll introduce you."

"I'd say we fit in with the crazy crowd at the bar. At least they seem to be having fun," I said.

"I agree," Dixon said, "but we've been invited into the back room."

Billy and I followed Dixon through a set of double doors into a smaller, more intimate parlor suite. A leather settee and two lounge chairs were arranged in a semi-circle in the center of the room. A brown-and-white cowhide rug covered most of the marble floor.

Dixon directed us to where two men set talking head-to-head in an intense conversation. The older man, a rangy-looking guy wearing a western-style suit and snakeskin cowboy boots bejeweled with silver studs, scribbled notes on a legal pad. The younger man, dressed more like a bank manager, appeared unhappy with what the other guy was writing. He slugged down his drink and slammed his glass on the table, a gesture that the older guy ignored.

Dixon cleared his throat and the older guy looked up. "You must be Sydney." He winked at Dixon, stood up, and shook my hand. He reached around me and shook Billy's too. "And this is Billy Ludlow? I'm Jackson Maynard. Folks call me Stringer. Sit here next to me, young lady. Edwin, find another chair for Mr. Ludlow and close the door. This is my nephew, Edwin Tatum."

The look on Edwin's face told me he was not happy with the interruption. He didn't bother with handshakes and looked as if he were about to protest our arrival, but he simply nodded and left to procure another seat. A waiter walked in with a tray of Oysters Rockefeller.

I was about ready to reach for one when our host spoke. "Not now," Maynard said to the waiter. "Bring in more drinks and make sure we're not interrupted." Then he turned to us. "I really appreciate you three meeting me on the spur of the moment, but that's how I do business. However, it took me some time to convince Ralph to take my case."

"Which I have not yet agreed to do," Dixon said. "Mr. Maynard came by the office this afternoon to leave us a retainer and to set up this meeting."

"Are you the one who called the office earlier today, refused to leave his name, and hung up?" Billy asked.

Stringer glanced at Dixon, and flashed me a true good-ol' boy smile. "Everyone, please call me Stringer. Yep, that was me. Please excuse my impertinence. I'm the first to admit I can be full of myself. My partner, Leland Tatum, will make an announcement" —he looked at his watch— "in just a few minutes. He's throwing his hat into the gubernatorial race. I'm his campaign manager. Lately, I've been concerned that Leland might be involved in something that could ruin his chances to win. I tried talking to him, but he assures me everything is fine. I know it's not. I want you to find out what's going on. I don't like surprises. We've been planning this venture for a long time. You don't get where I am by buckling under when a little problem arises."

"I think my uncle is overreacting." Edwin returned with a chair for Billy. Following behind was the waiter carrying a bottle of champagne and a bottle of scotch. The champagne was used to refill our glasses. Edwin took the bottle of scotch and refilled his glass, downed it, and poured again.

"Edwin doesn't share my reckless nature. Is that how you'd put it, son? Reckless nature? Anyway, unlike Edwin, I built my fortune from the dust that dirtied my boots. Poverty is a great motivator."

Edwin's eyes shot daggers at his uncle, who either didn't notice or didn't care. Stringer continued, "I made my fortune quickly, and now I'm headed in another direction. I plan for Leland to win this election."

"Can you be more specific about your suspicions?" I asked.

"I will, later."

I turned to Dixon whose slight smile never failed to relax my nerves. He shot me a knowing look and I held my tongue. Over the last few weeks, I'd learned to trust this man with the bon-bon colored eyes whom I'd met less than four months ago. In that short time, our relationship changed from adversarial to attraction to trust. It's also developed intimately, a development which I won't put into words. Until a month ago, I'd seen him only a few times, now hardly a day, or night, went by without me laying eyes on him.

"Why the urgency to meet now?" I asked.

"Yes, tell us why you are so eager to get this investigation started," Edwin said.

"We're late entering the race. The other candidates have had a head start. I've hired a company to handle the ad campaign, which starts tomorrow. So, you see, I can't waste any time. I need this cleared up as soon as possible. When Ralph told me you were down in the bar, I figured it would be a great opportunity for you to come to the party and mingle among the guests. Some of the people here are involved with whatever Leland is up to. I figured the sooner you can begin investigating the better."

"Seems like I just heard Dixon tell you we haven't agreed to take the case."

Edwin snorted into his glass, but said nothing.

Stringer waved a hand in front of his face as if my words were a mere annoyance that didn't deserve more than a shooing. He checked his watch again. "You will, once I tell you my concerns."

Well primed for Stringer to continue, we turned our attention back to him when the sound of a gunshot had us up and running. Stringer sprinted down the hall into a room next to the Yellow Rose Suite. Dixon was close behind. I edged my way through the crowd. Standing there in a small room furnished like an office was the woman named Eleanor—a gun in her hand and a body at her feet.

Stringer shouted for someone to call an ambulance. Dixon knelt down beside the body and felt for a pulse, but it was clear from the amount of blood and the damage to the back of the man's skull, he was beyond medical help.

"Who is he?" Dixon asked.

"Leland Tatum," Stringer said.

"Eleanor!" The woman named Fiona said, "What in God's name have you done?" Then she walked over and plucked the gun from her sister's hand. She turned to the crowd in the hall. "Someone bring my sister a scotch, straight."

Chapter Three

AFTER THE PARTY ENDED so abruptly, Dixon, Billy and I returned to our office on the eighth floor of the Scarborough Building where our two-room office sat overlooking the Colorado River. We'd signed the lease a month ago. Right now, the stenciling on the door simply announced the business as "Detective Agency."

I put on a pot of coffee, and soon its fresh-brewed aroma filled the room and brought with it a sense of clarity and normalcy, until I looked over and saw that Dixon had stripped off his shirt, the cuffs of which were bloodstained, and tossed it into the trashcan. He pulled a clean one out of the bottom drawer of the filing cabinet.

"Learned a long time ago to have a spare on hand. You look a little peaked." He reached for the bottle of brandy, also in the bottom drawer, and added a dollop to our cups.

"I'll never get used to seeing a dead body."

"No one does."

Billy walked in with a bag of Chinese take-out. "Figured we could use something."

Food was the last thing I wanted.

"What a day," Dixon said. "I was about to shut down the office and meet you at the hotel when Maynard showed up again as I was walking out. He invited me to join him at The Driskill's Citadel Club. I decided to see what he had to say before I met you in the bar."

"Did he give you any hint as to his suspicions about what Leland Tatum might be up to?" Billy asked.

"I don't know much more than you. When I got to the Club, the first thing Stringer told me was that he was trying to prevent a disaster. He didn't want to go into details and said we should meet in the morning at our office. I told him that you were downstairs in the bar, and he suggested I bring you up to the room so he could meet you. I thought it was a good idea. Give you a chance to get a feel for this guy in case we decided to take him on as a client."

"What's his connection to the beatniks?" I asked.

"Don't know that, either."

"Sounds fishy," Billy said.

Before we could consider Billy's remark, there came a knock on the door. I opened it and Stringer Maynard walked in.

"I figured you'd be here. Got another one of those?" He pointed to our cups.

"Sure." Dixon poured Stringer Maynard a cup and held up the brandy bottle.

"Perfect," Stringer said. "We're gonna get along just fine."

"There's no *we*, yet, Stringer," I reminded him. Something about this guy rankled.

"I didn't know who else to turn to. My sister-in-law just confessed to murder."

"Why did she kill him?" Dixon asked.

"Eleanor is not well. Over the years, she has suffered from depression. Sometimes it got so bad Leland had to admit her into the hospital."

"Leland?" I asked.

"Yes, didn't you know? Eleanor and Leland are...were married."

Stringer's news seemed to suck the air out of our tiny office. Why was I so surprised? You didn't look very far from home when murder was involved.

"That's how Leland and I met. It was back in college. I'd just started dating Fiona, and she suggested we double date with her sister and her boyfriend Leland. I liked both of them right off. Leland and I became instant friends; we married the Galloway girls, graduated, and started our own business. But because of Eleanor's mental problems, things haven't always been rosy. She's still under the care of her psychiatrist."

"Back to my question," Dixon said. "Why would she kill her husband?"

Stringer sipped his coffee and brandy before answering. "Eleanor snapped. She could be violent at times. I'd always feared that it would happen one day. I didn't want to mention details of this earlier at the party, but Leland had recently become involved with the wrong kind of people—the kind that could ruin his chances for winning the election. I'm sure this caused Eleanor additional stress, which she didn't need."

I glanced at Dixon, solemn and astute as always. I haven't yet figured out what goes on in that brain of his, but I swear I could hear the gears grinding. I didn't operate that way, so I plowed ahead. "Were the wrong kind of people in the Yellow Rose Suite tonight?"

"You noticed," Stringer said.

"Hard not to," I said. "Who were they?"

"A bunch of beatnik bloodsuckers who got their teeth into Leland." Stringer drained his coffee cup. "That's why I need a PI, and that's why I wanted you there tonight. Leland's dead, but I need all this straightened out soon. I still want Leland investigated. I don't want this hanging over my head with the upcoming election."

The three of us looked at one another, all of us thinking, I'm sure, that the man sitting in our office was the one who needed a psychiatrist.

"Don't look so startled," Stringer said. "Do you want the job or not? I don't have time to wait around."

"I don't mind telling you, Stringer, that this sounds farfetched," Dixon said.

Stringer stood up to leave. "That's the nature of your business, I presume. If there wasn't a seedy side of life, you'd be doing something else for a living, Ralph. I'll be here in the morning, and I'll want your answer. I don't have time to wait. The funeral is on Monday at ten at the Oak Hill Cemetery. Afterward, we're having the funeral meal at our ranch. I want you there. Nose around. See what you can find. I'm announcing my candidacy as governor the day after I bury my friend and brother-in-law. Like I said before, I don't let things stand in my way."

Since the Chinese take-out Billy brought had turned into a cold, gummy mess, the three of us drove over to The Nighthawk for late-night steaks. We hashed over the bizarre evening, discussed a few other cases that had come our way, and decided to call it a night. Dixon and I had gotten in the habit of seeing each other almost every night since he moved to town. My need to talk to him about my professional dilemma had waned after the excitement of the evening. But I had another early morning ahead of me, so we parted at the restaurant.

On the way to 444 Enfield Road, I wove my way down Twelfth through the narrow streets of Clarksville to my quaint West Austin neighborhood. I'd fallen in love with Tarrytown while attending the University of Texas. My windowless dorm room and my incurably messy roommate had me out on long hikes when I couldn't tolerate the ten-by-ten space. During my junior year, with a part-time job at the University's newspaper, I socked away some money and made plans to get my own apartment the following year. When a notice about an apartment on Enfield Road was posted on the student center bulletin board, I immediately called, and by the end of the day, had signed a lease to move in a week before school began in September. I found another roommate, one who appreciated my sense of order and love of nature. We got along fine. After we graduated, she moved on and I filled the empty space with my clingy poodle, Monroe, and my devil-cat, Mealworm. I've been there ever since.

I opened the front door and Monroe danced around on two hind legs, yelping with joy at seeing me. Mealworm, on the other hand, shot out like a cannon ball and disappeared into the holly bushes to take her frustration out on the neighborhood cottontails, I'm sure. I grabbed my flashlight and walked Monroe around the neighborhood. By the time I'd gotten back, my feet hurt and my head pounded. I drew myself a bath. Just as I eased down under the foam of blue bubbles, I heard scratching on the window screen above my tub.

"Hello, Miss Lockhart," a voice squeaked from outside.

I grabbed a towel and stood up.

"Don't worry I have my eyes shut."

"Good, then you won't be frightened by me holding a .38. Who the hell are you?"

"You keep a gun in your bathroom?"

"Don't you think that's a fine idea?"

"See your point. But it's probably not a good idea to answer your window when someone scratches."

"I thought you were my cat."

"You mean this one?" He held up an orange fur ball, and Mealworm's mug appeared in my window."

"Wow. She never lets strangers pick her up."

"I have a way with animals. I need to talk to you."

"You never answered my question."

"Name's Serge LaBeau."

"Sorry, doesn't ring a bell."

"How about Stringer Maynard?"

"You're getting warm."

"Can we talk without a screen in between us?"

"I get to keep my gun pointed at you."

"No problem."

"Give me a minute."

"Take your time. Fuzzy and I will get to know one another a little better."

"Her name is Mealworm."

Until recently, the idea of letting a strange man into my apartment, especially one who got my attention by scratching on my bathroom window screen, was unthinkable. But in the last six months, I've been suspected of murder, become the owner of a couple of guns, been kidnapped by a Cajun called Mongoose, shot at more times than I care to remember, and gained a detective for a boyfriend. I threw on a pair of blue jeans and a UT sweatshirt. I turned on the back porch light and opened the door.

"Stand back. Put your hands in the air and turn around slowly. I want to get a good look at you."

LaBeau did as he was told with Mealworm curling around between his ankles. Later I'd give her a lecture about talking to strangers. She's always had a thing for the unsavory types.

"Okay, now take off your jacket and set it on the patio table." That last comment got me an odd look, but he acquiesced. I wanted to make sure he wasn't packing heat.

A few minutes later, Serge LaBeau was seated at my kitchen

table. "Okay, what is this all about? And how do you know my name?"

"Listen, could I have a drink?"

I noticed his hands shaking and a bead of sweat on his brow. With my gun still pointed at his heart, I lifted a bottle of bourbon from the cabinet and poured him a shot.

"I found out today that Stringer Maynard hired your agency to investigate Leland Tatum."

"How?"

"It's not important how I know. I have to warn you about Stringer Maynard."

"Why didn't you come by the office? Why show up at my bathroom window?"

"I have to be careful. I don't trust Maynard and you shouldn't either. I found out your name and looked up your phone number and address. I called your apartment several times today. Some guy answered and told me he was your boyfriend. He told me if I called again he'd snip off my privates with hedge clippers and plant them in the flower bed."

"Damn."

"You got some tough guy for a boyfriend."

"Did this guy talk with a lisp and whistle his s's?"

"Yeah, he sounded like a teakettle."

The whistler was Mr. Grimwell, the wacky tenant who lives two doors down. When he retired about a year ago, he proclaimed himself the apartment complex's gardener. For the most part, he keeps the place manicured, but unfortunately, the position has gone to his head. He jokingly referred to himself as Burford Holly, since that thorny bush is his favorite. Now he has the name stitched on his work shirt. I made the big mistake of giving him a key to my apartment so he could water my plants when I travel. Seems his job description now includes taking phone messages.

LaBeau downed his bourbon and began his story.

"Leland Tatum was a close friend. As far as his partner, Stringer could fall off his horse tomorrow out in his pasture, break his leg, and I'd leave him there for the rattlers and coyotes to find before I'd lend a hand."

"Didn't much care for the guy?"

"Nope. Not that I knew him well, but I knew enough. He was Leland's partner and brother-in-law and a pain in Leland's ass."

"How so?"

"Demanding. It was either his way or no way."

"Most people in Texas consider that the normal qualifications for a successful business man."

"Maybe, but this guy went to extremes."

"But from what I understand, Leland and Stringer had been partners for years."

"Things change."

"How do you know Leland?"

"We met at an art-gallery opening a few months ago at the University. We struck up a friendship, and soon after, he became interested in helping me with a project."

"Go on."

"The Austin Art and Cultural Center."

"Art and Cultural Center?"

"Don't sound so surprised. Leland was an artist, a good one. But his art always took a backseat to the family business. Stringer often belittled Leland's talents, and I think after all these years, Leland decided enough was enough. Lately, he'd made comments like he wasn't getting any younger. When I approached him about financial backing for the Center, he jumped at the chance. We planned to sponsor some up-and-coming artists, give them a place to work, show, and sell their works. The Center would eventually stage cultural events like live theatre and music performances, offer workshops and classes. Leland always talked about giving back, and this was his chance."

"These artists, would they have been invited to the big party at The Driskill?"

LaBeau threw back his head and let out a chortle loud enough to send Mealworm under the sofa. "You're kidding me? They were there?"

"The group in the main room of the suite was not your coat-and-tie, fancy dress crowd."

"That's great." Suddenly his jovial mood darkened. "Leland

wanted me to attend. I refused to go. I can't stand to be in the same room with Stringer Maynard. Now I wish I hadn't been so stubborn. Yeah, those guys were probably our artist friends. I would love to have seen the look on Stringer's face when they showed up."

"What do you want from us?"

"Something happened today. I'm not sure what, but I'd never seen Leland so worried and upset. Leland was a good man. Stringer is a conniving, manipulating son-of-a-bitch. Listen, I've said enough."

"You haven't told me how you found out about our detective agency or how you found my name."

LaBeau merely tipped his hat, darted out the door, and disappeared through my honeysuckle.

Chapter Four

As I sipped my first cup of coffee on my patio the next morning, I tried turning my thoughts to my job at the newspaper. Lake Austin, with its plethora of water birds, lay about fifty yards away. This tranquil scene usually helped me focus, but all I could think of was Leland Tatum lying in a pool of his own blood. The ringing of my phone shattered that horrid vision. I figured it was Dixon calling to talk about the potential case. I was wrong.

"You and your bright ideas."

"Morning, Ruth. You're up early."

"I have to stay on my toes. Come to Dallas, now."

"I don't have time to go on a shopping spree to Neiman Marcus."

My cousin Ruth is a reoccurring pain in my butt. She liked to remind me that she stood by me many times when I found myself facing disaster. Unfortunately, having her by my side usually made the situation worse. She's a little rich girl who lives in a luxury apartment in the ritzy neighborhood of Hyde Park in Dallas. She inherited her money from her father and likes to fancy herself a philanthropist. A few weeks ago, her home for unwed mothers opened, and I had hoped that endeavor would keep her too busy to bother me. I should have known better. She had a knack for popping into my life during the most inconvenient time.

"Who the hell has time to shop? You need to straighten out Marcella."

Marcella is Ruth's half-sister who is in charge of running The Echland-Wheatly Home. We'd only discovered Marcella's existence a few months ago when she suddenly appeared in our lives. She was a hotshot lawyer from Houston who offered to represent me when I was suspected of murder while staying at The Luther Hotel in Palacios. She's also the illegitimate daughter of Ruth's father and mistress. Once Ruth accepted that fact, and with a little urging from me, she decided to hire

Marcella to run the home. She was perfect for the job. Marcella had brains, legal experience, and her *own* mother was unwed.

"I thought she was working out great."

"She's going to bankrupt me before the end of the year."

I hated to ask, but the word slipped out. "How?"

"She says I need to revamp my Articles of Corporation and have our own adoption service."

"Those sound like good ideas."

"Sure, take her side."

"Who drew up your articles?"

"I did."

"You? You drew them up? You, who made Cs on every college paper she ever wrote?"

"Funny, you're just too funny. It was easy. I found a form in this book in the library, filled it out, got it notarized, and that was it. I saved fifty bucks by doing it myself. It's not that I needed to save money, I just wanted the feeling of being self-sufficient."

"If you want to be self-sufficient, figure out what Marcella wants you to do rather than call me and complain. After all, she is a lawyer."

"Why are you so cranky this morning?"

"I attracted another dead body."

"Anyone I know?"

"Future gubernatorial candidate."

"No one important then. Listen, I can't waste any more time gabbing with you. I'm going to the Home and tell Marcella if she doesn't straighten up, I might have to send her packing."

After my cousin dismissed me, I was able to put things in perspective and went to see what lay in store for me at the *American*. I arrived at the newspaper in time for our morning editorial meeting.

I grabbed my pad and pencil and headed down the hall. Ginger, Ernest's secretary, four reporters, and the donut girl, all jockeyed for space around his desk. Ernest barked out orders; everyone talked at once; donuts were passed around, along with the coffee pot. The reporters argued, Ginger argued, Ernest told one reporter to shut up and get the hell out, to which the guy laughed and ignored his boss. Chaos, madness, upheaval—a typical day at the newspaper. I loved it and jumped right in.

Things settled down and Ernest told Jake Bradley, his veteran reporter, to follow up on the First National Bank robbery that took place yesterday. Another reporter, Rob Hadley, got assigned to cover an unscheduled meeting of the city council, and Ernest ordered me to get down to the jail and get the latest on the Tatum murder. The room went silent, donuts stopped on their way to hungry months, and all eyes turned to me.

Tweety Gilcrest raised his hand. "You forgot me, Ernest."

"No I didn't, Tweety, and don't call me Ernest. I'm expecting a call on a story and I want you here when it comes in." Tweety's face lit up with anticipation, even though the rest of us knew there was no phone call and no story. Ernest hated Twellen Theodore Gilcrest. He was the grandson of Herman Gilcrest, founder of the Gilcrest Group, a newspaper conglomerate that not only owned the *American,* but four other newspapers throughout the state. Tweety had been on the staff of all the other Gilcrest papers and this was his last stop. Herman called in a favor, and poor Ernest was obligated to hire the guy. "You got your assignments, now leave!"

We scurried from the office like mice when the light comes on. Jake nudged me. "Good job, girl. You got the top story."

"Much to the chagrin of some of my colleagues."

"Don't worry about it. You gotta be tough. Do your job." He winked and walked away.

I joined the *Austin American* team of writers as a soft-news reporter assigned to write travel articles for the Sunday paper. My first assignment took me to The Arlington Hotel in Hot Springs, Arkansas where I found a dead man in the bathtub of my hotel room. One thing led to another, and now whenever someone is murdered, I'm the one who gets to dig out the gory details. The Arlington Hotel was also where I met Ralph Dixon, who, at the time, was working as a detective for the Hot Springs Police Department. He was first on the murder scene. Since I was standing over the body, Dixon assumed I'd done the deed. But something kept him from slapping on the cuffs and hauling me downtown. Something kept me from slapping his face at the accusation of murder. That something felt like an electrical charge, a bolt of lightning, a shockwave like none other. That feeling was still there, although the desire to slap one another had disappeared.

Ernest interrupted my thoughts of Dixon by calling me back into his office. When he shut the door behind me, I knew I wasn't there to share the last donut. He parked his hip on the corner of his desk. He folded his arms and the wrinkles on his forehead bunched into one big crease. "Sit down."

I refused to get swallowed up in his intimidation chair. The springs were shot. When I went to see him for the job interview, I sat in that chair and almost gave myself a left hook with my knee. I walked over to the window and parted the blinds. "Shouldn't I get over to the jail?"

"You were at The Driskill last night. Not that it's any of my business what you do in your spare time."

"How did you find out?"

Ernest looked at me as if I were the dumbest reporter ever to walk into his office. "I'm in the news business. Spill it. You owe me that."

"You're right." I liked Ernest. He deserved to know the truth, and although I had misgivings about what I was about to say, I was also grateful for the chance to come clean. "A lot has happened over the last few weeks. I've sort of taken on a second job."

"I hope it doesn't involve hanging out in hotel lobbies at night."

"Actually, sometimes it does." I laughed. "It involves investigating. I'm setting up a detective agency with a couple of friends. It wasn't really planned, it just happened. Last night we were at The Driskill, meeting with a potential client, when Leland Tatum was murdered." I picked up his stapler and checked for staples just to have something to do with my hands so I wouldn't place them over my mouth to prevent the next words from slipping out. "I'll resign if you want."

"Put that damn thing down before you staple your finger. I need to think about this. Go get the story. We'll talk later."

I nodded and started for the door.

"And thanks," he said.

I turned around. "Thanks?"

"For leveling with me. Now get out."

A few seconds ago, I was sure I'd done the right thing. Now, I envisioned bills piling up on my desk at home, an empty icebox, a half-starved poodle, and an ornery cat, and worse yet, an empty gin bottle. How long would it take for the agency to bring in enough money to support three people? Thanks to a recent posthumous gift from my grandfather, and some sound advice from Dixon, I had a small nest egg.

We had an hour before our scheduled appointment with Maynard—time to drive over the city jail to find out the latest. When I arrived, I learned that Eleanor Tatum's psychiatrist had already managed to get his patient moved to his clinic. I made myself a nuisance until the desk sergeant asked me to leave. I drove to the office and hoped Dixon and I could glean more information from our meeting with Maynard. So far, I didn't have much of a follow-up story on the murder. Suddenly, a jolt of guilt struck, and my trepidations over my two professions came clear. Coming clean with my editor made sense, but what about my role as a detective? Wasn't there a conflict of interest? Shouldn't I come clean with my clients? Where was the boundary line there? I had to adhere to a code of confidentiality with our clients, yet I was obliged to report the facts to Ernest. I turned these thoughts over in my head as I stepped into the elevator of the Scarborough Building.

"Morning."

Startled, I turned to see Stringer Maynard step in behind me.

"Morning," I said.

"You look like I feel," Stringer said.

Mr. Jorgenson, the crotchety elevator operator, snickered. The man didn't like me.

I ignored Jorgenson and studied Stringer. Try as I might, I could not find one single sign of stress on Jackson Maynard's body: not a droop of the shoulders, no bags under his green eyes, no extra gray hairs on his head, no fading of his well-tanned face. For a man whose best friend, business partner, and brother-in-law was murdered the night before, Stringer looked as if he'd had a peaceful night's rest.

When I didn't respond to his comment, he said, "What's addled your cute little brain?"

What addled my cute little brain was not having the opportunity to tell Dixon about my meeting with Serge LaBeau before Jackson "Stringer" Maynard arrived.

I walked into the office first and Dixon met me with a hug and kiss before he realized I had our client in tow. A slight blush spread over his gorgeous face, but he kept his arm around my waist as if to affirm our romantic relationship. Dixon wasn't easily intimidated. I knew that from the moment I met him, but that fact was driven home when he stood up to my insane mother when I brought him to Galveston to meet my parents a few weeks ago.

Stringer took a seat before either of us could invite him to sit. He threw his hat on the desk. "Okay, let's get started."

Dixon plucked the hat from his desk and hung it on a wall peg. Billy walked in and the meeting began.

"I think you'd better start from the beginning," Dixon said.

I sat down behind the desk and pulled out my notepad.

"Like I said last night, several months ago Leland got involved with a bunch of artists, actors, theatre people, whatever you want to call them. You know the type, a bunch of liberal-assed Commies," Stringer began. "Some of them were at the party, as I'm sure you noticed. Ever since, Leland's been moody and difficult to deal with. A few weeks ago, we were scheduled to sign a contract with West Texas Oil Company to drill some land we own near our ranch in Oak Hill. This was a big-deal project for us. We'd been negotiating for months and things finally started to come together. Leland came into the office that morning. He wanted to back out of the deal. The papers were drawn up and our lawyers were on their way over. I was a bit miffed to say the least."

"Why did Leland want to back out?" I asked.

"At first he objected to the percentage West Texas Oil offered us. We worked through those negotiations—well, I did—and got us a slightly better deal. But Leland continued to pick through the contract. He got a bug up his butt and seemed to have issues with several minor points, none of which he understood. I finally had a talk with him about his stubbornness, and after that, he backed off and all seemed well for a while. But his moodiness continued. I confronted him, jokingly at first. I teased him about having a girlfriend on the side. He laughed it off, saying he was dealing with issues involving Eleanor. I questioned him, but all I got were evasive answers. Eleanor's depression and the problems it caused were never a secret. We're family. Leland, Fiona, and I often discussed Eleanor's situation. I knew he used Eleanor as an excuse."

"How can you be sure?" Dixon asked.

"I knew Leland well. He was like a brother to me. And his interest in our business had waned as soon as he began hanging out with those wacko artists."

"That's not much to go on," Dixon said. "Did you end up signing the contract with the oil company?"

"We did, but Leland wasn't happy about it. Damn, that contract will bring in the dough."

"Who keeps your books?" Dixon asked.

"Leland did."

"If we take the case, we'll need to take a look," Dixon said.

"No problem. I'll arrange everything for after the funeral luncheon on Monday. Anything else?"

"Give us some names and occupations of who will be at the luncheon so we can begin asking questions without sounding too intrusive."

"It'll be a small affair," Stringer said. "Mainly people who work for the ranch. There's Jones Digmire our ranch foreman, and Victor Nolan, neighbor rancher—they're pallbearers, along with Edwin—a cousin of Leland's from Midland, and my wife and Eleanor's father."

"What about the artists?" I asked.

"You think I'd invite those bloodsuckers to the luncheon? Not on your life." Stringer scoffed.

"Do you know any of them?" Dixon asked.

"Only that screwball, Serge LaBeau. Here are the directions to the ranch." He rose to leave.

"One more thing," Dixon said. "The room where Tatum was killed, was it joined to your suite?"

"Mine on one end and Leland's on the other. It's an office were I conduct business when I'm in town. So, you're taking the case?"

Dixon looked over at Billy and me. We nodded. Stringer thanked us and left.

"You don't like the guy, do you?" Dixon asked me.

"I have a funny feeling about him, that's all." I walked over to the corkboard we used to display notes for various cases. I wrote Jackson "Stringer" Maynard on an index card and stuck it in the middle of the board. "I hope we know what we're getting into."

"Billy, see what you can find out about West Texas Oil," Dixon said. "If Leland Tatum was reluctant to do business with them, see if he had a good reason. I don't think Maynard's telling us the entire story."

"Will do." Billy went into the other room and closed the door. I began scribbling more notes before they fled my brain.

"I say we go to the cemetery before the luncheon," Dixon said.

'Sure."

"I'd like to see who shows up."

"Sure."

"In my experience, funerals bring out the guilty."

"Right."

"Am I bugging you?"

"A little."

"Would you tell me if I were bugging you a lot?" Dixon walked up and pushed a strand of hair behind my ear. I hoped the gesture was more than just trying to see what I was writing.

"I might."

"Can you be more specific?" His hand left my hair and was now massaging my shoulder.

"Maybe."

With that last missive, he had me out of the chair and in his arms. See what I mean about needing to get my thoughts down on paper? Anything could happen in this office.

The door opened and Billy walked in. "I just got...whoops! I know you two like each other, but, really."

"We were just comparing notes," I said.

"Is that what you call it?" Billy grinned.

"Got something, Billy?" Dixon could go from romance to business quicker than he could take my breath away.

"Yeah, a guy named Gary Huffman was the one who negotiated the contract with Maynard and Tatum. He was out, so I left our number with his secretary."

"Good work," Dixon said, "Feel him out. Find out what you can without giving him too much on our end. You know what to do."

Billy left. And Dixon and I left one business and got down to another.

"Let's go over your notes," Dixon said.

"Whatever got Tatum killed seemed to have come to a head at the party. We need to talk to the wife."

"The woman's a nut case."

"That may be, but she was obviously upset. In fact, except for the beatniks, I'd say everyone there was tense over something. And that sister of hers, Fiona—talk about a nut case. Eleanor just murdered her husband and Fiona calmly tells the bartender to bring Eleanor another drink? I'd like to have a go at her too."

"You'll have your chance at the funeral. Any problem with getting off work to attend?"

The niggling thought of my two professions came crashing back.

"What is it?" Dixon said.

I told him about my concerns and about the conversation I'd had with Ernest. "I wondered about that too," he said. "Things have moved quickly since our exploits in Galveston. Are you having second thoughts about this? If so, Billy and I can run the agency ourselves for a while. Give you some more time to think it over."

"There will come a time when I'll have to decide. For now, I'll give Ernest the facts he needs without breaching client confidentiality."

"That's harder than it sounds. I wouldn't want to be in your shoes. Today's Saturday. I don't want to wait until Monday before we delve into this. Go back to your news desk and don't think about the case. I'm going to start digging. What time will you be home?"

"Around six. Stop by, and I'll have a copy of the want ads and a bottle of wine. We'll scourer the ads for an apartment for you. You can't stay in that Alamo Hotel forever."

Chapter Five

ON MY WAY BACK to the newspaper, I mulled over our conversation. Dixon was right. Things had moved rather quickly since the nightmare at The Galvez Hotel a few weeks ago. But I wasn't having second thoughts about our decision. I liked having Dixon nearby, but the poor man hadn't even had a chance to find a place to live. He and Billy rented two rooms at the infamous Alamo Hotel down the street from our office just a short walk from the state capitol. Rumor had it that more legislation got passed at Zeke's, the hotel's greasy spoon, than in the senate and house chambers. U. S. Senator Lyndon Johnson's younger brother, Sam Houston Johnson, lived at the hotel. His family arranged for a long-term lease for the troubled man whose older brother often lectured Sam on the evils of drink. I was eager to get Dixon out of the hotel and into more respectable quarters. He still had his furniture at his apartment in Hot Springs. Rather than deal with my professional dilemma over our new case, I decided to go back to the *American* and act like a reporter.

BY THE TIME I'D FINISHED my follow-up on the Tatum murder, Ernest, as well as most of the staff, had gone for the day. The society editor was, not surprisingly, still at her desk.

"Hey, Syd," she called as I walked by on the way to the coffee pot. "Someone just telephoned to see if you were here. The switchboard operator left so the call came to me."

"Male or female?"

"Female, she didn't leave her name. I told her you were still here. But she hung up."

"Thanks, Lilly. If it's important, she'll call back." It was either my mother or Ruth. I'd throw my money on Ruth. Whatever her latest crisis was, it could wait. If it was my mother, her crisis could wait until hell froze over.

I tidied my desk, dropped my work in Ernest's in-box, and

called it a day. On my way to my car, two images materialized in my mind—a bottle of gin and a bottle of red wine. Decisions, decisions. Maybe I'd serve both—martinis for us to unwind and later a glass of wine with dinner while we discussed Dixon's living arrangements. The last time I tried that formula, our steaks burned on the grill and the baked potatoes turned to rocks in my oven. We drank the wine with my homemade chocolate sponge cake and forgot about the business we needed to discuss. The same thing would probably happen tonight, not that I was complaining.

I pulled my keys from my bag, and as I neared my car, I saw someone looking it over. That wasn't unusual. My red Bel Air convertible often attracted attention. But the person peering inside looked familiar.

"You must make good money at the newspaper to afford this little jewel." She turned and smiled.

"I manage. I'm sure you're not here to talk about my income. How did you know it was my car, Mrs. Maynard?"

She looked around at the almost empty parking lot. The only other vehicle was a battered once-forest green pickup with four bald tires. No further explanation needed.

"You're right. Your income doesn't concern me."

"How did you know I worked here?"

"I read the papers. Don't worry, Stringer doesn't know I'm here. If he did, he wouldn't care. Believe me, the man's got more important things on his mind. Can you spare some time?"

I looked at my watch. "An hour."

"That's good enough. "Know where the Tarrytown Country Club is?"

"Sure, just a couple of blocks from my apartment."

"You do make good money. I'll see you there."

WE PULLED UP in the parking lot of the Tarrytown Country Club at the same time. I followed Fiona Maynard inside. She stopped briefly at the bar, gave orders to the bartender, and we headed for a table by the window. "Have a seat," she said.

"Are you always this bossy?"

"Yes," she laughed. "You'll get used to it. Most people don't, but you're a tough gal."

"That's true. You've used up twenty minutes of your hour. What do you want?"

"My sister did not kill Leland."

"She confessed."

"She was lying. After the incident, Dr. Richards gave Eleanor a strong sedative. She was little more than a rag doll. This afternoon after the drugs began to wear off, Eleanor and I were finally able to talk. I told her I knew she didn't kill Leland."

"But you thought she had when we found her standing over his body."

"Of course. It looked obvious at the time, but she's innocent. I'm sure of it. I asked her why she made such an absurd claim about killing Leland. She just said, 'I had to.'"

"Did she say why?"

"No. Eleanor clammed up. I know my sister is not capable of murdering her husband. She was drinking, which she's not supposed do to because of the medication she's taking. She was talking nonsense."

"She's unstable and violent."

"Violent? Who told you that?"

"Your husband."

"Eleanor often became distraught and emotional, flying off the handle at times, but I don't call that violent. Stringer thinks that any woman who loses her temper is violent. Anyway, things will be different now. Eleanor will be in my care now that Leland is gone."

That last statement caught me up short. "You didn't agree with how Leland handled your sister's situation?"

"Not at all. My brother-in-law and I didn't agree on much. I felt Eleanor needed to stay at Dr. Richards' clinic. She's too unpredictable. Leland believed that being in the institution, as he called it, was what caused most of her problems. Oh, don't look at me like that. You know I didn't kill him. How could I? I was hobnobbing at that damn party."

"You have to admit, that's a damn good motive."

"I suppose it is, but I don't need to resort to murder to get what I want. I need your help. My husband is already writing his acceptance speech. He doesn't wallow in the tragedies of the past. As far as he's concerned, Leland's dead, Eleanor killed him. Life moves on. I have money, Sydney. I want you and your partners to find Leland's killer. I don't want my sister in prison."

"Sorry, Mrs. Maynard. We're working for your husband."

"He's continuing with the investigation?"

"You didn't know?"

"Stringer and I don't talk business much anymore."

"Business? You call your brother-in-law's murder business?" But my surprise over her callousness was lost on Fiona Maynard.

"Of course he would continue the investigation," she mused, "but to find out what Leland was up to. He's concerned with the election. I'm not. Being the governor's wife isn't my idea of fun. I want you to find out who killed my brother-in-law. My time is up. You'd better go. Stringer will be here soon. Bill me for this hour."

DUSK HAD CAST A SHADOWY CLOAK over the neighborhood's oak-lined streets with their quaint cottages sitting side by side like a photo from a Currier and Ives greeting card. Azaleas, now in full bloom, splashed shades of magenta, violet, and white across lush lawns, announcing spring, just in case we hadn't noticed. My modest apartment complex, a rarity in this neighborhood, sat across the street from the Lions Municipal Golf Course and a few blocks from the Walsh Boat Landing, but far enough away from the country club to give the street a feeling of modest comfort.

When I opened the door to my apartment, Dixon was on the phone. "Don't cry, honey. I understand your anxiety," he said. "You've just accomplished one of the biggest feats of your life. It will take some time to smooth things out where you can sit back and be proud of what you've done."

I threw my bag on the coffee table. Monroe loped over and put her snout in my hand as if I didn't know my motherly duty. Mealworm sat on the windowsill, glanced over her shoulder and growled. It's the best welcome home I'd received from my cat in days. Dixon threw me a kiss and mouthed the word "Ruth." I motioned for him to tell her I wasn't home yet. He got the message and continued with his emotional support of my overly emotional cousin. "Non-profit is a good thing. Listen to Marcella. She knows what she is doing. I've an idea. Why don't you come to Austin for a few days? Let Marcella do her thing."

I violently shook my head, but Dixon continued. "Sydney and I are working on a case, but you can make yourself at home here. Go for a stroll along the lake, take the poodle. It'll be nice."

I flopped on my sofa, pressed my hands around my throat, and pretended to choke myself. "Or," Dixon said, "we can book you a room at The Driskill." He paused, and I heard Ruth chatting away like an excited squirrel. "Think about it. Okay, tell Marcella I said hi." He hung up.

"Have you lost your mind?"

"I picked up some burgers from Hut's. You've had a long day. Hope you didn't have your heart set on a gourmet meal."

"Burgers sound great. Your invitation to Ruth didn't."

"Once she finds out about this case, she'll come anyway. I knew if I invited her to stay with you and gave her the task of walking your poodle, she'd balk. Besides, having a plant at the hotel will come in handy. She's almost as good as you in digging out information."

"We're asking for trouble."

"What's new? Come here."

I walked over and he tangled his fingers in my hair. All thoughts of Ruth disappeared.

An hour later, we consumed cold burgers and soggy fries out on my patio. "We haven't had a chance to talk," I said. "I've had a couple of visitors. One at the newspaper and one at my bathroom window last night."

Dixon's brow raised a notch, a gesture that never failed to bring a flutter to my stomach. I was momentarily lost in our lustful endeavor of a few minutes ago when he said, "Tell me about the bathroom visitor first."

"His name is Serge LaBeau. He is, or was, a good friend, maybe even Leland Tatum's confidant." I told Dixon about how

Tatum became involved with the "beatnik bloodsuckers," as Stringer called them and how Leland wanted to help develop the Austin Art and Cultural Center. "Also, Tatum came to see LaBeau the day he was killed. LaBeau said something had happened to cause Tatum trouble. He claimed he didn't know what."

"Was this LaBeau character at the party last night?"

"He hated Stringer and refused to go."

"Why did LaBeau come to see you in the middle of the night, and how did he know you were involved in the case?"

"He wouldn't tell me how he found out, said it wasn't important, that he wanted to warn us about Stringer Maynard."

"Hmmm. And the other visitor?"

"Fiona Maynard. She was waiting for me in the parking lot of the newspaper when I got off work today. I feel like my life is an open book and the entire world knows about my double life."

"Things will work out on that front. Try not to worry about it now. What did Mrs. Maynard want?"

"She invited me for a drink at the Tarrytown Country Club. That's why I was late getting home. She wants to hire us to find out who killed Tatum. She's convinced her sister didn't kill her husband."

"She didn't. I had only a couple of minutes to view the murder scene before the cops made us leave."

"You didn't like what your saw?"

"No. Two things bothered me. Did you notice anything odd about the position of the body?"

"I couldn't see much in the crowd."

"From the looks of it, Tatum was facing the window when he was shot from behind, but his head and right shoulder were turned slightly upward."

"Maybe he didn't die immediately. Maybe after he fell, he tried to move."

"That was my initial thought until I saw the hem of Eleanor Tatum's dress. There was blood on it."

"How did that happen? When I saw her, she was standing over the body."

"She was when I saw her too. The only way for her to get

blood on her dress was to kneel down beside her husband."

"Then stand up again?"

"Exactly. She shoots him, kneels down to make sure he's dead, picks up the gun and stands there."

"Unless someone else shot him? But we heard the shot and then the scream immediately."

"We need to find out how much time had lapsed between Eleanor leaving the party and hearing the shot. Why is Fiona Tatum convinced her sister is innocent?'

"She knows Eleanor well enough to know when she's lying."

"That's convenient."

"She was surprised when I told her we were still working for her husband. Seems she and Stringer don't communicate much these days."

"Anything else?"

"That's about it."

"There's not much we can do tonight. We gather what information we can at the funeral and interview the hotel staff working the party. Find out if it's indeed possible for someone else to have killed Leland Tatum. Tomorrow's Sunday. First thing in the morning, I need to find a place to live."

For the next hour, we perused the *American* for rental ads. Dixon didn't require much more than a place to hang his hat and coat. We focused on apartments between the downtown area and my neighborhood, circled five ads, and ended the evening walking Monroe down to the boat landing. My high-strung poodle needed vigorous exercise so she wouldn't pace the hallway all night. As I threw a stick into Town Lake for the dog to retrieve, Dixon and I prioritized the rental ads and planned to spend Sunday afternoon checking out the possibilities. When Monroe finally got tired, we headed back to my place and spent the rest of the evening listening to my phonograph.

Chapter Six

AFTER A LEISURELY BREAKFAST, Dixon and I left on the apartment hunt. Our first stop was a garage apartment on Baylor just a block off Sixth. The location was perfect, not too far from my place and close to our office. From the outside, the place looked well kept. Dixon rang the doorbell of the main house while I walked back toward the apartment. Moments later, Dixon, joined by a grumpy man wearing workpants and a dingy undershirt under a faded robe, came around the corner. The guy looked as if he's just gotten out of bed. "The place is pretty small for a couple," he grumbled. "Just a shower. Ain't no bathtub. Small cook stove, one closet."

"It's just for me," Dixon said.

"Hey, buddy, it's none of my business. A tenant is a tenant."

We followed him upstairs. It took him a while to jiggle the lock open, and as he did, the smell of stale air escaped into the fresh morning. "Have to air the place out, get the wife in here to do a bit of cleaning, but everything works. I need twenty-five dollars deposit. The rent's due on the first and not a day after, and I don't put up with any wild parties or hanky-panky." He looked at me, and I smiled. Then back to Dixon, "What do you do for a living?"

"Police work," Dixon said, giving the place a thorough inspection. I was ready to scratch it off the list when he said, "I'll consider it. I just started looking. If you don't hear from me by later today, assume I found something else."

"Sounds fair. Police work, huh? Could be worse."

The next place on the list was a small apartment complex on West Tenth. The overflowing trashcans, row of rusty cars, and a mean-looking shepherd behind a rickety wooden fence, didn't deserve a stop. The dozen bicycles parked in front of the next complex on Windsor announced it as a college-student apartment, and we moved on from there. We drove down Morning Glory Road and noticed a for-rent sign in the front yard of a three-story Spanish-style home. We almost passed it by until we saw the words "cottage for rent." Behind the mansion stood a cute, square, cinderblock cottage with English Ivy trailing up one side. The door was opened, so we walked in. A red brick fireplace announced itself as the centerpiece of the living room, and off the hall was a small bedroom and a bathroom. The kitchen was spic and span and smelled as if someone had recently baked bread in the oven. French doors from the kitchen led out onto a patio shaded by fragrant mimosa trees.

"I expect Hansel and Gretel to arrive any minute," Dixon said.

Instead of the Grimm's two German kids, a dapper, elderly gentleman greeted us. "Sixty dollars a month," he said. "Place used to be the servant's quarters until my wife's mother moved in. She recently passed away. I'm Lester Granger, taught economics at the University before I retired.

"I'm Ralph Dixon and this is Sydney Lockhart."

"Will this be your first home together? You two make such a lovely couple." A tiny woman wearing a bright yellow apron, walked in. "I'm Mrs. Granger."

"Miss Lockhart and Mr. Dixon," Lester said to his wife.

"Hello," I said. "We're looking for a place for my...friend here."

"That's fine, dear." She acted as if my last statement was too inconsequential to comment on. "I always thought the house would make a fine place for a young couple just starting out. Lester and I seem to lose track of one another rambling around in the big, old house now that the kids have flown the coop. I've threatened to tie a bell around his neck so I could keep track of him. I'm so looking forward to having some activity here on the grounds. Do you work, Miss Lockhart? And what do you do for a living, Mr. Dixon?"

Dixon used his line of police work and told her I was a reporter for the *American*.

"A working couple, how wonderful! Come here, young lady, I want to show you something. We'll leave the men to talk business."

"Dear, they just got here. Give them a chance to look around."

Mrs. Granger ignored her husband and pulled me by the arm toward the big house. Once inside, we walked down a maze of hallways toward the back; Mrs. Granger chatting nonstop. It appeared as if the Grangers had a horde of offspring; pictures of whom I assumed were children and grandchildren consumed almost every inch of wall space. She led me into a room that burst with color: reds, pinks, golds, splashed across the wallpaper, furniture fabric, and rugs. Books filled shelves, more formed stacks on both sides of the sofa. A jigsaw puzzle, half-finished, covered a small table by the window, a basket of knitting supplies sat by the overstuffed lounge chair. The French Provincial furniture was authentic. This was clearly Mrs. Granger's own private paradise.

"Lovely room," I said.

"A bit cluttered, but it keeps my husband out," she giggled. "His need for order is not for me. I love the remnants of my hobbies spread around me, just like when the children were here. They were all over the place. We have eight. They're grown with families of their own, except our youngest. Emily is still in school at the University, studying archeology. Got some lofty ideas of exploring tombs in Egypt. Knowing that girl, she'll probably do it too. Here, this is what I wanted you to see." She pointed me over to an ornate desk littered with snap shots, shoe boxes of more snap shots, pieces of construction paper, and a pot of glue. "I'm working on a family scrapbook. I must have five hundred photographs here. Lester says I should pick out a few of the best ones and throw the others out, but I can't part with a single one. Here, this is Emily when she was two, digging up my marigolds."

"Her early archeological exploits?" I asked.

"Never thought of that," Mrs. Granger laughed. "Once you move in, come over any time. You can help me sort through all this. It's really consumed me lately. To tell the truth, I've gotten bored with all the community service clubs I belong to. Half the Bridge players fall asleep while they're playing. The Junior League seems to be taken over by a younger clan of women, and if I have to go to another church rummage-sale meeting where no one agrees on anything, I think I'll change faiths. I don't think Catholics are too much into rummage sales. I might give them a try. I heard they serve beer at their church bazaars. Do you think that's true?"

I handed back Emily's photograph. I assured her that she'd have the time of her life at any Catholic festival, but I didn't have the heart to mention again we were looking for a place for Dixon and not the both of us.

"We'd best join the men," she said.

Out in the backyard, Dixon and Mr. Granger were enjoying a smoke. When the man of the house saw us coming, he surreptitiously, tossed his cigarette into the fountain.

"I saw that, Lester." Mrs. Granger turned to me and said, "He's not supposed to smoke. He thinks I don't know when he sneaks one. You'll have to help me with this endeavor, Mr. Dixon. Don't let Lester bum cigarettes. You can move in as soon as you want."

"Caroline, he hasn't even said he wanted to rent the place," Lester said.

"Of course, he does! Why wouldn't he? It's perfect. Miss Lockhart loves it, don't you?"

"Well, I...yes, it's lovely, but I won't be—"

"It is nice." Dixon interrupted me with a smile. "But we have a few other places to look at. I can let you know as soon as possible, though. I know you're eager to rent it."

"Don't worry about utility bills. We've figured that into the rent," Caroline said. "Just write us a check at the first of the month. When you bring your things over, Lester will give you the key." With that, Caroline Granger bid us farewell and took her leave.

"My wife's a pushy little thing," Lester said. "No pressure. Let us know when you've made a decision."

Dixon and I thanked Mr. Granger and drove off. "Well, what do you think?" I asked.

"It is nice. Furnished too. I can move right in and get rid of my ratty furniture in Hot Springs."

"But . . ."

"I'm just wondering how private the place will be."

"I was wondering the same thing. I can see Mrs. Granger

hovering over you like a mother hen. She also thinks we're taking the place together."

"So I noticed. We have one more place to see."

I drove closer to downtown where the streets are named after the ten major rivers in Texas. They run north/south and are arranged in order of how they flow through the state. If you know anything about Texas geography, and are on Austin's Rio Grande Street, you'd know you're in west downtown; if you were on Sabine Street, you'd be in the eastern-most part of downtown. The San Miguel Apartments at 701 San Antonio (as in river) Street were close to the middle. Dixon could walk to the office. The apartment for rent was on the corner on the second floor. It overlooked a string of elegant historic homes built in the 1800s and a block away was The Alamo Hotel. The manager had a "be back in 15 minutes" sign posted on the door, so we walked over to the hotel and ordered coffee at Zeke's Grill. The smell of bacon grease and pancakes competed with the aroma of garlic and fried fish.

"The San Miguel looks good from the outside," Dixon said. "What do you think?

"Look at the pros and cons of each. The San Miguel Apartments are close to the office, and probably cheaper than the cottage, but there are a few bars near here. It could be noisy at night."

"The cottage is quiet and closer to your place," he said, "but then there's Mrs. Granger. What will she think when she realizes that I'll be living there alone and you'll be a frequent visitor?"

"It's not like I didn't make a concerted effort to tell her. Let's see what the apartment looks like first. What about Billy? Has he been looking around?"

"Not that I know of. I think he kind of likes it here," Dixon laughed. "It suits a young man like him."

As if the mere mention of Billy's name could conjure him up, the handsome guy walked in. I did a double take. Billy was dressed in a suit and tie, shoes shined, and hair combed neatly off his forehead. When he saw us, he looked slightly embarrassed.

"Pull up a chair," Dixon said and motioned the waitress to bring another coffee. "Huffman ever call back?"

"Nope."

"See if you can get a home number from the operator. Where've you been on a Sunday afternoon?"

"After I struck out with Huffman, I decided to go to church, the New Light Church, to be exact. There was a note on the door that Reverend Lindy had suddenly taken ill and there would be no service today. I walked around to the back of the building and looked into a couple of windows. From what I could see, no one had been in the church for a while. Looks fishy. I'll keep checking. Found a drugstore diner open and had lunch. I like Austin, the downtown area. I can get around on foot. It's starting to feel like home. In the past year, I've been little more than a nomad."

I hadn't given much thought about the young man's living arrangements. When I met him on New Year's Day, he'd only recently moved from Houston after graduating from the police academy. He'd taken a job as deputy sheriff in the small town of Palacios. By the end of my stay at The Luther Hotel, his boss, Sheriff Lynol Fogmore, who was determined to make a murder wrap stick to me, even if it meant tampering with evidence, resigned. Dixon was there helping me out of the mess and was impressed with Billy, so Dixon took the young policeman back to Hot Springs where they began, unbeknownst to me, their detective agency.

Dixon threw some change on the table. "Come on." He looked at me and winked.

The three of us strolled back to the San Miguel Apartments. The manager showed us apartment number 201. It was simple, fairly clean, and to our surprise, furnished. All a person needed to move in was a set of sheets, bathroom linens, and a stock of groceries. We heard Billy flush the toilet in the bathroom. He announced that the plumbing worked. Dixon laughed. "I've made my decision. I'll take the cottage and Billy can have the apartment."

"You mean it?" Billy said.

"That is if you like it," Dixon said.

"Sure. It's perfect."

"The place won't be available until next week," the manager

said. "We have to paint. You can sign the lease and put down the deposit today."

"Anyway I can get in any earlier?" Billy asked. "The walls look pretty good to me."

"We might be able to work something out, but the place has to be painted. Rules, you know."

We left Billy and his new manager to work out the details, and drove back to the Granger place to do the same there. By the end of the day, Dixon and I and the poodle were back at the lake watching the sun set beyond the Hill Country. A productive day on the domestic front. Dixon found a place to live. Billy would soon have his own apartment. Monroe had two swims in the lake. Not bad for a leisurely Sunday. I would have enjoyed it more had I known what lay ahead.

Chapter Seven

DIXON, BILLY, AND I stood away from the large crowd gathered around Leland Tatum's final resting place. We weren't actually invited to the graveside service. Stringer glanced over and looked surprised to see us, but nodded his approval. Fiona stood on one side of Eleanor, and a man whom I'd not seen before stood on the other. He wore a dark brown cashmere trench coat. A bit warm for this weather, but the fashionable look went well with his professional manicure and chic haircut. He reminded me of the mannequins used to display Brooks Brothers suits in Scarborough's Department store window. He glanced at Fiona, and I saw a silent message pass between them. Fiona placed her arm around her sister's waist and the guy held her by the elbow. Had it not been for their support, Eleanor would have crumbled. Behind the family stood two men who tried their best not to look like cops.

I spotted the beatniks the same time Stringer did. The scowl on his face and the expletives I read on his lips were no surprise. Had the service not been about to begin, I believe Stringer Maynard would have marched up to Leland's new friends and had words.

The beatniks stood together in a colorful cluster that, for me, added a touch of gaiety to the solemn affair. A lime-colored polka dotted scarf, a navy blue sequined vest, a coppery satin jacket, all worn by the men, competed with a fuchsia cap sprouting a peacock feather, a swirly yellow skirt with a red geranium print, and a skin tight black leather pantsuit all worn by the ladies, who had accentuated their attire with bangles, beads, and boas. This mélange of color and fabric looked like a giant human bouquet. The only one who looked funeral appropriate was Serge LaBeau in his black turtleneck sweater, dark pinstripe sport coat, and gray slacks. But fashion eccentricity had not escaped this guy. On his feet were red and white wingtips.

I nudged Dixon. "The guy in the candy-striped wingtips is Serge LaBeau."

"Interesting."

We watched as the funeral director opened the back of the hearse. The pallbearers slid the casket out, hoisted it up, and ambled over to the grave. Besides Stringer and Edwin, there were four others. I attempted to put names to the men Stringer had described to us. The two guys with tan, leathery skin who looked strong enough to hoist the casket themselves, I figured to be the ranchers Victor Noland and Jones Digmire. The older man was probably Stringer's father-in-law and the other Leland's cousin.

As they approached the gravesite, Eleanor came out of her trance and screamed. The man helping hold her up, whispered something in her ear, but Eleanor began sobbing uncontrollably. He tried again to calm her only to cause her to wail even louder. Fiona turned her sister around and slapped her face. The man, as well as the rest of the crowd gasped, but Fiona merely rolled her eyes and shook her head. As soon as the casket was placed on the frame, Edwin rushed over and put his arms around his mother. He held her until her hysterics turned to quiet sobs.

"Jeez," whispered Billy.

My thoughts exactly. I studied the faces of those attending, for what, I wasn't sure: a guilty, frightened, hateful, remorseful look; someone whose nervousness might look suspicious? No one gave up a clue.

The preacher read one of the Beatitudes. "Blessed are those who mourn, for they shall be comforted." He then took a breath and began to interpret, just in case we weren't intelligent enough to grasp the message. Suddenly, I felt a presence behind me, and before I could turn around, that presence whispered and nearly sent me into the hole with Leland.

"Sorry, I'm late."

I turned to see Ruth, looking like a model on the cover of a *Widow's World*. She wore a jet black tailored suit, stylish pillbox hat with a black veil pulled over her face, and an expensive pair of Ferragamos.

"Close your mouth. You look ridiculous," she said "Don't you know how to dress for a funeral? Slacks and a jacket? Really! You look like you just walked out of a bar. Why didn't you tell me about poor Leland's death? I always have to find out second hand." She stomped her tiny foot. "I barely had enough time to find an appropriate outfit. I had to leave before dawn to make it in time" Then she turned her attention back to the ceremony as the preacher gave the final blessing. Even though it wasn't a Catholic service, Ruth made the sign of the cross and managed to let a tear drop. Before I had a chance to utter a word, Ruth pushed in front of me and joined the group standing behind the family.

"Did you tell her we'd be here?" I asked Dixon.

"I'm innocent," he said.

"Miss Echland looks fantastic," Billy said.

"When doesn't she?" I huffed.

The preacher led Leland Tatum's family and friends in a sweet, but mournful rendition of "Amazing Grace." The casket was lowered into the ground, and then, one by one, the family grabbed a handful of dirt and sent Leland to the afterlife. Stringer chose his words carefully and invited the family and Leland's *family* friends to the ranch for lunch. He turned and shot a stern glare at Leland's odd *compadres* as if to warn them away. The crowd of mourners began to disperse to their cars.

Edwin looked up and cried, "Ruth Echland? Ruthie, is that really you?" He rushed over, grabbed her by the arms and gave her a peck on the cheek. Ruth pulled a black lace hanky from her clutch and dabbed her eye. "Oh, Ed, I was reading my way through the financial section of *The Dallas Morning News* yesterday when I read about the death of your poor, dear father. I'm so sorry. How are you holding up?"

"As best as can be expected. It was a shock. But you look wonderful. The last time I saw you was on campus right before graduation," he said. "I tried to stay in touch, but, well, you know how things go."

"I guess you heard that my father passed away about a year ago," she continued.

"No, I hadn't heard. You have my condolences. That must have been difficult."

"It was horrible. My mother and I sold the ranch soon after. We just couldn't go on living there with Daddy gone."

"One day you should tell Edwin the entire story of your father's demise," I said. One hot and humid afternoon when Uncle Martin was supposed to be at a cattle auction, he died in the arms of his mistress.

"You two know each other?" Edwin asked.

"We're cousins," I said.

Having gotten his answer, Edwin turned to Ruth. "Please come by the house for the luncheon."

"Oh, I couldn't," Ruth said.

"I insist. You're just what I need today; a bright face, a delightful memory. The gloom over the last couple of days is beginning to choke me. Come on, I'll walk you to your car." Ruth looped her arm in his and they left without saying goodbye.

"I told you it was a good idea to invite her to Austin." Dixon said as he came up behind me.

"I didn't know they published death notices in the financial section of the newspaper. But what do I know? I've only been a reporter for a short while."

"You can tell me all about it later. Maybe after a drink."

"Explaining Ruth takes more than one drink. You'll owe me at least two."

Chapter Eight

A THREE-STORY COLONIAL sat facing a pasture of rolling hills surrounded by a white fence. Horses grazed lazily, raising their heads to stare as we motored down the gravel road leading up to the house. The drive curved around a cluster of oak trees, and I caught sight of another house—this one less pretentious—a one-story brick ranch, which sat nestled between an enormous red barn and a well-tended orchard. The fifty yards separating the two houses were dotted with a string of white-washed buildings. Dixon parked behind a row of cars, and as we followed the other guests around the side of the house, someone blasted their horn. We all turned and saw a dark green roadster speeding down the drive. It skidded to a stop and the beatniks spilled out.

"This should be fun," I said.

Mrs. Maynard greeted us when we walked into the garden. A spread of food covered a long table set up by the pool, and people were filling their plates. Waiters walked around handing out cocktails and refilling glasses.

"Nice service," I said to her.

"Such a waste," she scoffed. "Funerals, I mean. The person who died is gone. What does it matter—all the ritual, prayers, hymns? I have no patience for it. People stand around saying things like, 'He would have wanted it this way,' or 'She would have loved all the flowers,' or some other such nonsense."

"Funerals are for the living," Dixon offered.

"If you say so. You're Mr. Dixon, aren't you? We didn't have a chance to meet formally the night my brother-in-law was killed. I'm Fiona Maynard, Stringer's wife."

"I'd say something like, 'I'm sorry for your loss, Mrs. Maynard,' but you'd probably considered it a waste of words."

"I understand the attraction between you two." She smiled at me. "You both possess wit and a certain effrontery." She turned to Billy. He held out his hand and introduced himself. "My husband is waiting for you in the library through those French doors."

We started to head in that direction when she grabbed my arm. "Sydney will join you soon."

Dixon glanced at me.

"I'll catch up with you later," I said.

When Dixon and Billy were out of earshot, she whispered, "I want you to keep me abreast of your investigation."

"You're not the one who hired us, Mrs. Maynard."

"Call me Fiona. I'll pay you twice what my husband's paying you."

"We don't operate that way. I'm sure you understand."

For the first time, Fiona Maynard looked me in the eye, and I saw the depth of her unease. "I told you Stringer is only concerned with how Leland's murder will affect Stringer's future. He talks a good talk about family, friends, but it's just talk. Do what you can, Sydney. Please. I care about my sister, and even if she doesn't spend time in jail, I don't want her labeled a murderer."

I wondered about the relationship between Fiona and Stringer Maynard, a husband and wife who didn't talk, who had their own motives, who kept secrets from one another.

"Where's your sister?" I asked.

"Dr. Richards was under orders from the cops to take her back to the clinic."

"Think it's possible for me to talk to her?"

"What good would that do?"

"She might remember something."

"I'll talk to her again."

"She's guarded with you. If I talk to her, she might be more forthcoming."

"I'm not sure you seeing her is a good idea."

"You came to me for help. Do you want it or not?"

"She is too drugged right now. Besides, the cops won't let anyone but the family near her. I'll see her later today. I've given specific instructions to Dr. Richards to cut back on the sedatives. She was almost comatose during the service."

"Until she began screaming."

Fiona ignored my comment. "Grab some food before this crazy crowd Stringer refers to as friends gobbles everything up."

I wasn't ready to be dismissed, so I plowed ahead. "Are you always so cynical?"

"I was raised with two wisecracking parents," she laughed. "The first words my father said to me after I was born were, 'What took you so damn long? If you're ever late again, I swear I'll send you back to the stork.'" A waiter walked by, and Fiona lifted a champagne cocktail off his tray. She took a sip, giving me a chance to get in a few words.

"Let's say your sister is innocent. Do you have any idea who would murder you brother-in-law and why?"

"Eleanor *is* innocent. And, to tell you the truth, I can think of more people who would want my husband dead rather than Leland."

"Why?"

"Leland, for all my disagreements with him, was a wonderful man. My husband less so."

"If you don't mind my frankness, why are you married to him?"

"I'm sure I'm not the first woman to make a mistake. Don't get me wrong. Stringer and I are good together in certain aspects of our marriage. But for the most part, we go our separate ways."

"How did Eleanor feel about her husband running for governor?"

"Reluctant. It hasn't always been smooth sailing with Leland and Stringer's business. There have been a lot of ups and down. That's to be expected. During those down times, Eleanor and I have always been able to talk about it. Since she's been out of the hospital the past few months, we've grown apart. But I know she's been troubled, especially lately."

"It would be a big responsibility on her shoulders if her husband had won the election. Could she handle being the wife of the governor? Did Stringer consider it when he began this venture?"

"You mean would people vote for a man whose wife was in and out of a mental hospital? I'm sure my husband planned for Leland to get some sympathy votes out of that."

I glanced over at Leland's artist friends. "Could Leland have been seeing another woman?"

"I can't picture Leland doing that."

"If there was another woman, Eleanor had a motive for killing him."

"Trust me, it wasn't Eleanor." Suddenly, the woman's stern bossiness returned. "My sister will not spend one moment in jail. Not one moment. I'll see what I can do about you seeing her. I'll let you know. Excuse me. I've got guests to attend to." She started to leave and then added, "I'll say it again; it wasn't me, so get that absurd thought out of your mind. Now, who is that woman batting her eyes at Edwin?"

I watched her walk away, more puzzled than ever by her attitude toward her sister.

I spotted Ruth on the far side of the garden entertaining Edwin Tatum, and she was indeed batting her eyes. When she saw me, she gave Edwin a little hug and dismissed him. She strolled over. "I can't believe the things I stoop to doing to help you," she said. "Prostrating myself is simply disgusting."

"You mean prostituting."

"That's what I said."

"You are so good at it, though, and you looked like you were enjoying yourself. Now cut the act. How well did you know Edwin in college?"

"We dated a while."

"And his family?"

"I'd never met them, but I remember Ed talking about his father and an Uncle Stringer. I tried to get a room at The Driskill before driving over, but I can't get in until tomorrow night. I went down to the Stephen F. Austin Hotel, but they were booked too. Seems there's a convention in town, engineers. What do a bunch of train drivers have to meet about anyway? I refuse to stay with you and that devil cat."

"My heart is broken. And Mealworm was so looking forward to stalking you."

"Funny." She pulled out her menthol cigarettes, screwed one into a holder, and lit up. "You'll have to find me a place to stay tonight, and it had better be acceptable."

Dixon and Billy joined us. "Hello, Miss Echland," Billy cooed. "It's always good to see you."

"I'm glad someone feels that way."

"Ruth and Edwin knew each other in college." I explained my cousin's presence.

Dixon gave her a hug. "How are things going at the Home?"

"Fine," she said, "once you were kind enough to explain the nonprofit thing." She shot me a dirty look. "I felt I could leave the business to Marcella, at least for a few days. So, I'm here to help. But I need a place to stay tonight. Most of the hotels are booked. It's the pathetic story of my life."

"I think I can find you a room, Miss Echland," Billy said. "I just need to make a phone call."

"Call me Ruth, since we're practically family." She grabbed his hand and pulled him toward the buffet table. "Let's get some food and you can tell me what you have in mind."

"Find out anything?" I asked Dixon.

"Not much. Stringer is going to show me the business's books and I'll see what I can dig up. How about you?"

"I'm just getting started. Fiona Maynard is adamant her sister didn't kill Leland."

"The evidence is circumstantial. No one actually saw her pull the trigger. Nevertheless, she was upset that day, and linking that with her mental problems offers a prosecutor a damn good case. Before we can eliminate her as a suspect, we need to see if she had a motive."

"Fiona is going to see about getting me into the clinic to talk to Eleanor."

"Good. Keep mingling before these people leave. Talk to some of Tatum's friends. The guy in the brown suit is Jones Digmire, the ranch foreman. The one next to him is Victor Nolan. Good luck. We'll meet up later."

Dixon wondered off. I noticed Serge LaBeau talking to some guy near the buffet table. The two men appeared to struggle to keep the conversation going, so I thought I'd butt in.

"Hi, Mr. LaBeau, nice to see you again." I introduced myself to the other guy as a family friend. He introduced himself as Tony Gill, Leland's cousin. He shook my hand and made a lame excuse to leave.

"I noticed some of Leland's artist friends, but I'm surprised to see you here, Mr. LaBeau."

"You didn't tell anyone about me coming to see you, did you?" He swayed and grabbed hold of the nearby chair to steady himself. The drink in his hand was not his first.

"Only my partners."

"I don't want it getting back to Stringer."

"Why are you afraid of him?"

"Afraid? That's a good word." He finished off the rest of his drink. "Excuse me, Miss Lockhart. Afraid—I'm not."

I watched Serge LaBeau push his way through the crowd and into the house. This was the second gathering Stringer Maynard invited me to, and I hoped it wouldn't end as tragically as the first. I started to follow LaBeau to see where his anger would take him, but Tony Gill walked up.

"That's one odd person," he said. "He doesn't fit in with this crowd."

"It takes all kinds. Are you from Austin, Mr. Gill?"

"Midland area. Leland and I grew up together, but after college, we saw one another only during family gatherings, which grew infrequent as time went on. Seems once Leland met Stringer and the *sisters*, he didn't get back up home much. I regret not making more of an effort to see my cousin when I had the chance. He came to town to do some banking recently and called to see if I could meet him for lunch. I was too busy. I missed my chance and will never have another. How can anyone be too busy for family? Were you a friend of Leland and Eleanor?"

I had to be careful here. "I'm actually a friend of Fiona's."

"Fiona? I didn't know she had friends. Sorry, that was a tacky thing to say."

"I wish, though, that I'd had the chance to know Leland better. He seemed like a wonderful person, and I heard he was a talented artist."

"Leland had such great potential. He used to talk about going to Europe to study."

"What happened?"

"Oh, life, you know. He met Eleanor, got married, went into business with his brother-in-law."

"Did you know he was planning to finance an art and cultural center in Austin?"

"That's more like the Leland I knew—the entire governor thing— that was so unlike my cousin."

"Seems odd someone would take on a huge project and campaign for governor at the same time."

"You may be able to figure that out better than me." Gill paused, and I got that same hard stare that LaBeau had given me. "...since you're a friend of the Maynards." The edge in his voice was sharp enough to slice through this conversation. "Enjoyed talking to you, Miss Lockhart, but I've got a long drive ahead of me." He tipped his hat and left.

I went in search of LaBeau, wondering what business he'd plan to take care of when shouts from inside the house erupted.

"You'll pay for this, Maynard! I'll make sure."

The patio doors were wide open and I caught sight of Stringer and LaBeau facing off in the den.

"Get out of here, you drunken son-of-a-bitch." Stringer looked as if he were about to pop a vein. He tried to grab LaBeau's arm, but LaBeau's right hook struck Stringer and sent him flying. Victor Nolan and Jones Digmire rushed over to break it up. LaBeau pushed them aside and kicked over an end table. He shoved his way through a small crowd that had now gathered at the door, but turned back. "Your name won't be on that ballot if I have anything to say about it."

Dixon rushed out of the library just as Jones Digmire ushered LaBeau toward the front door. He managed a couple more wild swings and caught Digmire below the eye. His reaction was one that surprised me. He looked more hurt than angry. The following short exchange surprised me too.

"Jonesy," LaBeau said. "Man, I didn't mean to do that."

"Go home, Serge. Sleep it off before Stringer calls the cops. I'll call you later."

"Oh, man," LaBeau said and ambled off.

I watched as Dixon scanned the room. When he caught Billy's eye, Dixon motioned for our young partner to follow LaBeau. Before the front door closed, I saw Billy catch up with LaBeau and offer him a cigarette. The young detective had a way with disgruntled people, and hopefully, he'd discover the cause of the guy's aggression.

Dixon came over. "If the tension at this funeral luncheon gets any worse, I'm afraid we'll have a good ol' Texas brawl on our hands."

"I'll talk to Jones Digmire," I said. "Seems he and Serge LaBeau know one another well."

"Good idea. I'm not finished going over the books. We'll be a while. After I leave here, I'm going back to the office. I'll see you there later." Dixon handed me his keys. "Take my car. I'll get a ride with Billy. Good luck talking to Digmire."

"First, I'm going to see to Ruth."

"You make me sound like a sack of chicken feed," Ruth said, walking up behind me. "I'm here by invitation of your boyfriend, remember?"

Ruth had the uncanny knack for materializing out of the fog even when there wasn't one. "As if you had anything else to do with your time. Speaking of helping, see that guy over there?" I pointed to a husky, middle-aged man with an angular, chiseled face and wavy auburn hair. "His name is Victor Nolan. He is a neighboring rancher. See what you can find out from him concerning Leland Tatum. Think you can turn on the charm?"

"In this outfit? Piece of cake."

"Be circumspect."

"Circumcised; that's my middle name."

I'd like to believe that Ruth wasn't the bubblehead she pretended to be, but I could never be sure.

Jones Digmire was next on my list. I found him in the den, digging ice out of a champagne bucket. "Here, let me." I found a napkin, placed a few cubes inside, and touched it gently to Digmire's now-swelling eye.

"You're that detective woman."

"Sydney Lockhart. How did you know?"

"Hell, Stringer called me in yesterday and told me he hired some private detectives to investigate Leland. I don't know who Stringer Maynard thinks he is."

"He's your boss."

"Leland was my boss. Maynard is a meddling asshole."

"I've known Stringer Maynard a short time and I've heard him called several awful names."

"No surprise. And now he's trying to find some dirt on anyone who worked with Leland. He was the best friend and the best boss a man could have. There was nothing odd going on with Leland. I've been running this ranch for ten years, but I'll be damned if I stick around and take orders from Stringer Maynard and watch him run this place into the ground. Now that Leland is gone, there's no holding back that lunatic."

"Stringer must have his reasons. He said that Leland was acting strange lately, moody, argumentative."

"Well knock me over with a feather. If Leland wanted any sort of life of his own, he'd have to make sure his partner wasn't aware of it, otherwise, Stringer would have his nose into that business too."

"Like the Art and Cultural Center?"

"Yeah, like that."

"Mr. Digmire, Stringer contacted our agency only a few hours before Leland was killed. He was concerned about Leland's involvement in their business and how it would affect the gubernatorial race. Maybe that involvement led to Leland's murder."

"Leland no more wanted to be governor of Texas than my pet duck. I've been over this with the police. Why should I discuss it with you? You're working for Stringer Maynard, and for that reason, I'd rather not have any dealings with you." He threw the ice cubes in the bucket and stormed out.

I left the house and went in search of my cousin. On the front lawn, I found Fiona and the mannequin-looking guy in the cashmere trench coat in a heated exchange, except he no longer appeared stoic and self-centered. His face was white, and I could tell he was talking through gritted teeth. Fiona smirked and walked away.

I found Ruth looking intently under the hood of her Caddy. She pointed to something and folded her arms. That's when I saw Victor Nolan fiddling with the engine, chatting a mile a minute. He took his handkerchief from his jacket pocket, wiped his hands, and slammed the hood shut. He and Ruth exchanged a few more words and he left. I walked over as Ruth wiped a smudge off her shiny hood.

"Did you know my car has a V8?" she said.

"You mean you didn't ask that when you bought the car?"

"The Caddy has four tires, a steering wheel, a radio, and a color that matches my eyes. What more is there to know?"

"Did you learn anything from Nolan?"

"I most certainly did. We almost got off to a bad start, though. I was about to slap the guy before I even started my interrogation. I saw him standing here, ogling over my Caddy. I offered him a cigarette. He pointed to the car and said, 'Snazzy. I wonder who owns it.' I said I did. He said he'd like to look under my hood. Imagine that! I may look sweet and innocent, but I recognize a pickup line when I hear it. I was momentarily shocked until I realized he was talking about the car."

"It's a good thing you're so swift."

"Damn right. Did you know *I* have a fuel pump?"

"You're joking!"

"Well, it's true. And there's this huge accordion-looking thing that has water running through it to cool the engine. Now I understand why the car was so expensive. I really got my money's worth."

"Did you interrogate the guy or not?"

"It was difficult directing the conversation away from dip shits and hoses to murder."

"Dip stick."

"That's what I said. But I found my cue when he asked if he could listen to the engine. I said sure go ahead, that I'd like to hear it too. But I couldn't hear a damn thing. I leaned closer and I still couldn't hear anything. He just laughed and told me to start the engine first. I would have felt stupid, except that I'm so above that. Anyway, I started the engine and he asked me to gun it. I told him that I certainly would not 'gun it.' The car is barely six months old. Why in the hell would I blow a hole in the motor? Besides, I told him, I'd left my antique Derringer in my other purse. So, I said, 'speaking of guns,' and told him how awful it was Leland was murdered before he even had a chance to run for governor." Ruth raised her chin and smiled. "How about that?"

I looked across the fence at two horses grazing in the field. They looked so peaceful; I wanted to join them.

"Well, aren't you going to say something?"

"I'm speechless."

"That's okay. I amaze myself sometimes. Do you want to know what I found out or not?"

"I'm listening." God help me.

"After we talked for a while about how shocking Leland's murder was, I asked if he had any idea why Leland's wife would kill her husband. Great question, huh?"

"Brilliant."

"I thought so. Anyway, he said he was as surprised as anyone, but that she did have mental problems."

"We know that."

"Stop interrupting me. Then I asked him how he thought Stringer could run the business by himself."

"That's a good question. What did he say?"

"He scoffed and said that no one could replace Leland Tatum and that Stringer was in for a shock if he thought he could manage things on his own. I get the instinct impression he dislikes Stringer Maynard."

"Distinct."

"That's what I said."

"What else?"

"He said he'd enjoy nothing more than watching Stringer Maynard fall on his face and lose everything."

"That seems to be the consensus of most of everyone here. Anything else?"

"That's not enough?"

"It only adds to what we already know. Tatum was a good guy and Maynard is not."

"Oh, here comes Billy. Hey, handsome," Ruth called.

"Everything okay with your car, Ruth? I saw you had the hood up."

"Everything is dandy. I needed to check on the fuel pump and a few other things. Did you know my Caddy has —"

Listening to Ruth wax eloquent about her Caddy, I was not willing to do. "Billy, did you find out what that scuffle was about?"

"LaBeau was too angry and too drunk. He said he'd had

enough and planned to stop Stringer in his tracks; that it was the least he could do for his friend. I couldn't get much more out of him. How about you? Find out anything?"

"I did, but I don't want to discuss it here. We'll meet at the office later."

"Count me out," Ruth said. "Billy's found me a room at his hotel. I'm going to check in and then Edwin's taking me to dinner."

"He's not spending the evening with his family?" I asked.

"You heard him. He needs some cheering up, and who better to do that than me."

"See if you can do a better job getting information out of your date than you did with Nolan. Something was definitely bothering Edwin Tatum at the party."

"Just leave it to me." Ruth tapped her forehead. "I'll put this fabulous brain to work, don't worry."

"Ever thought of using jumper cables on that brain?" I asked.

"Go ahead and joke, since you get such sadistic pleasure out of insulting me. I'll call you tomorrow, Miss Smarty Pants."

I smiled at the thought of Ruth staying at The Alamo Hotel tonight. I should have felt guilty about my sadistic pleasure in that regard, but I didn't.

The crowd had thinned. There wasn't much else to be gained by hanging around, so I headed for Dixon's car when Fiona called my name.

"Here's the address of the clinic. I've arranged for you to see Eleanor tomorrow at two."

Before I could thank her, she walked away.

Chapter Nine

AFTER I LEFT THE RANCH, I drove to the *American* and put in an afternoon of work. For once, it was quiet around the newsroom. I typed up my notes from the funeral and worked on a small follow-up piece on the Tatum murder, finessing the facts while trying to avoid including too many of my personal suspicions. After a couple of drafts, I had a final and was about to put it in Ernest's inbox when I heard him in his office arguing with someone. I had assumed he was gone for the day since his door had been closed all afternoon. I heard him slam down the receiver and moments later he jerked open the door, hat and coat in hand, ready to walk out.

Caught in an awkward moment, we stood there for what seemed like forever when he finally said, "Sydney."

"I'd just finished the follow-up on the Tatum murder," I said holding up the story as proof I had not been eavesdropping.

"The Tatum murder, yes, right. I guess you heard that." He nodded toward his office.

"No, well, just a few curse words before you hung up the phone."

He put on his coat and checked his watch. "Time for a drink?"

It was almost time to meet Dixon at the agency, but seeing the look of someone who desperately needed an ear, I said sure.

Henry's Place was two doors down. It was a news reporters' hang out, and that's where I assumed we were heading. When Ernest passed it by and turned into The Eli Club, I knew whatever was bothering him was personal. We took two seats at the bar.

"Hey, Ted," Ernest said to the bartender. "I'll have a draft. Sydney?"

"Make that two," I said. When Ernest remained silent, I suddenly realized I had it all wrong. He didn't need someone to talk to. He'd made his decision. I feared I'd just written my last story for the paper.

"It's okay, Ernest. I understand."

"You do?"

"I'll clear out my desk in the morning."

"Clear out your what? For Christ sake, girl, not everything revolves around you."

"Then what is it?"

"After twenty-six year of marriage, I'm living alone." He downed half his beer. "I don't know why I'm telling you."

"What happened?"

"Usual stuff. Long hours, cancelled weekend plans. Vera told me she was tired of it all; told me I was married to my work. What could I say? She was right. She wanted us to see a—what do you call it?—marriage counselor. When I refused, she went herself. After a few weeks of seeing this counselor guy, I told her she was wasting my money and the guy was a quack."

"Well, hey, Ernest, I'm sure she thanked you for being so understanding."

"She moved out last week and is staying with her sister in Waco. I finally called her today. That was the argument you heard. I told her she was being stupid and to get her ass back home. I don't think that was what she wanted to hear."

"Honestly, I seriously doubt she's packing her bags to come home."

"You think?" Ernest threw four bits on the bar. "I'm sure you got places to go and people to see, and I got a lonely dog to feed. Thanks for listening."

"Maybe you should do that."

"What?"

"Listen to what Vera has to say."

"In my business, who has time to listen? If I did that, nothing would get done."

"Sounds like nothing's gotten done on the home front, either." I thanked Ernest for the beer and left, feeling damn lucky I had a man in my life who, although I didn't always know what he was thinking, listened to every word I said.

WHEN I WALKED INTO THE OFFICE, Billy was on the phone, and

Dixon was poring over his notes at his desk. They looked as haggard as I felt.

"How's it going?" I asked. "Find anything in the books?"

"Not a damn thing. Edwin came in after a while and helped me. We scrutinized every ledger, correspondence, memo—nothing. Everything looks legit."

"What was Edwin's take on the situation?"

"He thinks his uncle is paranoid."

"I wouldn't call him paranoid. I'd call him obsessed. I know everyone seems to believe the sun rose and set with Leland Tatum, but Stringer must have his reasons," I said. "Could there be two sets of books?"

"That's certainly a possibility. Billy's in the back room on the phone now talking to Huffman at West Texas Oil. How about you? Learn anything?"

"Digmire let go of an interesting tidbit of information," I said. "He claimed Leland Tatum did not want to run for governor. Digmire refused to say more because he knew we were working for Maynard, but the guy was hacked. Oh, I have an appointment at the clinic to see Eleanor Tatum tomorrow afternoon."

Billy came in and tossed his notebook on the desk.

"What did you find out?" Dixon asked.

"Huffman pretty much confirmed what Maynard had told us about having to renegotiate the contract. But he said it was Maynard who was the one picking over the contract, not Tatum. Huffman wouldn't say much more, company confidences." Billy sat down and tilted his chair back against the wall. "What now?"

Dixon threw down his pencil and rubbed his face. "I never, for one, believed Stringer told us the entire story. He's not leveling with us. There's not much more we can do today. I'll give Maynard a call first thing in the morning. How about the old man's will?"

"I'm heading back to the New Light Church now," Billy said.

"Fine. I've some unpacking to do at the cottage." He came out from behind his desk with that look in his eye.

"I'm out of here," Billy said and he was gone before he had a chance to blush.

"Want to come along?" Dixon asked.

"I do, but I'm beat. I'm going home to take a nice hot bath and get to bed early."

"Good luck with Eleanor tomorrow, hon." He nuzzled my ear and said something that sounded like dove, or shove, or glove. I uttered something that sounded like me too, and I fled in Billy's wake.

I went straight home, walked Monroe, fed the demon cat, and poured myself a glass of wine. On the way to the bathroom to draw a hot bath, the phone rang.

"Sydney, it's Marcella."

"What's up?"

"You're a busy lady. I tried calling your apartment several times and then the newspaper, but couldn't catch you. I thought it better I talk to you first."

"Uh oh," I said.

Marcella laughed. "Don't worry, it's not that bad. We've had an expectant mother check in a couple of days ago. She insists on talking to Ruth. She wouldn't say why. When I held tight to my refusal, she finally told me she and Ruth were best friends in high school and that she desperately needed a friend. She and Ruth had lost touch, but she said Ruth was always someone she could turn to."

"That doesn't sound like my cousin."

"My thoughts too, but Mary Thompson will not take no for an answer. Maybe if Ruth could call the Home and have a quick chat with the woman, it would be enough to calm her down. She's pretty distraught."

"When is she due?"

"Very soon."

"I'll pass along the message. Otherwise, how are things going?"

"Fine. We have five young women here, and Nurse Abernathy is working out well. But, there's another issue. I've tried talking to Ruth."

"Say no more. What is it?"

"She set us up with an adoption service. The agency is one of the best around, but their fees are exorbitant. They mainly cater to the wealthy who will pay anything to find a child to adopt. I don't think we are ready to take on that expense."

"She told me about that. What do you suggest?"

"I'd like to provide our own adoption service. We could cut out the middleman. Sure, we'd have to add extra staff to care for the babies, but we have plenty of room, and instead of our money going to another agency, we could invest it here and offer more complete care."

"And Ruth won't listen. Let me work on her. You can't put too much into that brain at once. With meddling in my business, maintaining her wardrobe, and starting up the Home, she's running on all eight cylinders. I'll see what I can do about Mary Thompson too. You're a Godsend, Marcella. Ruth's lucky to have you, not just to run the Home, but as a sister."

"Thanks, but it's a two-way street. I needed a break from the law practice. How's the detective business?"

"Shaping up, maybe too quickly. We've been hired to investigate this guy's business partner, but before we could add a label on the new file, the partner was murdered."

"This wouldn't be the future gubernatorial candidate I read about, would it?"

"One and the same."

"Nothing like starting off your business with a notorious case. I'm sure my half-sister will be a big help to you."

"Your sarcasm is so subtle, Marcella. Be careful, or I'll send her back to Dallas."

"Whoops. Me and my big mouth. I'm hanging up before I invite more trouble."

Marcella was partners with another lawyer in Houston. Their business was booming, but the work had taken its toll on Marcella's health. When Ruth asked her to run the Home, Marcella turned the law practice over to her partner and moved to Dallas to take charge.

I don't remember Ruth mentioning a friend named Mary Thompson, but we went to different high schools. It's not unreasonable that Ruth would have a best friend, however, being a comfort and confidant seemed unlikely. Ruth was always the one who needed comforting, and I was the one she turned to every time.

I'd deal with Ruth tomorrow. Right now, my only concern was a hot bath. I poured in a good helping of bubble bath and eased myself into the tub when my doorbell rang. I knew it wasn't Dixon, and there was no one else I wanted to see. I shut off the water and listened. Another ring, and all was quiet. It was probably Mr. Grimwell, my neighbor, wondering when I'd pull the weeds out front of my apartment. I was past due for his weekly yard-maintenance lecture. Last time he came over complaining about my dead geraniums. I handed him my hand shovel and told him to help himself. I'd just turned the water back on, slid under the lavender-scented foam, took a sip of wine, and contemplated Dixon's last intimate remark. We'd had a hot and heavy courtship the last few months, but the mention of love had not come up. I closed my eyes and allowed those words to resonate in my head. Suddenly, my bathroom door flew open.

Chapter Ten

"WHAT THE HELL ARE YOU DOING?"

I dropped my wine, turning my crystal blue bubbles a blood red. "What the hell does it look like, and what the hell are you doing here?"

Ruth put the toilet seat down and sat. "Hurry up and get out. I could certainly use a bath after traipsing all over that dusty ranch today. You should see my stockings and shoes—brown with dirt. Here," she handed me a stack of envelopes. "Don't you ever check your mail? You have a bill from the light company and a letter from your dad. Finish up while I pour myself a glass of that wine. It had better be a good vintage after what I did for you today."

"How did you get in?"

"That weird neighbor let me in. If he has a key, why can't I have one?" She kicked off her shoes and walked into the kitchen.

Had the most desirable man on the planet not been my boyfriend, I would have drowned myself. I fished out my glass, drained the tub, and donned my robe. I found Ruth in the living room, reading a magazine and drinking my wine. Then my breath caught when I saw her luggage by the door.

"This sofa is comfy. You should sleep well," she said. "And it's a good thing I brought my own magazines. You have nothing of value to read. Those women in *National Geographies* have the fashion sense of a pagan. They don't even bother with blouses."

"*National Geographic*; and they are pagans. Let me guess. The Alamo Hotel wasn't up to standard."

"Hardly! The door was opened to the room next to mine, and there was this half-naked man passed out on the bed. His snores rattled the walls. The sheets on my bed were dingy yellow, and there were no hangers in the closet. Staying with you isn't much better, but it will be for one night only. Thank God I will be at The Driskill tomorrow night once those train guys leave."

"Billy will be crushed. He had to pull some strings to get you a room."

"I'll make it up to him."

"Did you ever think I might have plans tonight?"

"Go ahead with your plans, you won't bother me. Just make sure the poodle and that cougar stay out of the bedroom." The cougar, hearing her sobriquet, slunk into the room, tail high, ears back, eyes focused. In one smooth jump, she positioned herself on the arm of the sofa and locked her eyes on Ruth.

"Tell her to go away," Ruth said, sliding away from the cat.

"She won't."

"Pick her up and take her into the kitchen, then."

"She'll come back."

"Lock her in the damn closet."

"She'll just flatten herself and slide under the door."

"She hates me."

"She hates everyone except Dixon. Me, she tolerates."

Once her position of authority was established, Mealworm bounded off the sofa and planted herself under the kitchen table where she could keep an eye on her domain. She folded her paws neatly under her chest and began tail-twitching, back and forth, like a metronome keeping time until the humans would disappear and leave her in peace.

Relieved, Ruth grabbed her magazine. "Cats are supposed to be warm and cuddly. That one needs to live in the jungle."

"Now that you're here, tell me about your dinner date with Edwin."

"We went to El Rancho, a tiny little restaurant on East First Street. This husband and wife ran it. They were so cute. She was in the kitchen cooking and he was serving out front. There were only a few tables. I had a cocktail made with fresh lime juice and tequila. They called it a Margarita. And get this, the guy used to be a boxer. He was so good, they gave him golden gloves. Can you imagine that? They must be worth a fortune."

"I'm not interested in some quaint, little eatery you discovered. Did you learn anything from Edwin?"

"Of course. He said the oddest thing. Do you have a pencil?"

"A pencil! What the hell did he want with a pencil?"

She rolled her eyes and reminded me again how dense I was. "It's for me."

I pulled a pencil off my desk and pitched it over, thinking she wanted to make some notes. Instead, she scribbled something on the magazine.

"Anyway, Edwin said what he felt more than anything about his father's death was regret."

"Regret?"

"Because of his mother's mental problems, Edwin spent a lot of time with the aunt and uncle. When he was at home, it was hard for him, growing up with his mother's depression. He always felt he was walking on eggshells, fearful something bad would happen. His thoughts were always with his mother and not with Leland. That's why he feels regretful and sad he didn't spend more time with his parents."

"Understandable. At least his mother's been home for the past few months. Evidently, she was doing better."

"Phooey. Edwin said she almost had a breakdown the day before Leland was killed. He wouldn't say any more and changed the subject. Do you have any tequila? The wine is not up to my standards, either. While I finish this, you can make me a Margarita and draw me a bath. You need limes and sugar. I like lots of bubbles."

Ruth could string together four different subjects all in one sentence. The scary thing was I've learned to understand much of what she said.

"No tequila, no limes. Draw your own bath." I refilled my wine glass and drank half of it down. "What are you doing, anyway?"

"I'm answering questions for this sensitivity survey in this month's issue of *Vogue*. How would you rate my listening skills on a range of one to ten?"

"Uhhh...one."

"No, stupid. One is the worst and ten is the best."

"Oh, uh...one."

"Okay," she took her pencil and filled in an answer. "Nine. I'll be the first to admit I'm not perfect. Next question: how sympathetic am I towards friends who are in trouble; one to ten?"

"Two."

"Ten," she said.

"It's a good thing your listening skills are so sharp."

"Okay, that was the last question. Let's see. I scored in the top range and am considered the best possible friend any one could ever have." She shot me a perky smile and tossed me the magazine.

"I'm not doing it," I said.

"You don't have to. I took the survey for you, and you scored a three."

"That high?"

"Well, I cut you some slack on a few questions."

"How am I classified, then?"

"Self-centered and untrustworthy. But don't worry. I'll always be here for you."

"I'm blessed."

"I hope you didn't drain the hot water heater." She opened her suitcase, pulled out her bathrobe and headed for the bathroom. "You can put my stuff in your bedroom."

When she closed the bathroom door, I banged my head against the wall—hard—four times.

"Whoever's knocking, I'm not here." I heard Ruth giggle. I made up the sofa and opened a second bottle of my substandard wine.

Chapter Eleven

I HAD HOPED TO SLEEP later than usual, but having Ruth staying over meant I needed to get up before she did or I wouldn't see the inside of my bathroom until next week. I finished my ablutions and went into the kitchen. Ruth was seated at the kitchen table. She tried to talk me into making her Eggs Benedict. I ignored her request and set a box of cornflakes in front of her. The toast had popped up just as the phone rang. "Hello? Oh, hi. Yes, Billy, she's right here."

Ruth shook her head as I handed her the phone. "Oh, Billy, honey, I'm so glad you called." She pulled a tissue from the box I keep on the phone table. "I'm so sorry I had to leave the Alamo Hotel." Tears sprang from her eyes like a deluge from a thundercloud. "No, no, it was a lovely room. But Sydney called and woke me up around midnight. She said she was deathly ill and pleaded for me to come over and stay with her. So, I checked out, I paid for the room of course, and rushed over here." She blew her nose. "No, she's fine now. Just overreacted. It was probably something she ate. She was carrying on so badly, I thought her spleen had burst."

"Appendix," I said.

"And her appendix. I thought her spleen and appendix had burst. You're right, it doesn't sound like Sydney." She lowered her voice to a whisper. "To tell the truth, I think my cousin had a wee bit too much to drink last night. But everything is fine now. Yes, yes, I'll tell her. And thanks so much for your help. You're such a sweetheart." She hung up and lifted her coffee cup. "Refill, please. When you go to your detective office today, try to look a little pale, will you. Billy is such a darling young man."

"Your lies don't surprise me, but you need to be careful with the honey and sweetheart stuff. Billy might get the wrong idea." I drained the coffee from the pot into *my* cup.

"Oh, you're right. I don't want to encourage the young man. I can certainly understand his attraction. Such a boy, and boys are so...what's the word? —vulnerable."

I was impressed with her correct use of vocabulary, but did not pass on the compliment for obvious reason. "Billy's only a couple of years younger than you."

"I'll do my best to gently discourage him."

"Oh, I almost forgot. Marcella called last night before you barged in. Do you know a woman named Mary Thompson? She claims you were best friends in high school."

"Mary Thompson?" Ruth slammed her coffee cup on the kitchen counter.

"She's just checked into the Home and is about to deliver any day now. Marcella said Mary insists she talk to you because you were such a comfort to her in high school."

"Mary's in the Home? I'm not surprised. She had such a rep. She was always hanging around me trying to butt in on everything I did."

"Well, you'd better call. According to your *Vogue* survey, you're 'the best possible friend any one could ever have.'"

"We were not best friends."

"She thought you were. Just call the damn woman."

"I'll put it on the top of my list with a big red star by it. Now, since you refuse to be more hospitable, I'll pack my things, check into The Driskill, and go to work."

"See if you can get a room on the fifth floor. Don't do anything until Dixon and I have had a chance to discuss it."

"Sure, I'll just nose around a bit."

"Ruth!"

AN HOUR LATER, I had my apartment to myself. I dressed quickly, fed the animals, and left. I stopped by the office before I went to the newspaper. Dixon and Billy walked in right behind me.

"How are you feeling, Sydney?"

"Better this morning. Thanks for asking, Billy."

"You were ill?" Dixon said.

"Possible rupture of the spleen and appendix. Once Ruth left, the symptoms disappeared."

"Amazing," Dixon smiled and gave the first of what I hoped would be many displays of affection for the day. I grabbed my notes, and we gathered around the table to discuss the case.

Billy walked up to the corkboard and pulled off an index card with "Paul Noonie" written on it. "We can close the missing-will case," he said. "I went by the New Light Church again. The office was open and a secretary asked if I was there to leave a donation. I told her I'd like to speak to Reverend Lindy. She informed me Reverend was still ill. I drove out to the West Side Country Club, and guess who I found?"

"The good reverend playing tennis with his buddies?"

"*Her* buddies. Reverend Lindy is Susan Lindy. She was tan and healthy and gorgeous. I nosed around and discovered that Lindy spends a lot of time at the country club schmoozing wealthy old codgers."

"Who are easily talked into writing checks to save their souls?" Dixon asked.

"It was clear to me that Mr. Noonie was not as interested in saving his soul as much as spending time with Miss Lindy. I managed to spend a few minutes with her in the clubhouse. Her eyes lit up when I told her one of her parishioners had recently died. She turned crestfallen when I mentioned he'd been married. She said he told her he was a widower. At this point, she dropped the nice-lady façade and wanted to know who the hell I was and why I was asking questions. I showed her my license. Her tennis partner came up and asked if I was bothering her. She introduced him as her lawyer and told me to leave before she called security. On my way out, I mentioned the words "scam" and "will" and told her I was happy she was feeling better, and that maybe I'd see her in church on Sunday. The lawyer caught up to me in the parking lot and said he'd drawn up the codicil himself and it was ironclad. I told him our client, Mrs. Noonie, would be glad to discuss the situation in court."

"I hope Mrs. Noonie has a good lawyer," Dixon said.

"Better than that," Billy said. "I stopped by to see her and give her the news. Her brother is the state's assistant attorney general. I predict the light in the New Light Church will soon go out. Here's Mrs. Noonie's check for double the amount."

"Great work, Billy," Dixon said.

At moments like this, I was certain I'd made the right decision to turn investigator. I hated swindlers and thought back to the mess my grandfather had stepped into in Galveston almost twenty years ago; the mess that got him killed and years later led to three other murders. I shook those thoughts from my head. "Where do we start today?" I asked.

"Let's go back to the beginning," Dixon said. "Stringer Maynard called the office to hire us to investigate his partner because of his reluctance to sign a new contract with an oil company and because of his involvement with the artists. Later that afternoon, Tatum was murdered. We need to start checking alibis for any loopholes."

"One thing puzzles me," Billy said. "Stringer didn't mention to us that Tatum didn't want to run for governor. Do you think Stringer knew how Tatum felt?"

Dixon thought for a moment and then said, "I'm sure Stringer knew, but it probably didn't matter to him."

Billy began making notes for the board.

"When Billy and I walked into the Yellow Rose Suite," I said, "Eleanor and Fiona were talking with a group of people. Eleanor was upset, and Fiona made an offhanded comment about her sister being off her stride lately. Eleanor rose to leave, saying that was a funny way of putting it. Fiona tried to stop her from leaving, but Eleanor pulled away. Moments later, we heard a shot, and she was standing there with a gun in her hand. It *looked* like a simple murder."

"From my experience, murders are usually cut and dried," Dixon said. "Whenever there's something that doesn't look right, it most likely isn't."

"Like the blood on the hem of her dress and the body being moved slightly, " Billy added.

"What do we do now?" I asked.

"I want to know if Stringer was aware how Tatum felt about running for governor," Dixon said. "Billy, pay another visit out to the ranch. Digmire knows something. See if you can shake him down." He turned to me. "Go see Eleanor at the clinic, Syd, and see what you can find out. Serge is yours, too, if you want him. Seeing as how he turned up at your bathroom window, I say you two have a rapport."

"Sure. My life needs a bit of color. Ruth's at The Driskill. I'll stop by there first."

"Have her start with the housekeepers," Dixon said. "Let's meet back here at five. And be careful, hon."

Billy headed for the door and I was right behind when the phone rang. We both paused while Dixon answered. "Detective Agency, Dixon here." He waved us back in. "What's this about, Mr. Digmire?" I sat back down and Billy closed the door. "I see. Yes, right. See you later this afternoon." He hung up. "Looks like you don't have to make a trip out to the ranch after all. Jones Digmire wants to see us. Said he needs our help. He didn't say much else except that he'd be here around six. Now I really want to talk to Stringer Maynard before Digmire arrives. I'll see if Maynard can meet me here in town. I don't want Digmire to see me on the ranch. He might change his mind about talking to us. Billy, stick around. I could use you here."

"Good luck," I said. "See you guys later."

Chapter Twelve

THERE WAS A NOTE from Ernest on my desk. I'd been summoned again. His door was open, so I didn't bother knocking. It appeared as if my boss had had a rough night. His gray hair stood up and the bags under his eyes had slid down another inch.

"You look bad," I said.

"Love you too. Have a seat. Got an anonymous call this morning about some questionable accounting practices in the business office over at the University. Two guys were shot last night at the Crooked J, and there's another bacteria outbreak at Barton Springs. The city health department had to close the pool to swimmers for the next few days, not to mention, I had to make my own breakfast."

Had Ernest not looked so bad, I would have lectured him on proper expectations in a marriage and then kicked him in the shin to make my point clear. But I didn't. "Which story do you want me to take?"

He tossed his pencil stub in the air and gave me that look. "None. I want you on the Leland Tatum case. The cops don't know squat. What's your take on it?"

Our staring contest lasted a total of five seconds before I shifted my gaze out his window. I walked over and closed the door. "That coffee smells like it was made last week." A glass percolator sat on a burner, a thin layer of dark sludge bubbling in the bottom.

He hit the button on the intercom. "Ginger, we need coffee." He released the button in the middle of Ginger's complaint about not being his personal maid.

"This puts me in an awkward position," I said.

"No, young lady, you put yourself in an awkward position."

"Then why me? Put someone else on the Tatum story."

"Because this is right up your alley. I trust you, Sydney. I want this story. As far as I'm concerned, you are my reporter and I'm giving you an assignment. Your other dealings are something you will have to figure out yourself. Did Stringer Maynard know you were a reporter when he called your agency?"

"I'm not sure. If he did, he didn't let on."

At that moment Ginger barged in, a behavior that annoyed the hell out of our boss.

"Knock next time!" Ernest barked.

"You want coffee, I bring coffee. This ain't no English manor and I ain't no parlor maid." She changed pots and walked out.

"She ain't no Della Street, either. You didn't answer my question. What's your take on this murder? Is the wife guilty?" He handed me a cup.

"I don't think so."

"Any leads?"

"We're just getting started. Seems like Leland Tatum was liked and well-respected, but recently stepped into something foul. Whatever that was most likely got him killed."

"Get the story. We'll work things out. And, Syd, be careful."

"I have too many men in my life telling me to be careful."

"It's what we do."

I nodded and rose to leave. Then, before I knew it, the words flew from my mouth. "Henry's Bar is open early and serves breakfast." I quickly closed his office door behind me, but not before I heard a few of Ernest's favorite expletives.

I rushed to my desk, my mind on murdered men and wayward wives, when I ran smack into Tweety Gilcrest, knocking his visor askew and sloshing coffee over my hand. The little twerp didn't seem to notice. He brushed past me and barged into Ernest's office. "Here's my latest, Ernest. It's the story about the ninety-one-year old woman who swam naked across the Colorado River to show her dissatisfaction over Governor Shivers turning Republican."

I heard Ernest bark, "Don't call me Ernest. If this story is full of filler, I swear, Tweety, you're rewriting it and I don't give a damn if it ends up shorter than my little toe. You understand?"

"Yes, Ernest— yes, Mr. Turney." Tweety backed out, stumbled over the door jam, and moped back to his desk. I sort of felt sorry for the guy, but not much.

WALKING INTO THE MAIN ENTRANCE of The Driskill under the watchful eye of Jesse Driskill's sons, Bud and Tobe, whose limestone busts sit above the entrance door, never failed to give me the shivers. But once inside, I was swept away by the airiness of the lobby. The rotunda, which reaches up four floors to the glass dome, gave the place a solarium feeling. The quietude made me wonder if Ruth had checked in yet. Her presence usually had the staff scurrying around like neurotic mice.

"I'm here to see Ruth Echland," I told the desk clerk. "She checked in this morning. Can you call her room and tell her Sydney's here?"

He picked up the phone, delivered my message, then paused and looked at me. "Sydney who?"

"Jeez. Lockhart, her cousin."

He delivered that message, too, then gave me the once-over. "Tall, long red hair, looking disheveled and slightly angry. Yes, ma'am. Should I?" He hung up. "She's in room 543. You can go on up. And she told me to tell you that Scarborough's Department Store was having a sale tomorrow and that maybe you could find something decent to wear."

"I'll contact my banker about a loan for a new wardrobe."

He had the good sense to laugh.

Five minutes later, I pounded on her door.

"Who is it?"

"Open the damn door!"

I heard the moving of furniture, the deadbolts clicked, and the door opened a crack.

"Did you have to drain the moat?"

"We should have a secret code so I know it's you."

"You're insane. Undo the chain lock."

"I can't be too careful with a murder committed in the room across the hall."

"You're right." I walked into a room with a twelve-foot ceiling, crown molding, and a fireplace. I'm sure one night here cost more than my monthly rent. "Did you have any trouble getting a room on this floor?"

"Not at all. Because of the murder and the ghosts, seems not many people want to stay on the fifth floor."

"It's a good thing you don't believe in ghosts."

"I heard The Driskill ghosts are harmless. This man named Peter Lawless lived here until 1931. He liked the place so much, his spirit stayed after he died. And the housekeeper told me about Samantha Houston, a four-year-old girl who died when she fell down the grand staircase while chasing a ball. Now she plays tricks on the fifth floor guests and is often heard running down the hall, giggling. Now, what do you want? I have an appointment at the hair salon in forty-five minutes."

"Are you here to help us or pamper yourself?"

"Both. I like mixing business with pleasure. Besides, what better place to find information than a salon?"

"Good point."

"After the housekeeper told me about the ghost, we had a nice chat about other things too. After a while, I brought up the murder. I said it was too bad about the man who was killed. And she said she wasn't surprised. I asked if she knew him, and she blushed and said that he often stayed here at the hotel, and that he was one of those pushy, demanding guests."

"That doesn't sound like Leland Tatum."

"That's because it wasn't. You think garlic would help?"

"In solving the murder?"

"No, you idiot. Pay attention! In keeping ghosts away."

Ruth's mind worked like a ping-pong ball. You could never be sure where it would bounce next.

"Garlic only works with vampires. What do you mean, it wasn't Leland Tatum?"

She held up one finger to silence me and picked up the phone. "Could you send up another pot of coffee to room 543?" Putting her hand over the receiver, she said to me, "I'm getting to that. Are you hungry? I better eat something before my hair appointment." Not waiting for my answer she continued with her order. "Please bring two slices of apple pie. Thanks."

"Go on with your story."

"Anyway, she thought it was Stringer Maynard who was murdered. Evidently, she doesn't read the newspaper."

"So, Stringer's a frequent visitor to the hotel."

"Not just the hotel, but the Yellow Rose Suite."

"Meetings, liaisons?"

"She didn't say, just that when she heard about the murder, she assumed it was Stringer who was killed."

"Did she remember Tatum ever being here?"

"I showed her his picture from the newspaper and she didn't recognize him. I wanted to keep her talking, but she had to get back to work."

"Have you called Marcella?"

"Is it really necessary?"

"Ruth, this is your business. Be responsible for once. Besides, I told Marcella you'd call."

"Okay, I will, but later."

Our pie and coffee arrived. We refueled and Ruth went to the salon, although how any beautician could improve her stunningly glamorous appearance, was beyond me. My only attempt at improving my appearance was to stand next to Ruth.

After she left, I took a look around. The fifth floor was a maze with one hall leading into another and another. After ten minutes of wondering around, I was back at Ruth's room, which was situated across the hall from The Yellow Rose Suite and the room where Leland Tatum was shot. I closed my eyes. The noise of that murderous night—laughter, conversation, clinking glassware—echoed through the hall. My eyes shot opened when the image of Tatum lying in a pool of blood flashed before me. I shook away the image and tried not to think about ghosts while I tried the door to the office suite where Tatum was killed. Naturally, it was locked. I straightened a bobby pen and jiggled it around in the lock until I heard a click. I stepped inside. Initially, I thought this suite had another exit door, but now I realized that this was the corner of the hotel. The only way for the killer to leave the murder scene was through the main door into hallway, unless they climbed through the window and down the fire escape.

What I needed now was an ally.

Chapter Thirteen

THE STAFF AT THE FRONT DESK was friendly enough, but also acted as a barrier to anyone who didn't belong, so I headed to the niche of the hotel where I was most comfortable—the bar. On the way up the stairs, I noticed a familiar green face studying an oil painting hanging on the wall outside the bar. I couldn't resist. "Most news people only wear those in the office," I said.

Tweety jumped and jerked off his visor. "Oh, hi, Miss Lockhart. I forgot I had it on."

"Are you interested in art, Tweety?"

"Uh... I'm waiting for my mother. I'm taking her to lunch. She loves this old hotel. I was—"

"How nice. Gotta go. I have to meet someone too. See you at the news office."

I went in and took my usual seat at the bar and was happy to see Joey on duty.

"Afternoon, Miss Lockhart." He reached for the martini shaker.

"Not right now, Joey. How about a Royal Crown Cola?" He seemed disappointed over the lost opportunity to mix and shake, so I asked for extra ice and a cherry. He wiped down a sparkling clean bar and sat my drink on a napkin.

"Slow this time of day," he said. "I don't often get stuck with the day shift, but we're shorthanded right now, so I'm pulling a double. Hey, the last time you were here was the night of the murder."

"Afraid so. In fact, I was at that party on the fifth floor."

He leaned over and lowered his voice to a whisper. "Is your new agency investigating the case?"

"Looks that way. Up for answering a few questions?"

"Sure, fire away."

"The guy who was checking invitations at the door, any idea of who he was?"

"Could have been any one of our security staff, or sometimes the hotel uses someone from the restaurant or catering. What did he look like?"

"Medium build, about thirty, sandy-colored hair. Although he was standing sentinel, he looked like a pushover, not too authoritative."

"Sounds like Jasper Noells. You're right. He's a waiter. Probably his first time bouncing a door. Want to talk to him? He clocked in right behind me."

"That'd be great, Joey."

Joey picked up the phone, and a few minutes later, Jasper was behind the bar. Joey made the introduction. "Miss Lockhart is okay. It's safe to talk to her."

"I remember you," Jasper said. "I almost didn't let you in. You didn't have an invitation. I thought you might have been one of those beatniks."

"Think nothing of it. I'm sure the cops questioned you, but since then, you've had time to ponder that night."

"Hard to think about anything else. Not often a wife shoots her husband in one of our hotel rooms."

"What time did you arrive at the party to begin working?"

"I helped set up. We had to have everything ready to go at five, so we began setting up around four."

"Did you see anyone going or coming from the other rooms that the Maynard/Tatum party had reserved?"

"I saw Mrs. Tatum go into her room about half an hour or so later. I didn't exactly stop to look at my watch."

"Where did she come from?"

"How would I know?"

"I mean, did she step out of the elevator or another room."

"Oh, the elevator. She was a bit tipsy."

"See anyone else?"

"Mrs. Maynard arrived around five and went and knocked on Mrs. Tatum's door. She went in and I heard them arguing. They came out a few minutes later and went into the Yellow Rose Suite."

"You didn't happen to hear any of that argument, did you?"

"Nope. But right before they walked into the Yellow Rose, I heard Mrs. Maynard say, 'You'll regret this, Eleanor.' That was when the real fun started."

"Real fun?"

"Yeah, you should have seen Mrs. Maynard when the beatniks showed up. There were four of them. She came over before I had a chance to say anything. She pushed me aside and told them they were at the wrong party. They laughed and showed their invitations, and I thought she was going to have a stroke. She turned to her sister, who had walked up behind her, and said something like, 'did you know about this?' The Tatum woman said that her husband invited them. She told them to come in and took them to the bar and told the bartender to make their drinks. Mrs. Maynard called her a fool, right there in front of everyone. You could have heard a pin drop. Mrs. Tatum said, all cool like, 'aren't we all, Fiona.' She ordered a double scotch on the rocks and began chatting with some lady dressed in a bunch of scarves. I didn't pay much attention after that. I was too busy checking invitations."

"Did you notice anyone in the hall after the partying got going?"

"A few people milling around. Mrs. Maynard came by and told me that if I let anyone in without an invitation, she'd have me sacked. That's why I gave you a hard time. Sorry."

"Anyone leave the Yellow Rose Suite?"

"Mrs. Tatum, pretty tight I might add, shoved past me and headed down the hall. Next thing I knew, a shot is fired, and she's screaming."

"How long was it from the time she left the party to the time you heard the shot?"

"Are you kidding? Right away."

"Ten seconds, sixty seconds? Think."

"I was busy, but it couldn't have been much longer and a minute."

"You didn't see anyone else go into that room before his wife?"

"No. Oh, wait. I did see this one guy. I didn't actually see him go in, but he must have been in there."

"What do you mean?"

"He was standing back by that entrance area."

"The alcove?"

"Yeah, whatever you call it. He was just inside to the right."

"Then how were you able to see him?"

"The mirror. I saw him in the hall mirror. Anyway, a couple of minutes later, I looked up and he was gone."

"Could he have gone into Tatum's suite or the office room where the murder was committed?"

"He could have. The office room in the middle connects those two bedroom suites. If he went into one of those rooms, I didn't see him come out. I could have missed him, though. We were busy setting up."

"What time was this?"

"Why do you want to know? I already told all of this to the cops."

I shoved a fin into his coat pocket.

"Right before the guests began to arrive. I'd say about 4:45 or so."

"What did this guy look like?"

"I figured him to be one of beatnik guys. Dressed all in black except for his shoes. He wore red-and-white wingtips."

My radar went off. "His age?"

"In his forties. Nice looking guy, but too cool for my taste. Listen, I've got to get back to work."

I thanked Jasper, finished my cola, and left Joey a big tip. So, Serge LaBeau was lurking outside the room where Tatum was murdered. Funny, Serge failed to mention that fact to me. I left the bar and made a hasty retreat to the elevator to have a look at that mirror on the fifth floor when a pair of shiny lavender shoes stole my attention. Attached to the pair of small shoes, was a pair of thin ankles. Most of the rest of the body was hidden behind an open newspaper. I sat down in the chair next to her.

"I like your overalls, but don't you think those shoes deserve a more sophisticated outfit?"

Lydia, the young girl whom I'd meet under the blue moon the night I was chasing Jelly's bartender, put down her newspaper and smirked. "Who cares? Certainly not you." She eyed my slacks and saddle shoes. "I'm surprised they let you in here."

"You should talk. Is this your usual haunt? The Driskill lobby?"

"I come in and do what I do every afternoon around this time, read the newspaper. My father is too cheap to have it delivered. Besides, he claims the publisher is a moron. How else is one to know what is happening on the scene?"

I peered over at the article she had been reading. "The Tatum Murder?"

"I like to keep abreast of the latest things happening in my fair and quaint city."

"I would love to chat, Lydia, but I'm in a hurry."

"You know where to find me." She folder her paper, tucked it under her chicken-wing arm, and marched out of the hotel.

As soon as I stepped out of the elevator on the fifth floor, I noticed the mirror Jasper had mentioned. I was surprised I hadn't seen it before. It hung on the wall in the alcove leading into the room where Tatum was found. If Serge were standing just right, he would easily be seen from the hall. I pulled out my notebook and made a quick sketch of the hall layout and the position of the mirror. As I turned to leave, a guy stumbled into me. He wore a scarlet dinner jacket. His hair was stark white and his eyes the color of gin; clear and shimmering. I grabbed his arm as he slowly sank to the floor.

"Hey, mister, I think you've had one too many. Where's your room?"

He waved his hand in a wide arch. "Pick a room, any room." His head slumped down to his chest and he began to wail. "I'm such a fool. I have no right to be in this hotel, but I had to come up here. I had to." He clutched at the crown molding, which divided the wainscoting from the wallpaper above and tried to stand. I helped him up. He pulled out his handkerchief and blew his nose.

"She's not here," he said. "I gotta find her before it's too late."

"I can't help you, sorry."

I left him there, leaning against the wall and sniffling. I stepped into the elevator and told the operator there was a drunk guy in the hall. "It was probably Mr. Lawless. He tends to tie one on every now and then."

I was half way to the salon when I stopped. Lawless—the ghost? Surely, not.

Chapter Fourteen

Ruth sat under the hairdryer, admiring her magenta-colored nails. I jotted a note down on the salon receptionist's pad and held it in front for my cousin to read. She smiled and waved me off.

Dr. Richards' clinic was located near the University in a modern L-shaped building made of concrete blocks and hundreds of small, fixed-glass inset windows. At first glance, it appeared to be two-story, but the high clerestory wall with a row of rectangular windows running along the top gave a false impression. Bright red concrete steps led up to a red door with a small brass plate that read: The Andrew Richards Clinic. The place was beautifully landscaped with azalea bushes, wisteria, and mountain laurels. The sound of trickling water caught my attention, and I saw the entire area to the right entrance had been turned into a garden with benches, birdbaths, sculptures, and a rock wall over which the water tumbled into a pool of goldfish. The place reminded me of something Frank Lloyd Wright would have designed.

The reception area didn't look like any reception area in any doctor's office I'd ever been in. The light filtering through all the windows and the masonry walls gave the place a light, airy feel. A hundred-gallon aquarium filled with tiny florescent fish, swimming through small castles and pieces of colored coral, bubbled in the corner. The sofas and lounge chairs were made of blood-red leather, and the Persian rug was woven in various shades of red. The color red is associated with passion, love, anger, danger, sex, and blood. I wondered if being surrounded by the color was supposed to stir up the emotions. I guess Dr. Richards wanted his clients well primed before they made it to his couch.

A well-groomed woman sat behind a desk that looked as if it belonged in a corporate office of the company's president. There were no weeping women, no guys who looked as if they needed a drink, and no unhappy couples anywhere. I've never been into a psychiatrist's office, although after spending time with my parents, I'd often thought I'd needed psychiatric help, but it was evident that Dr. Richards' clients weren't the usual down-and-out crazies.

"May I help you?" The receptionist looked down her nose at me and scanned my attire with disapproval.

"I'm waiting for someone. I'll just have a seat."

"Please sign in, ma'am." She handed me a clipboard. "We have to keep a record of who comes in. I'm sure you understand."

I didn't, but what the hell. I signed in and handed it back.

"Always efficient, aren't you, Sarah?"

"Mrs. Maynard. Nice to see you today."

I turned around to see that Fiona Maynard had walked in behind me. "I can vouch for Miss Lockhart. She's here to see my sister."

I followed Fiona to a side door, which Sarah had to unlock to let us in.

"How is Eleanor?" I asked.

"How do you expect? She's suspected of murdering her husband."

"A murder she confessed to."

"My crazy sister is sticking to that crazy story. You realize you won't be able to talk to her alone. I'll be in the room with you."

I expected a cop would sit in, or maybe Dr. Richards, but Fiona was the last person I wanted to join us. One raised eyebrow, cock of the head, clearing of the throat, and I feared Fiona would control whatever came out or didn't come out of Eleanor's mouth.

I was right about the cops, there were two, a man and a woman, standing outside her room. The woman patted me down and then opened my bag. Inside was my .38. I handed her my permit. I must have met with her approval. She grinned and told me she'd keep my bag until I was ready to leave. She shot Fiona a look that said she was not happy with this arrangement. She unlocked the door, and Fiona barged in without knocking.

Eleanor sat in a winged-back chair staring out the window. The room was small, but otherwise, furnished with all the comforts of home, if one didn't count the bars on the window. I noticed a food tray setting on a table next to her chair. Eleanor's back was turned from the door, and without looking back to see who'd come in, she said, "Fiona, don't you have anything better to do than walk in here every few minutes?"

"My sister is a bit grumpy today," Fiona said. She lifted up the silver tray and studied the uneaten slice of prime rib and green beans. "I don't suppose you plan to eat any of this."

"It's been sitting there for two hours," Eleanor said. "Take the damn thing away and don't make excuses for me." She turned around to see who else was in the room. Fiona introduced me as a friend.

"Cut the crap," Eleanor said. "I know all your friends, and she's not either one." Eleanor studied me from top to bottom. "I saw you at the party and at my husband's funeral. Sit down. You must be from the detective agency my brother-in-law hired."

This was not the woman I saw at either event. This Eleanor Tatum was as brazen as her older sister. Fiona rolled her eyes, but for once held her tongue. She took the food tray into the hall and came back in.

"What do you think about my cell, Miss Lockhart? I get room service, I have a view of the garden and two nice guards outside my door. What more can a prisoner ask for?" She reached over and touched the side of a silver coffee service. "Coffee's still hot. Would you like a cup?"

I took her up on her offer and pulled a chair over by the window.

"How can I help you?" She handed me a china cup.

Silver coffee service, china cups; sure bets the hell out of the city lockup. "I need to ask you a few questions."

She studied my face for several seconds over the rim of her cup and said, "What's there to ask? I shot Leland."

"Why?"

Eleanor merely shrugged. "It doesn't matter."

"Your sister doesn't believe you killed your husband."

She sipped her coffee and stared out the window.

"You were upset at the party. Why was that?"

She sat her cup down hard enough to crack the saucer. "It was over this governor fiasco plan that my brother-in-law was trying to shove down my husband's throat."

I looked at Fiona, stoic as a piece of wood.

"What I don't understand is why Mr. Maynard didn't run himself?" This question went out to both sisters. Fiona started to answer, but Eleanor cut her off. "Because my husband was more electable. Stringer had connections, but he was smart enough to know he wasn't well liked in the political arena."

"Why did your husband allow himself to be talked into it in the first place?"

"Leland had his hands full with me, and Stringer has a way with finagling things. My sister knows how I feel," Eleanor continued.

"Tell me what happened when you and Leland arrived at the hotel?"

"After we checked in around noon, Jones Digmire and Victor Nolan came in. Leland had asked them to come. They talked a while, and then the three of them went to Stringer's room to tell him Leland was not going to run. But things didn't quite work out. When Leland came back to our room a few minutes later, told me he'd changed his mind and was going ahead with the announcement as planned."

"Did he say why?"

Eleanor looked at Fiona. "No, he just said for me not to worry. That he'd fix things eventually and that he'd explain later. It was the same thing over and over. I begged him not to do it. I pleaded for us to leave the hotel, but Leland said it wouldn't be a good idea."

"Is that why you killed him?"

Eleanor jerked around and looked at me for the first time. "I couldn't take it anymore. I...I just lost it." She twisted her napkin into a tight coil.

"He wouldn't stand up to Stringer and leave the hotel, so you shot him?"

"It...no. Leland left to go see Serge LaBeau. He owns the theatre down the street. I...left too. I couldn't stay there, so I walked around downtown for a while."

"When did you come back to the hotel?"

"I'm not sure." She picked up her cup and took a few sips. "With all the medication I take, things sometimes get foggy, plus I had a few drinks. Let me think. I came back right before the party started."

"Where did you get the gun?"

"Leland always carried one. It was in his suitcase. I...I took it and put it in my purse. I couldn't let Leland ruin everything for us by agreeing to Stringer's plan once again."

"You took the gun, put it in your purse, and right before your husband was to walk in and make the announcement, you went after him and shot him."

"Yes," she whispered. Suddenly, her cup slipped from her grasp, splashing coffee on her lap and down her legs. I grabbed a tea towel.

"Oh, for heaven's sake," Fiona said.

"I've got it," I told her. "Are you okay, Mrs. Tatum?"

She took the towel from my hand. "How clumsy. I think I'd better lay down."

Fiona walked me out to the lobby. "I told you talking to her wouldn't help. She was just talking out of her head."

"I have a question for you. Someone overheard you and Fiona arguing right before the party started. What did you mean when you hold your sister, 'You'll regret this, Eleanor?'"

"She said she'd do whatever she could to keep her husband from running for governor."

"Sounds like she did."

"She's out of her mind. Work on the case, Sydney. She didn't kill him."

Once outside, I unfolded the note Eleanor had surreptitiously slipped into my hand. It said:

Talk to Serge.

BEFORE RETURNING TO THE NEWSPAPER, I made a pit stop at my

apartment. Mr. Grimwell was standing at my front door brushing cobwebs from my mailbox.

"Do you really think that's necessary, Mr. G?"

"Gotta keep the place up to snuff. First its spiders, and before you know it, termites. Oh, a woman named Marcella called. I told her you didn't know any Marcella and hung up."

"You should not have done that."

"It's no bother, glad to help. I'll be in the back tending to the Althea trees if you need me."

"I don't have any Althea trees."

"You will by the end of the day."

I went inside and locked the door with the deadbolt and made a mental note to change my locks. Then I called Marcella to apologize for Mr. G's rudeness.

"I assume Ruth hasn't called you."

"No, she hasn't, and it's probably not necessary. Looks like Mary has checked herself out. When she didn't come down for breakfast, Nurse Abernathy went to see about her and found her and her suitcase missing. I am a bit worried. She was in such a state when she came in."

"Damn, Ruth."

"Well, don't worry about it. If Mary comes back, I'll let you know."

Ruth's problems have a way of becoming my problems, but for once, I was going to take Marcella's advice and not worry about it.

Chapter Fifteen

S. J. LABEAU was the only LaBeau listed in the Austin phone-book. When my call was answered, I fell back on my sofa, not believing what I'd heard. "Tell me it's not you."

"Sydney with a *y*?"

"Lydia with a *y*?"

"I knew you'd call sooner or later. We don't have much time. If they arrest my father, I'll have to go on the lam. Living in an orphanage or a foster home is so beneath me."

"How did you know—"

"I'm good of figuring things out."

"So, Serge LaBeau is your father?"

"If you plan to make your living as a private eye, you're going to have to be more observant. Are you at home?"

"Let me see. I have a gin in my hand, a sympathetic poodle on my lap, an ornery cat draped over my typewriter, and a neighbor whose ear is plastered to my backdoor. Yep, I'm at home."

"Good. The number fifty-nine bus stops two blocks from your place. I'll be right there."

She hung up and I refilled my glass. Before I added another ice cube, my phone rang. "Lay off the booze. We have a lot of work to do."

Fifteen minutes later, I was listening to a noise coming from my sofa that was unlike anything I'd ever heard. Mealworm was curled up like a tight cinnamon roll in Lydia LaBeau's lap, purring like a well-tuned Harley.

I pulled my glass of gin from the icebox and used it to wash down four aspirin. My life was too weird. I opened a box of Oreos and a fresh bottle of chocolate milk.

"Oh, by the way, Mealworm doesn't like her name," Lydia called from the living room.

"She told you that?"

Lydia traded my cat for the cookies and milk. "Yep. One of the reason's she's so cranky is because she is jealous of your poodle."

"My pets get along fine."

"The cat puts up with the poodle because she doesn't have a choice. She's put out because you gave your poodle a glamorous name like Monroe and named her after an insect larva."

"How do you know my poodle's name?"

"That dog food dish with 'Monroe' printed on the side."

"What would she rather be called?"

"She likes Ava."

"As in Gardner?"

"Yep."

"I'll think about it. Mealworm took to your father too, when he paid me a visit a few nights ago."

"He was here?"

"I'm surprised you didn't know."

"It's maddening keeping up with him and the theatre and all of his business dealings."

"But you knew he was at the party at The Driskill the day Tatum was murdered."

Lydia dipped a cookie into her milk, studied it for a brief second, and then shoved the entire thing into her mouth. She chewed. I stared. Mealworm purred. Finally, Lydia swallowed.

"I told him not to go. I told him there'd be trouble."

"We need to start from the beginning, Lydia. Your father led me to believe he wasn't at the party. I just found out that he was there."

"He's scared. Mr. Tatum came to the theatre just a few hours before he was murdered. He was angry with his brother-n-law."

"I know this. Mr. Tatum wanted to help your father with the Art and Cultural Center instead of run for governor."

"That was old news—the governor thing. Mr. Tatum was never happy about that. He often came over to talk about it with Dad. This was something different."

"What was it?"

"I don't know, but it was bad. At first, I thought he was sick. He was white as a marshmallow and kind of stunned like he's just come from a horror show. I told Mr. Tatum that he should sit back and put his feet up before he passed out."

"You were in the room?"

"Of course. Did you think I would stoop to eavesdrop from behind the curtains? Actually, Mr. Tatum didn't know I was there until I spoke. What is it about adults? They seem to fill a room and cast shadows over everything around."

"What did he say?"

"He looked at me for a long time, and then a weird smile spread across his face. He said there were things he could never change, but some things he could. He stood up and left. Dad paced around awhile and then said he was going after Mr. Tatum, but that I shouldn't tell anyone where he was going."

"Why would he not want anyone to know?"

She shrugged and dipped another cookie.

"Mrs. Tatum shot her husband while several people were in the suite next door. She also confessed. Why do you think the police will arrest your father?"

"I don't know. It's just a feeling."

"You're lying."

"I'm good with feelings."

"I'm sure you are, but there's more you're not telling me. If you want my help, you're going to have to fess up."

"I read the newspaper. Mrs. Tatum doesn't seem to have a good motive for killing her husband."

"The only motive she needs is that she's his wife and she had the opportunity. Several witnesses can vouch she was angry that afternoon, so start talking, Lydia."

Lydia reached for another cookie and then drew back her hand. She stared at the plate, and for the first time since I laid eyes on her, she looked like a little girl. I even saw a slight tremor in her lower lip.

"When Dad came back later that afternoon, he was scared stiff. His hands were shaking. I've never seen him like that before. He went into the office and closed the door. I...heard him crying. Later I discovered blood on his clothes. Will you help us? I know my dad would never kill anyone!" She looked me in the eye. The worry I saw a moment ago had turned to desperation. "Please help."

Lydia wasn't the only one in the room letting her guard

down. Maternal instincts I didn't know I had, assaulted me. I put my arms around the girl and told her not to worry.

I DROVE LYDIA HOME and made her promise she'd stay put. My next stop was the Next to Nothing Theatre where I found Serge arguing with a man who was dressed in a Davy Crockett outfit. I plopped down in a theatre seat and waited. I loved old theatres. These venues were not foreign to me. My mother used to act in community theatre when I was growing up in Houston. After school, I would sneak in to watch the rehearsals. They were much more entertaining than the stage presentations, especially when my mother was at odds with the director.

The Next to Nothing, although somewhat shabby and smelling of mold and barbeque, maintained its architectural integrity. Three stories of ornate seating tiers curved from the main balcony and spilled down both sides of the theatre, stopping halfway to the stage, giving the audience a feeling of watching the performance from a cloud. Faded murals of Texas' historic battle scenes covered the walls where the tiers ended. Deep maroon brocade curtains flanked the sides of the stage and cascaded over the center. Knotted turquoise-colored tassels hung at the bottom of each cascade. But the centerpiece, a domed ceiling painted in a gold background, left no doubt as to what state this theatre was located. A cut-glass chandelier hung in the middle of a plaster seven-point star. In the space between each arm of the star were more murals. Each one depicting the various landscapes that spread across our state: high-desert plains, agricultural valley, coastal bend, pine forest, hardwood forest, black-land prairie, and the hill country.

I picked up a discarded playbill from the floor. Last night's production, *Hamlet at the Alamo,* showed a sketch of a guy wearing a bloody military uniform with an older ghostly figure hovering behind him.

"It's a comedy," Serge said. He sat down in the seat next to me.

"I had the impression you produced live variety shows."

"You mean like the old, raunchy, vaudeville stuff?"

"Right."

"We do that too. Anything that will bring in a crowd. The Hamlet show; a lot of music, dancing, actresses in scant costumes, whatever works. Although the Hamlet thing didn't draw much of a crowd last night. How's the investigation going?"

"It's taken some interesting turns. There's a possibility that Eleanor Tatum didn't kill her husband."

"I don't believe she did."

"Did you?"

"Me!"

"You're in the acting business, Serge. I figured that's the reason you're such a good liar. You were at the hotel the afternoon Leland was shot."

"Who told you?"

"It's not important. If I found out, how long do you think it will take the cops to figure it out? And when they do, they'll be on your tail. So, start talking."

"Okay, okay, I was there. Leland came to see me after he checked into The Driskill. He was in a fit when he walked into the theatre. He was too angry to say much of anything. I think he just needed a place to cool off before he went back to deal with Stringer again."

"About not running for governor?"

"About dissolving the partnership."

"What?"

"That's what I told you the other night. Things had been brewing between Leland and Stringer for a few days before Leland was killed. The day of the party, everything came to a head. Leland said he had contacted a lawyer that morning to draw up the papers to dissolve the partnership immediately. He wouldn't say why. I'd never seen Leland so agitated. He was always calm and self-assured. Something about him wasn't right. I was worried, so a short while after he left, I went after him."

"You went to the hotel?"

"I did. He wasn't...there. I waited a while and then left and came back to the theatre."

"What time was that?"

"Hmmm, around three, I think

"Three?"

"Or thereabouts."

So far, Serge hadn't told me anything that would have caused him to rush back to the theatre, close himself in his office, and cry, so I knew he was holding back as well as lying about the time he was at the hotel.

"You were on the fifth floor and you didn't see anyone?"

"That's what I said. Listen, you got to help Eleanor. She would never kill her husband."

"But the case against her is strong. She was upset with him. She was drinking."

"You didn't know Leland, and you don't know her."

"Serge, you tell that fool director that I will not play the part of Colonel Travis' ghost too. I don't care if it is a non-speaking part." The man in the Davy Crockett suit was rushing down the aisle waving a white sheet at Serge. Behind him came an attractive young woman with auburn hair and bright green eyes. "I keep telling him, Serge, that there's more to the costume than the sheet, but he won't listen," she cried.

Serge turned around. "What happened to Melton? He was supposed to play the ghost."

"He never made it back from Matamoras," the woman said. "He's probably sitting in some Mexican jail, nursing a hangover. I doubt if we'll ever see him again."

"One of my actors and my costume designer/assistant," Serge informed me. "Miss Lockhart, I'm glad we had this little talk. Please stay in touch and let me know how things are progressing." Serge and his frustrated actor, a guy whom I now recognized from the group of beatniks at The Driskill the night of the murder, disappeared backstage.

I let Serge escape into his fantasy world to stew for a while, hoping it might loosen his tongue.

Chapter Sixteen

I FOUND THE NEAREST PHONE BOOTH and called Ernest to let him know I was still alive. I told him about my conversation with Lydia, about my plan to visit Eleanor, and my surprise visit to Serge.

"Do you think this LaBeau fellow plugged Tatum?" Ernest asked.

"Maybe. I'm not finished with him."

"Good. Keeping snooping. See you in the morning." He hung up. I pushed the door open and stepped out into a rain shower caused by one of those afternoon cloud formations that flee across Texas on any given, cool, spring afternoon. Lying on a bench was a discarded newspaper. I unfolded it, placed it over my head, and hoped I'd make it to The Driskill before the ink ran down my face.

Ruth should be nice and done and in a chatty mood after her salon treatment. As I walked through the lobby, I shook out the paper and was about to drop it in the trash when I noticed someone had circled a curious item in the classified section. By the time the elevator door opened to the fifth floor, my plan was well formed.

I GOT THE THIRD DEGREE at the door. "Georgia," "Claude," and "how in the hell do I know?" were the answers to: "What was my maternal grandmother's middle name; What was the name of Ruth's mother's French gigolo; and how many pistons are under the hood of Ruth's Caddy." I waited while Ruth decided whether or not to open the door and let me in. Finally, the lock clicked, and there she was; my cousin, looking like a million bucks—nails polished and hair coiffed to perfection.

"New outfit?" I asked. "How did you find the time?"

"There's a boutique next door. I'll have to take you there. I'll buy. Anything to get you out of slacks and those awful Mickey Mouse shoes."

"Never mind about my wardrobe. Find out anything at the salon?"

"I was there for two hours, and not once did the conversation turn away from the Tatum murder. Stringer Maynard was not exactly a stranger to this hotel, like the housekeeper said."

"More than just business?"

"Maynard was reputed to have entertained a flurry of ladies in the Yellow Rose Suite."

"Catch any names?"

"No. Seems he didn't have a steady girl."

"Prostitutes?"

"Most probably. How about you?"

"You look too good to sit in this room. Let's go down to the bar and I'll fill you in."

WE CLAIMED TWO lounge chairs near the piano, and I went to the bar to order our drinks. I found Tweety seated on a stool, attempting to hide behind a menu. "Another date with your mother, Tweety?"

He turned and feigned surprise at seeing me. "Hi, Miss Lockhart. Just having a little refreshment." He glanced over my shoulder. His usual dopy expression turned dopier. "You spend a lot of time here at this hotel."

"Same can be said of you."

I turned around to see what he was gawking at, and except for Ruth, whose face was beaming into her compact mirror, the lounge was empty of anything deserving attention. Joey had my drinks ready. I laid a couple of bucks on the bar and told him to keep the change. "Enjoy your cocktail, Tweety." As I walked away, I heard Joey say, "Hey, buddy, you gonna order anything or set here all afternoon reading the menu?"

I made sure I strung out the report of my investigation until Ruth's second martini was halfway finished. I excused myself to visit the ladies room and rushed into the lobby, slipped a dime into the rack, and pulled out a newspaper. By the time I returned, Ruth was swirling her olive and looking serene. I gave her the exciting news, causing a good amount of gin to shoot up her nose.

"You want me to what?" she sputtered.

"It'll be fun." I circled the ad and handed it to her.

"I can't cook! You know I can't cook!"

Don't I know it. The last time I visited, she tried to served me vanilla wafers and watery lime Jell-O for breakfast. "You won't be doing any real cooking, just chopping and stirring. The ad is for a prep cook, not a chef."

"I'm staying at the hotel. Someone will recognize me."

"I know where to get a disguise."

"I'll bet you do."

When she took another look at the ad, I knew she was hooked, but to be sure, I said, "You're so good at this."

"I played Lady Macbeth in our high school play."

"I didn't know that."

"'Out, damn spot! Out I say!'"

"That's good, Ruth. Do you know what it means?"

"Something about blood, but who cares. It says here interviews are held tomorrow between one and three. What if they don't hire me?"

"Make sure they do. Pour on the charm. Once you're in, you'll be our mole."

"Can I wear one of those tall white chef's hats?"

"I'm sure it's a requirement."

"How do you think I'll look?"

"Taller."

"Do you really think I can pull it off?"

"How hard can it be? Besides, with your brains, you'll pick it up in an instant."

"You're right."

"There's a bookstore down the street. Buy a couple of simple cookbooks, like *Better Homes and Gardens*. Look for some with plenty of tips and focus on that rather than recipes. You might even call your maid Sophie and get some advice from her. Speaking of phone calls. You never called Marcella, and Mary flew the coop."

"I'm not surprised. That girl was so flighty, a real featherhead."

"Ruth, that girl is eight months pregnant. She checked into your Home for help."

"And she left. Is that my problem?"

"Your name's on the sign out front; the Echland-Wheatly Home."

"That's right. Echland-*Wheatly* Home. I hired *her* and put *her* name on the business too. I also hired a nurse. I can't be expected to help you and every wayward girl who's gotten herself into trouble."

"But she was your friend." Trying to make Ruth feel guilty was like trying to shove the moon off its orbit. "Just forget it. Let's go to the office and I'll type up your resume."

THE RESUME WAS SO HOT it smoked as I rolled it out of the typewriter. I listed three references: Marcella at the Echland-Wheatly Home where Ruth had been in charge of planning menus, Ralph's Diner (coincidently with the same phone number as our agency) where Ruth had worked as an assistant chef, and Sophia's Restaurant in Dallas (coincidently with the same phone number as Ruth's apartment where her housekeeper Sophia hangs out all day eating bonbons when she's not helping herself to Ruth's liquor cabinet). I was reading it over one more time when she snatched it out of my hands.

"Read it carefully," I said. "You need to be familiar with everything on it."

"I know who I am."

"Maybe, but you don't know squat about Adele Adleburg."

"I can never pass for an Adele. Thirty-six! I'm only twenty eight. All the makeup and frumpy clothes in the world will not make me look ten years older."

"It's a good thing you're not applying for a bookkeeping position."

"And why do I have to be a prep chef? Change this and put me down as a head chef at Ralph's."

"You're not applying for a position as head chef, so why tell an even bigger lie? Chopping, slicing, stirring soup. You should be able to handle that. If you had to do any serious cooking, you'd be fired as soon as the staff realized that you don't even know how to light an oven."

I picked up the phone and made a call. I was pleased to know that Lydia had followed my instructions and stayed home. I wrote down the address for the Next to Nothing Theatre. "Lydia will meet you at the backdoor with all the supplies you need to turn yourself into Adele Adleburg, prep chef. Tomorrow, I'll be at your room at noon to help you get dressed. Once you get back to the hotel, you'll have to keep a low profile. Do not change into your disguise in your hotel room. Someone might see you going in as Ruth and coming out as Adele. Go downstairs to the lobby restroom and change there—or better yet, a bar down the street."

When Ruth skipped out the door, she was whistling.

A moment later, Dixon walked in carrying a box tied with a green ribbon. "I met Ruth in the hall. She said she came up with a grand idea that would help in digging out information. Know anything about that? Wait, tell me later. You're a sight for sore eyes."

"What's in the box?" I asked.

"Chocolate chip cookies from my new landlady. I was arranging my clothes in the dresser when Mrs. Granger handed me this little housewarming gift. She baked them this morning. Are we alone?" He locked the door, dropped the box on the desk, and had me in his arms before I could answer.

"We have a lot to do," I said.

"I'm trying, but you keep talking."

Ten minutes later, I fluffed my hair, Dixon straightened his tie, and we resumed our professional relationship. "Jackson 'Stringer' Maynard?" I said. "How did the meeting go?"

"I was with him for only a short time before he made an excuse to leave because of another meeting."

"He agreed to come to the office?"

"Uh...no. We met at the hotel—the Citadel Club. When he's in town, he usually conducts business in the office suite on the fifth floor, but since Tatum's murder, he wanted to meet at the club. We spent the first fifteen minutes squaring off like a couple of street thugs, flinging threats at one another. When he threatened to have my license revoked and shut me down, I finally laughed, and so did he."

"Let's get the stuff on the board. Billy should be here soon."

"You talk, I'll write. What do you have?"

"An interesting story from Serge La Beau, and according to Ruth, some scandalous information from the housekeeper on the fifth floor."

I handed him a stack of index cards. "She thought it was Stringer who was murdered since he's the one who conducts a lot of business at the hotel. She also said Stringer engages in private entertaining in the Yellow Rose Suite—ladies of the evening. Ruth said the beauticians at the salon downstairs were aware of this Stringer's philandering too." I paused to allow Dixon to catch up.

"Okay, got it," Dixon said. "Go on."

"Jasper, the guy checking invitations the night of the party, said the two sisters had words when the beatniks began arriving. Fiona tried to get them to leave, but Eleanor was adamant they stay. Fiona called her sister a fool right there in front of everyone."

"Some family," Dixon said. "Anything else?"

"Serge lied to me. He was indeed at the hotel that afternoon, lurking outside of Leland's room. Jasper saw him shortly around 4:45, although Serge claims he was there around three. "

"Go on," Dixon said, writing furiously like a mad English professor.

"I spoke to Serge at the theatre this afternoon after Lydia paid me a visit at my apartment."

"Lydia?"

"Serge's twelve-year-old daughter."

"Maybe I should hear everything first; otherwise, we'll need to get another corkboard in here."

"That's probably best, since I haven't even gotten to my visit with Eleanor."

At that moment, the door flew open and an excited Billy came in and slapped the afternoon paper on the desk. "Stringer Maynard wasn't kidding. Read this."

Dixon picked up the newspaper and glanced at the front-page story. "Jackson Maynard has announced his bid for governor. The man doesn't waste time, does he? Take a seat.

Grab a cookie, Billy. Sydney's about to get to the good stuff. Your turn to write."

"I need to back up to Thursday night when I chased Jelly Bluesteen's bartender into the warehouse district and you found me in the alley behind that building?"

"How could I forget?" Dixon smiled.

"Okay, anyway, that building was the back of the Next to Nothing Theatre owned by our friend Serge. Right before I came out and encountered you in the alley, I encountered Lydia, Serge's daughter, playing dress up in the prop room. I saw her again in the lobby of the hotel this morning. She used the excuse that she was reading the paper, but she was waiting for me. We exchanged a few pleasantries, well, I did, she threw me a few sarcastic remarks. As soon as I got home, she called and told me she was on her way over via the bus. Over cookies and gin, she told me she's worried the cops will arrest her dad for murdering Tatum. She said that Tatum came to the theatre the day he was shot, and after he left, Serge left too. When he returned, he was scared. He closed himself in his office and cried."

"Cookies and gin?" Dixon asked.

"Gin, me; cookies, Lydia." I poured myself a cup of coffee and grabbed a cookie. "You know, I think you've been adopted by Caroline Granger," I told Dixon.

"It's my irresistible charm," he said. "Back to Serge LaBeau."

"After Lydia's visit, I headed over to the theatre and had a heart-to-heart with Serge. He confirmed what his daughter had told me. And get this, Tatum told Serge he was not only going to refuse the governor thing, he was severing the partnership."

"Damn!"

"My thoughts exactly. Imagine Stringer's surprise when his partner tells him all their plans and their thirty-year partnership is over. Serge said that Tatum would not say why he was doing it."

"Stringer is sticking to the story he told when we first met," Dixon said. "He swears Leland was into some sort of shady business and that shady business had to do with the art center, because until Leland got involved with Serge LaBeau, everything was fine."

"Looks like Stringer Maynard and Serge LaBeau are pointing fingers at one another," Billy said.

"Since Stringer conducts business at the hotel, I think I'll pop up to the Citadel Club," I said. "I assume they have a bar in the club."

"No, I mean, yes," Dixon said. "I'll handle the Citadel Club." He bent down to tie his shoelace that had not come untied. "It's uh...well, the club's not that easy to get into, and since I've been there as Stringer's guest, I'll take care of that."

I didn't often see Dixon hesitant and unable to look me in the eye. I was about to call him on it when the phone rang. Dixon grabbed the receiver and handed it over to me.

"Oh, Jeez. Where are you?" I mouthed the word *Lydia*. "Stay put, I'm on my way." I hung up the phone. "The cops picked up Serge. Lydia called from the police station."

Dixon grabbed his hat and jacket. "Let's go."

Chapter Seventeen

WE WALKED INTO THE STATION to find Lydia, standing in front of the sergeant's desk. She was dressed as Sherlock Holmes, complete with a pipe stuck between her teeth.

"We were rehearsing when the cops blew in," she said. She looked at Dixon and then Billy. "You must be the partners."

Before I could make the proper introductions, the sergeant said, "Are you her mother, ma'am? Please take this child out of here before I lock her up."

"Sergeant Nibbles." Lydia nodded and rolled her eyes.

"That's Neddles, young lady."

"We're leaving," I told the sergeant. I took Lydia by the arm. "There's a diner down the street. We can talk there."

"Sergeant Nibbles, if my dad gets released, tell him I'm at the Tip Top."

It was dinnertime, and the Tip Top Diner was crowded. Luckily, Dixon spotted a booth in the back and we grabbed it.

"You're the boyfriend," she said to Dixon as she slid into the booth.

"I don't know how she knows this," I said in my defense. "I haven't said a word."

"It's my business to know what other people don't." Lydia said.

"Hey, that's pretty good," Billy chimed. "It's from *A Study in Scarlet.*"

"Nope, the Christmas story, "The Adventure of the Blue Carbuncle.""

I laid my head on the table and mumbled, "I'll have something strong. I don't care what."

"You drink too much," Lydia said.

"I wonder why."

The waitress came by and we opted for three coffees and a Dr Pepper for the thirty-year-old child sitting next to me.

"Okay, start talking," I said.

"We were rehearsing and the cops came in and wanted to

talk to Serge. We, him and me, and the cops went into the lobby. They said they had some questions about the Tatum murder and took him to the station."

"Did they cuff him?" Billy asked.

"No, they only wanted him for questioning."

"Did he call a lawyer?" Dixon asked.

"No, but I did. He's in there with him now."

"Good thinking. There's not much we can do until we find out what's going on," I said. "What's with the Holmes outfit?"

"I'm in the play," she said.

"*Hamlet at Alamo?*"

"We changed it. It's now *Holmes at the Alamo.* I'm Holmes. Melton was our only actor who could handle the Shakespearean dialect, so we dropped Hamlet. The cast has been quiet about Melton's whereabouts, but I pieced things together and figured he's still holed up in some brothel in Mexico."

"Why aren't you in school?" Billy asked.

"Looks like she is pretty well educated," Dixon said.

"Serge!" Lydia cried. "Over here."

We looked up to see Lydia's father walking in the door. When he arrived at the table, his only comment was directed at me.

"You're a coldhearted woman, Miss Lockhart. You went to the cops."

"I didn't," I said. "Bring that chair over and sit down. My partners, Ralph Dixon and Billy Ludlow."

"Ralph's the boyfriend," Lydia said, "We call him Dixon."

Serge turned the chair around and straddled it. "What a mess this is."

The waitress came by, slapped a cup down in front of Serge, refilled ours, and left.

"Sydney filled me in on your story today," Dixon said. "What did you tell the cops?"

"As little as possible, thanks to the lawyer. I was told the usual stuff, not to leave town, blah, blah, blah."

"Your lawyer's not here, so maybe you should try the truth on us," I said.

"What's that supposed to mean?" Serge huffed.

"You lied about the time you were at the hotel."

"I wasn't sure *exactly* what time I was there. I had a lot on my mind."

I looked over at Lydia. She was doodling on her napkin, pretending not to listen, but I knew she was absorbing every spoken word, every word not spoken, and every nuance of everyone's facial expressions.

"I visited Eleanor Tatum this afternoon," I said. "Want to tell me about how well you know her?"

"What the hell are you getting at?" Serge sputtered.

"She gave me a note that read, 'Talk to Serge.' She secretly stuck it in my hand so her sister wouldn't know."

"Leland and Eleanor were my friends. She didn't trust her own family. I guess I'm the only one she can turn to. If I could help any more than I already have, I would, but there's nothing more to tell."

"Then there's nothing more we can do for you," said Dixon. "We're working for Maynard, so we're still on the case. We'll dig until we find the answers we need. In the meantime, take care of that daughter of yours. And if you truly believe Eleanor Tatum is innocent, maybe you can come up with some viable suspects."

Our party broke up and Dixon, Lockhart, and Ludlow, Private Investigators, left.

We returned to the office to wrap things up and wait for Jones Digmire. Dixon went back to the corkboard and we added more index cards with the information concerning Serge LaBeau.

"By the way, what else did you learn from Eleanor Tatum?" Dixon asked.

"At first, she was forthcoming, not at all reluctant to talk. She said she and Leland checked in around noon. Leland asked Jones Digmire and Victor Nolan to meet him there at one. He wanted their support when he broke the news to Stringer about not running for governor, and, as we found out later from Serge, dissolve the partnership. Eleanor said things didn't work out like Leland had hoped. He was going to let Stringer make the announcement after all and told Eleanor he'd fix things and not to worry. She begged him not to, but he told her to trust him. He left the hotel and went to see Serge. Eleanor left too. Later that afternoon, Leland returned to the hotel and was murdered. I asked Eleanor where she got the gun. She said she got it from Leland's suitcase earlier that day. I asked her what time she returned to the hotel. At first, she claimed she couldn't remember and then said it was right before the party started. At that point, Eleanor pretended to have a spell. She dropped her coffee cup, and when I went to help her, she stuck the note into my hand."

I pulled it out of my pocket and stuck it on the board.

"Interesting," Dixon said.

We were interrupted by a knock on the door. "I'll get it," Billy said and walked into the outer room. We heard Billy usher in Digmire and went out to see what the man had to say.

"Can I get you a drink, Mr. Digmire?" Dixon offered.

"Yes, that would be great." He lifted his handkerchief from his pocket and wiped his forehead. "Bourbon straight, if you've got it."

Dixon handed him a glass with three fingers of bourbon. "What can we do for you?"

Digmire took a swig. "I didn't want to come here. I don't want it getting back to Stringer that I talked to you, understand?"

"If you know something that will throw light on the case, we may have to go to the cops," Dixon said.

Digmire looked as if he were about to bolt. "The cops. Oh, God." He took another healthy swig and emptied the glass. "I can't believe this is happening, but you gotta know. The day before Leland was killed, Thursday, I went to see him in his office. We had planned to meet about some cattle he wanted me to look into buying. I could tell something had happened. I've never seen Leland look so down and out. I asked him what was wrong and he stammered and said it was nothing. Then, he really surprised me by asking me what I wanted. I reminded him that we had a meeting, but that we could talk another time. He said that might be better, that he'd call me later that day. Something had really upset him. As I walked out of the office, I saw him pour himself a stiff shot of whiskey. That wasn't like the Leland I know."

"Did he ever call?" Dixon asked.

"Yes, but we didn't talk about cattle. He said to meet him at his suite at The Driskill the next day at one. He said to bring Victor. He wanted to discuss a matter with us, before Stringer and Fiona showed up. When Victor and I got there, Leland told us that he decided not to run for governor and that he'd planned to end his partnership with Stringer as soon as possible."

"Did that surprise you?" Dixon asked.

"Not running for governor, no. Learning he wanted to end the partnership was a big surprise."

"He didn't say why?"

"No."

"Go on."

"We went with him to tell Stringer. I was proud of Leland. He laid it on the line, plain and simple. Stringer just sat there— that smug look on his face. It was all I could do not to walk over and knock it off. Finally, Stringer said he understood, but he wanted to talk to Leland alone. Leland told us to leave. We waited in the hall. The anticipation was killing us. Ten minutes later, Leland came out boiling mad. He told us he needed to talk to his wife, so we left and went to some bar down the street— Bluesteen's."

"What hold did Stringer have over his partner that he could convince him to do his bidding?" I asked.

A nerve twitched right over Digmire's lip. He glanced away and rubbed his jaw. "I haven't the foggiest."

We were silent, each in our own thoughts, when we were interrupted by someone knocking and jiggling the doorknob. "Dixon, you in there?"

Digmire turned as white as his shirt. Billy grabbed him and ushered him into the back room, turned off the light, and came back in to let Stringer Maynard into the outer office.

"Hate to barge in on you like this," he gasped and paused for a breath. "Had to take the stairs."

"Sorry, Mr. Maynard," Billy said. "The elevator operator goes home at six."

"No problem. The climb did me good. Glad you're all still here. I wanted to let you know that Edwin called me at the

Citadel. He's uncovered something in Leland's personal records that looks suspicious. He wouldn't say what, but he'd like to meet with you tomorrow. In fact, we both would."

Dixon glanced down at the calendar. "Two o'clock?"

"We can make it," Stringer said. He took a white handkerchief out of his pocket and polished a smudge from one of the silver studs on his boot. "Uh, hey, you three come down to The Driskill. I'll buy you dinner. You look like you've had a tough day."

"We have," Dixon said. "Thanks, but we'll take a rain check."

Stringer looked around, acted as if he had something more to say, but nodded. "Okay, then. See you tomorrow."

"I'll walk down with you, Mr. Maynard. I was on my way out," Billy said. I smiled at the cleverness of our young partner who had intended, I suspected, to make sure Maynard had left the building.

Dixon and I waited several minutes and then brought Digmire back in.

"I hope you know that son-of-a-bitch is lying. Leland was too much a gentleman to be involved in anything shady."

"Go home, Mr. Digmire," Dixon said. "We'll contact you if we find out anything. You do the same. When you reach the second floor, you'll find another set of stairs that will take you to the alley. This way you can avoid your boss."

"He ain't my boss!" Digmire shook his head and left.

"Digmire confirmed what Eleanor and Serge had told me about Leland being upset the day he was murdered," I said. "But this is the first time we learned whatever upset him possibly happened the day before."

"We're making some slight headway, but it's not enough to lead us in any sort of direction. I'm still curious about what I saw at the murder scene. I want to check into that further. See if I can learn anything from the cops. I've been on this case for fifteen hours today and so have you. Let's call it a night and go over to my place. Mrs. Granger said she'd have a roasted chicken warming in my oven."

We'd shut off the lights and Dixon was about to lock the door when the phone jingled. "I suppose we should answer," I said.

"Let me." Dixon picked up the phone, and before he had it halfway to his ear, he jerked it back, sighed, and handed it to me.

"Lydia is a twelve-year-old!" Ruth shouted.

"I didn't tell you that?" I asked.

"No, you conveniently forgot that little bit of information."

"It doesn't matter how old she is. Lydia knows what she's doing."

"You should see the outfit she gave me! It's disgusting! It makes me look like Betty Crocker. Frumpy and fat!"

"That's the idea. You don't want to look too glamorous."

"The last time I wore a disguise for you, my skin broke out because of chigger infestation."

"It wasn't chiggers. It was the sequins."

"What about lice, then? That theatre prop room smelled horrible, just the sort of environment lice love. I was about to object to the entire idea when she got a phone call and rushed out."

"Her dad was brought in for questioning concerning Tatum's murder. That's why she left. Did you take the costume?"

"What choice did I have?"

"You're a trooper. How about the cookbooks?"

"I bought four from the bookstore down the street. It was difficult to choose. I had no idea there were so many on the market. I mean, how difficult is it to cook a meal? And there were books for all types of cooking: Chinese cooking, outdoor cooking, cooking in a pressure cooker—whatever the hell that is. There was one with three hundred recipes for mixing drinks."

"So what did you decide on?"

"*Easy Recipes for Gals Who Want to Impress Their Mother-in-Law: Dishes That Make Men Swoon*, and, my favorite, *Cooking While Wearing Your Mink*. You know, Syd, this will be fun. I might even take up cooking."

God help us. "I'll see you at noon tomorrow, and we'll make the best of your disguise. Remember to keep a low profile. Dixon and I are heading over to his new house. Want to come?"

"No, I'm going back to my room to prepare for my interview."

Chapter Eighteen

I WENT BY MY APARTMENT to check on Monroe and Mealworm before I headed over to Dixon's place. All was well on Enfield Road. I fed the girls, brought in my mail, and avoided Mr. Grimwall.

The smell of roast chicken assaulted me as soon as I reached the patio. Dixon was sitting on a bench under a magnolia tree, sipping a glass of red wine. Mine was poured and on the table.

"How are your wards?" he asked.

"Monroe was asleep in the middle of my bed and Mealworm pretended she hadn't ripped one of my ivies to shreds. All and all, seems like they both had a good day."

Dixon gave me that contemplative look. "Have I ever told you you're the best thing that's ever happened to me?" He handed me my wine.

I sat down beside him. "Is it my sense of humor, superior intellect, gorgeous looks, or my wacky family?"

"All of the above and more."

"I was worried," I said.

He pushed a strand of hair behind my ear. "About what?"

"You, mainly. A few months ago you were working as a detective for Hot Springs Police Department. Your life was simple."

"Is that what you think? That life in Arkansas was choking me. I wouldn't have been there much longer, even if you hadn't come along."

"We never really talked about the mushy stuff."

"Are you happy?"

"Yes."

"Hungry?"

"Starved."

"Let's eat. We can talk later."

THE MORNING WAS TOO BEAUTIFUL to be inside, so I filled my Thermos with coffee. Monroe and I walked to Walsh's Boat Landing. It had been close to midnight by the time I arrived back at my apartment last night. It was tough to leave Dixon's cozy cottage, but we decided an overnight stay should wait since he'd just moved in. Mrs. Granger's roast chicken was superb, the wine mellow, and the talk minimal.

While my poodle sniffed every bush and tree around, I pondered all that had happened since Dixon walked into my room at The Arlington Hotel. Up until that moment, the idea of being involved with a man was out of the question. I'd just started my new job at the *American*. I saw myself as a single, working woman. I was still a single, working woman, but now I had two new jobs and a new boyfriend. Sometimes I wasn't sure about all this. The relationship between Dixon and me flowed so naturally, it frightened me sometimes. I leashed Monroe, screwed the lid back on my Thermos, and went back to my apartment.

I had a few minutes before I had to leave for work. I placed a long distance call before I could talk myself out of the expense.

"Hi, Mom, is Dad there?"

"You don't want to talk to your mother? Why do you always ask to speak to him?"

"Because he likes me."

"You're a hoot, Sydney Jean Lockhart, a real hoot. George, it's your smartass daughter."

"Syd? What's up?"

"I called to see how things were going."

"You could have asked your mother that."

"I wouldn't have gotten a straight answer."

"You're right. Well, things are back to normal. Before our feet hit the cold, hard floor in the morning, we're bickering, by the time breakfast is on the table, you mother tells me she's never speaking to me again, and by the time I gather my fishing tackle and head out the door, she's throwing something against the wall. How I managed to live without that woman for six weeks, I'll never know. Now, let's get to the real reason you called."

"I'm scared."

"You're not involved with another murder are you?"

"Yes, but that's not what frightens me."

"That's a relief. What is it then?"

"It's Dixon."

"I like the young man."

"So do I, but you see...well, I'm not sure how to put this. It's just that you and mom are my parents."

"Say no more. I understand perfectly. I heard that insanity skips a generation."

"That doesn't help much, considering my grandfather—*your* father—ran with a shady crowd before his murder."

"Listen, Syd, I don't know where you got it, but you have a level head and your instincts are right on the money. You've always been the one who took risks too. There are no guarantees. You do the best you can. It's that simple."

"Dixon seems pensive lately and at times jumpy. I asked him about the sudden changes in his life and he said those changes were long past due. But I think he might be keeping something from me."

"Men do that, Syd. Ask him, now, before any bad habits develop."

"You're right. Thanks, Dad."

"Call anytime. Oh, for crying out loud! You're mother's backing the car out of the garage. She just ran over the lawn mower."

BEFORE I LEFT for the newspaper, I called The Driskill to see if Ruth was preparing for her interview. It was only seven-thirty, and I was looking forward to rousing her awake with the phone call, but she wasn't in. My cousin, up before dawn? I called the front desk to see if she'd checked out, thinking that the assignment was too much for the girl, but the desk clerk assured me she was still registered. I told him to give Miss Echland a message that I'd be by to see her around ten.

TWEETY GILCREST was seated at my desk, pawing through a stack of papers. At first, I thought he was looking for a notepad or pencil since he often borrowed my supplies, having lost his. But when he surreptitiously slid open the bottom drawer, I knew he was up to something.

"I keep a loaded mousetrap in there," I said.

Tweety slipped out of my chair and banged his head on the corner of the desk. "Sydney! I was looking for...your tape dispenser."

I picked it up and handed it to him.

"Thank you." He scurried away to his desk, set down the dispenser, and flew out the door.

I didn't know what Tweety was up to, but I was damn tired of the twerp snooping around. If he was trying to scoop one of my stories, he should know that I wouldn't leave any valuable source information lying around. I intended to find out what game he was playing, but first, I had a heap of paperwork to dig through before it was time to meet Ruth at the hotel. I looked at my messages first; one from Ernest and one from my mother. Ernest reminding me to check in sometime today and my mother demanding I call her immediately. I placed Ernest's note in my must-do-today pile and tossed my mother's into the trash. I'm sure it had something to do with it being my fault she ran over the lawn mower. Next, I had two proofs to look through and a few phone calls to make. When I finished, I ran into Ernest's office, gave him a quick update, and headed for The Driskill.

This time Ruth answered on the first knock. She was wearing her mink and the chef's hat. "Where did you get that?" I asked.

"You've seen my mink before."

"No, the hat."

"There's a restaurant supply place down the street."

"You're not wearing that to the interview."

"I want to make an impression."

"Oh, you will. You'll have the human relations director in stitches before she shows you the door. Where's the outfit Lydia gave you?"

"I can't wear it."

I expected Ruth would balk. Arguing with her would only solidify her stubbornness, so I tried a little reverse psychology.

"Have it your way, but you won't get the job, and you won't be able to help, which is okay by me. Besides, you're needed in Dallas at the Home. I'll help you pack."

Ruth tossed her hat and mink. "Okay." She pouted. "You spoil everything."

An hour later, we had her wig in place, most of her makeup wiped off, her garters loosened so her stockings sagged around her ankles, and the hem of her homely dress shortened two inches. She did look like Betty Crocker, but with a frown.

"Now tell me what you've learned from the cookbooks."

"Men love catsup, Worchester sauce, and lots of garlic. When you cook in your mink, your menu should include mainly cold cuts, and be careful of mustard. A Gin Rickey is named after some guy named Joe Rickey. You want me to make you one?"

I opened her closet and started removing her five suitcases.

"What are you doing?"

"You're going home. You were supposed to prepare for an interview for a prep cook, not a food columnist. You need to know how to hold a knife, how to chop vegetables, and to make salads. Your interview is in fifteen minutes and all you can do is make a sandwich, no mustard, and a Gin Rickey."

"You're so pessimistic. I'll fake it. By this time tomorrow, I'll be chopping up a storm. Don't be surprised if I'm promoted to head chef." She slipped on her shoes.

"Not *your* shoes. Wear the ones Lydia gave you."

"No one will notice. See you later."

Before I could wrestle her out of her Ferragamos, she was gone.

WHEN I ARRIVED AT OUR OFFICE, Dixon was leaning back in his chair with his feet propped up on his desk, pondering the notes on the board.

"Connecting the dots?"

"Following the trail is more like it."

"And where does that trail lead?"

Without turning his head, his eyes floated from the board over to me. His gaze began at my ankles, traveled up to my knees, paused momentarily, and continued slowly upward. By the time they stopped at my lips, I was out of breath and my mouth was dry.

"I know where I'd like it to lead," he said.

"Later, maybe?"

"Not too much later." His feet came down with a plop and he plucked his hat from the peg. "We have little over an hour before our appointment with Stringer and Edwin. Let's go see Serge, shall we?"

SINCE THE NEXT TO NOTHING THEATRE was only a few blocks away, we decided to walk. "Did Ruth make it to her interview?"

"She did. She was off to chop and slice up a storm. Create one is more like it. I don't hold much hope she'll get the job."

"You of little faith. Don't worry. If she doesn't, we'll come up with a new plan."

Dixon saw the marquee before I did and stopped dead in his tracks. "Looks like we need that new plan right now."

I looked up. Across the marquee announcing "Holmes at the Alamo" was a banner, which read CANCELLED: THEATRE CLOSED UNTIL FURTHER NOTICE. The front door was padlocked, so we went around to the back and found the stage door open. A few people were milling around inside, stacking chairs, removing props from the stage, and boxing up what looked like hundreds of freshly printed playbills. The actor who refused to play the part of Colonel Travis' ghost appeared to be in charge.

"I'll take the office staff," Dixon whispered. "You have a go with this guy."

"What's going on," I asked. "Where's Serge?"

"Gone."

"As in—"

"As in scram, vamoose, flew the coop, did a runner. In other words, he ain't here. Hey, you're the redhead from the party at The Driskill." He snapped his fingers as if to jog his memory.

"And you were here at the theatre talking to Serge. What do you want with him anyway?"

"Information. You have any idea of where I can find him?"

"Wish I knew. I came in this morning expecting to rehearse my lines with Lydia, she's Holmes, of course, I'm relegated to play Watson, and there was a notice to close up the theatre."

"Permanently?"

"With Serge, who knows? I gotta get back to work."

"ANY LUCK?" DIXON ASKED once we were back out on the street.

"Looks like Serge LaBeau skipped town. How about you?"

"There was an angry young woman in the office, shoving papers in files and cursing like a longshoreman. She said Serge called her this morning and told her he was going out of town for a while and to shut down operations. She didn't know where he went or why it happened."

"Maybe Stringer was telling the truth after all," I said. "If LaBeau did a disappearing act, he must have something to hide."

As we passed The Driskill, I asked Dixon if he minded getting the meeting with Stringer and Edwin started without me. I was eager to see if Ruth was now a member of The Driskill kitchen staff. I told him I'd stop by later.

Before I could knock on her door, it flew open and Ruth, in her Betty Crocker outfit, flew out. "Out of my way. I'm on my way back to work." She stormed down the hall toward the service elevator. "Don't follow me, someone will get suspicious."

"You got the job?"

She stopped and turned around. "Don't be so surprised. I not only got the job, but Helen wants me to start immediately."

"Who's Helen?"

"Helen Corbitt, the restaurant and catering manager. She used to run the teahouse at Joske's Department Store in Houston. Before that, she taught cooking classes at UT here in Austin. She's a real classy lady, and she likes me."

"I've heard of her."

"Sure you have. Now get out of my way."

"You did good, Ruth."

"Damn right," I heard her say as the elevator doors closed.

Miracles never cease. With Dixon busy with our clients and Ruth undercover, I decided to stop by the LaBeaus' apartment and see if they were there, although I doubted they would be.

The front door was padlocked just like the theatre. I went around to the back and it was also locked, but not with a padlock. I jimmied the lock, and soon the door popped open. It seemed like eons ago when I met Lydia on that blue-moon night. The prop room looked much the same. Dracula still smiled, showing his canines, and the guillotine sparkled. I walked upstairs to the apartment. The door was open. The radio was playing.

"Lydia? Serge?" No answer. I walked on in. A dirty skillet sat on the stove. The beds were unmade. Clothes were gone from the closets. I felt sad for the young girl. Wherever she and her father took off to, it must be hard on her. I went back down to the prop room, and as I headed for the backdoor, I noticed Lydia's lavender shoes on top of the bureau. I was surprised she'd left them behind. They are the only footwear I'd ever seen her wear, even when she was dressed as Sherlock Holmes. When I got closer, I noticed something white sticking out of the left shoe. I pulled out a piece of paper and unfolded it.

> *Sydney with a Y,*
> *The cops came around again asking more questions. I told Serge we needed to stay and fight, but he's such a coward. Don't worry about us. I'll contact you when I get a chance. In the meantime, keep working on the case and take care of my shoes.*
> *Your new friend,*
> *Lydia with a Y*

What the hell was wrong with me? Tears welled in my eyes, and before I could wipe them away, I was blubbering like Ruth when she missed a sale at Neiman Marcus. I had no idea why there wasn't a mother in Lydia's life, and that thought brought on more tears. The only thing to do was to take Lydia's advice and keep working on the case.

Chapter Nineteen

WHEN I GOT BACK to the agency, it was just after two. Stringer, Edwin, and Dixon were gathered around the table in the conference room. Stringer's face lit up when I walked in. "Well, if it isn't my favorite gal!"

I was in no mood for his false flattery. "I'm not your gal, Stringer." I turned to Dixon. "What have you found out?"

"We were getting to that," he said. "Go on, Edwin."

"After we went over the books on the day of the funeral and found nothing out of the ordinary, I decided to have a look at Dad's personal bank accounts." He opened a thick manila folder and leafed through the papers. "I actually had to go through everything anyway to settle his estate. Dad made me executor years ago since Mom is not capable. In the last couple of months, Dad had written several large checks to Serge LaBeau. At first, I thought they were donations to that damned art league nonsense."

"That was something your father seemed passionate about." I didn't know why I felt the need to defend a man I'd never met, but having Stringer, and now Edwin, in this small room gave me the willies.

"That's true," Edwin said, "but there were a steady stream of checks totaling five hundred thirty thousand dollars. That's some passion. What's worse is that I phoned LaBeau's theatre this morning and got word that the slime ball has left town and the theatre is closed."

"We discovered that too," Dixon said.

"It looks to me like Dad's dear friend squeezed him dry and took off. Dad has some stocks and bonds and a few other investments, but his Austin bank account is almost depleted. How could he do that? Mom's care is expensive. I might have to put their house on the market."

"Don't worry, son." Stringer placed his hand on his nephew's shoulder. "Your mother will be well taken care of. Fiona and I promise you that."

Edwin shook off Stringer's arm. "With all due respect, Uncle, if I need your help, I'll ask for it."

Stringer paid no attention to his nephew's rebuff. "I told you Leland was in some sort of trouble," he said. "He obviously got taken in by these artsy Commies. Leland wasn't the best businessman, that's why I ran the operation. Oh, Leland was fine working directly on the ranch, managing the cattle, handling the workers; he had a knack for that sort of thing, much better than me. I guess you could call Leland the PR man and me the money guy. But Leland could be easily taken in. He was a pushover for every needy cause that came his way. I'm sure LaBeau figured this out right away."

The words were on the tip of my tongue, but Dixon was quicker, and it was probably better that the question came from him. "My partner made a call to the West Texas Oil Company and spoke to a guy named Gary Huffman. He said it was you, Stringer, who had a problem with the contract and not Leland. Care to explain that?"

"Certainly. I play hardball, Ralph, when dealing with West Texas Oil or any other business. In the beginning, I went toe-to-toe on several contractual points. We settled those quickly. That was what Huffman referred to. This disagreement about the contract was between Leland and me. Listen, I'm sure I seem like a callous son-of-a-bitch. I mean, with going ahead with the gubernatorial race. Leland would have made a much better governor than me. He had that electable charm and charisma. And yes, you could say I used him, but it was a two-way street. We both had our own talents, and the partnership worked fine for thirty years. Then, all of a sudden, Leland gets involved with these crazy people and storms into the my room moments before we were to make the big announcement and refuses to go ahead with the plans. Look how foolish we both would have looked in front of our investors, our connections, and politicians—in front of half the wheelers and dealers in the state. Now, I ask you, who was the callous one?"

Edwin slammed the folder closed. "Damn it, Stringer! I didn't like Dad's involvement with the art center either, but Dad had his hands full and was going through a lot lately! How can you think he would pull something behind your back?"

"I'm sorry, son," Stringer said. "Your father had not been leveling with me lately. Initially, I thought it might have had something to do with the contact with the oil company. I was grasping at straws, I know. What was I supposed to do? I needed to find out what was going on. He was the closest friend I had, but his recent moodiness and his work with the art center was puzzling."

"Did you know that Leland contacted a lawyer that morning and had planned to end your partnership?" Dixon asked.

"That's absurd." Stringer sputtered. "Where did you hear that?"

"From two different people," I said.

"I'm sure that LaBeau fellow was one of them. See what I mean about his influence over Leland."

"Mr. Dixon, do you think you can locate Serge LaBeau and find out what he did with my father's money?" Edwin asked.

"This has turned out to be a much bigger job than I anticipated," Stringer said. "I'll pay more. It's only fair."

That last comment got a snicker from Edwin.

"We'll talk about money later," Dixon said. "We'll get to the bottom of this, or you owe us expenses only. That's only fair too."

"Good man," Stringer said. "I knew I could count on you. Let us know if you turn up anything. I'm going back to the ranch."

"There's one other thing," Dixon said. "We need to talk about your sister-in-law again."

"Mom?" Edwin said.

"That's the one," I replied. "Fiona believes she is innocent."

Stringer slumped down in the chair. "I know it looks damn bad for Eleanor. But Dr. Richards feels sure she won't spend much time in prison, if any, considering her condition."

"So you believe she's guilty?" Billy asked.

"I know my wife has been talking to you. I know she believes her sister did not kill Leland, but Eleanor has a history of instability."

"Why would she kill him?" I asked.

"I have to agree with Aunt Fiona," Edwin said. "Mom would

never do such a thing, and with the odd things that have been going on with Dad...I hate to point the finger, but it seems that with all the money disappearing so quickly, I can't help suspect Serge LaBeau."

"Do what you can, Ralph. Discovering that Eleanor did not kill Leland would definitely help the campaign." Stringer said. "Keep me abreast of everything." He got up to leave. "Edwin?"

"You go on. I have some business in town and then I want to see Mom later today. I haven't decided to tell her about the money, yet."

"I wouldn't say anything now," Stringer said. "She's got enough to deal with."

After Stringer left, Edwin stuck his folder in his brief case. "LaBeau's behind all of this. I know he was my father's friend, but we don't know much about the guy. My father could be naïve. Please find LaBeau. I'm flying to Midland tomorrow to check on Dad's bank accounts there. I'll be in touch."

Once we had the office to ourselves, we added the latest information to the board.

"Five hundred thirty thousand dollars. That's a lot of dough to give to a good cause, especially if it leaves you without much," Billy said. "Do you think LaBeau was blackmailing Tatum? We only have his word for it that he and Leland were good friends."

"Jones Digmire and Victor Nolan seemed to trust LaBeau," I said.

"Maybe all three guys were in on things together," Billy said.

"That's certainly a possibility," Dixon said.

"Except that Eleanor trusted LaBeau also," I added.

"We need to sniff out LaBeau," Dixon said. "Billy, go back to the theatre. Someone knows something. Talk to that dame in the office. She was damn hacked, and I have a feeling it was over more than just the closing of the theatre. I'm going to try to get Digmire back here for another little talk; ask him to bring Victor Nolan along too. See if I can rattle 'em."

"I'm going back to the clinic to see Eleanor without her sister being in the room," I said.

"How are you going to manage that?" Dixon asked.

"That, I haven't figured out yet. Oh, guess what? Ruthie May

Echland a.k.a. Adele Adleburg is now employed by The Driskill as a member of their kitchen staff."

"I told you she'd pull it off," Dixon said.

"The day's still young. See you guys later."

WHEN I DROVE UP into the parking lot of Dr. Richards' Clinic, I was relieved to see that Fiona's car was not there. I also needed to make this quick before Edwin arrived. I parked toward the back of the lot next to a food delivery truck. As I walked up the red steps, someone said, "You back to see Mrs. Tatum?"

I looked around and saw the female cop sitting on the bench near the waterfall enjoying a smoke. I walked over and joined her. "Mind if I bum a cigarette?" I asked.

"Not at all." She shook one loose and pulled out her lighter. "I admire any woman who carries a gun in her purse." She laughed and lit my cigarette. "Fancy place, don't you think? A sanitarium with a sculpture garden, waterfalls, shiny little fish swimming in their very own ocean."

"Dr. Richards must be doing well."

"Rumor has it that his wife's the one who footed the bill for his clinic, but what do I know. If my alcoholic grandmother could afford a place like this, she might have given up the bottle before she gave up on herself."

"Sorry to hear that," I said.

"It happens."

I wanted to say more, but she made her point so I let it drop. "How long have you been on the force, Officer?"

"Officer Crowley. About five years. It took four and a half to work my way to the other side of the desk. This is my first real assignment. It's not the most exciting police work, but it's a start. How about you? Been a PI long?"

"Unofficially about four months, officially about four weeks."

"I heard about you and that murder in Galveston. Now that must have been some excitement."

"Too much. I almost got my head shot off and my friends and entire family blown to smithereens."

She inhaled and a longing expression told me she envied my

near tragedy. "Think she killed him?" She nodded toward the building.

"I'm not sure. That's why I'm here. I doubt I can get in. I don't have an appointment and Mrs. Tatum's not here to escort me."

"That bitch! Fiona Maynard has been nothing but trouble. You'd think she owns this clinic. She has the staff hopping. 'Bring my sister this; bring my sister that. Take the soup back and heat it up.' Blah, blah, blah. Whoops. I hope you're not friends."

"What do you think? To tell the truth, I'm glad Mrs. Maynard's not here. Eleanor Tatum is pretty forthright with her thoughts and opinions, but I think she would have more to say if her sister weren't in the room."

Officer Crowley stood and stretched. "My break is over. I need to relieve my partner. There's a backdoor right next to Mrs. Tatum's room. How about you walk around there before my partner comes out and notices you? Once the coast is clear, I'll let you in."

"You mean it? I don't want you to get into trouble."

"Hey, I didn't get where I am today, guarding a rich lady who is accused of murdering her husband." She laughed. "Besides, I have a hunch about Mrs. Tatum too."

"You honestly don't think she did it?"

"Nope. Around the back. That way. See you in a few minutes."

My wait by the backdoor was no more than ten minutes when the door cracked open and Officer Crowley peered out. She motioned for me to come in. "I spoke to Mrs. Tatum, and she is eager to see you, but you have to make it quick. Mrs. Maynard usually shows up in the afternoon, and my partner will be back from break in about fifteen minutes."

"I owe you, Officer Crowley."

"Call me Madge. Now hurry."

Eleanor was standing by the window when I walked in. "Glad you came back. Sorry about what happened last time. Sometimes everything that's happened washes over me and I...well, it's difficult to comprehend. Did you talk to Serge?"

"Yes and no. I saw him a couple of days ago at the theatre

and he told me your husband came to see him right before he went over to The Driskill." I told her the rest of my conversation with Serge. "Half of what he said was a lie. He told me he wasn't at the party that night, which was true, but he was at the hotel and on the fifth floor right before the party started."

"When?"

"Apparently before your husband was shot. Before I had a chance to talk to him again, the cops scared him off and who knows where the hell he is? Were you aware your husband wiped out his bank account and gave the money to Serge?"

"Yes. Leland and I discussed it at length."

"Care to tell me why?"

"Leland and I had enough of Stringer. Leland had been losing interest in the business for some time. He tried on several occasions to get out, but each time, Stringer held something over Leland's head."

"Blackmail?"

"I'd call it that, yes. Stringer had a way of making my husband feel responsible for the welfare of the company. Making Leland believe that if he didn't go along with Stringer's plans, the business would fail. We realized that if we wanted to break from my sister and her husband, we would have to do it secretly, at least get the ball rolling. We decided to withdraw our money, give it to Serge to deposit in his company accounts for safe keeping."

"That's a lot of money to give to someone whom you haven't known that long."

Eleanor laughed. "Oh, Serge is trustworthy. Besides, we have a lawyer handling things too. After the money went to Serge, most of it was then transferred to our bank in Midland. Everything was going according to plan until a couple of days before Leland was to break the news about not running for governor."

"But why wait to tell Stringer only minutes before the announcement?"

"Actually, the plan was not to tell him until Leland made the announcement. Don't look at me as if I were mad."

"Let me get this straight; Stringer gathers everyone together, hands Leland the microphone so he can announce his candidacy for governor, and instead he says he's sorry to disappointment everyone, but he's changed his mind?"

"I would love to have seen Stringer's face when that happened." Eleanor pulled several tissues from the box and sat down. "Oh, God, Leland . . . "

I sat down next to her. "I know this is difficult, but I'm here to help and we don't have much time before your sister shows up."

She wiped her tears. "You're right. Please forgive me. Okay, yes, we did plan it that way."

"That would make Stringer look pretty foolish."

"That was the only way we could do it. If we told him ahead of time, he'd have pulled another one of his tricks and Leland would have been forced to go along with it."

"What could Stringer do?"

"He threatened to tie up all of Leland's assets so that it would take years to unravel everything, and in the meantime, Leland and I would be strapped financially. This way, with our personal finances protected, we could manage nicely. We'd planned to move from the ranch to a smaller place in town and live a much simpler life. We were not going to tell Stringer about dissolving the partnership until after the fiasco at the hotel."

"But Leland told him before the announcement. Why?'

"I don't know."

"Why did you want me to talk to Serge?"

"Serge and his art center deserve a chance. It's what Leland wanted. I don't want Stringer to prevent that."

"You don't sound like a woman who murdered her husband."

"I'm not happy about shooting my husband, Miss Lockhart. I wasn't myself when it happened. Drugs and alcohol don't mix."

"True, but I learned that you were off the drugs since you left the clinic a few months ago."

"I kept a few tranquilizers. I certainly needed them that day."

Before I could press her on the issue, Madge stuck her head in the door and told me it was time to leave.

"You'd better go before you get that nice lady police officer in trouble," Eleanor said.

"I'll be back," I told her.

"I wouldn't bother," she said. "What's done is done. Tell Serge he has my blessing and I will do what I can to get the art center up and running."

I rounded the corner of the building and ran smack into Fiona.

"You could have just called and I would have let you see her."

"I should have. Not very smart of me. It's like Fort Knox in there. I knew the receptionist wouldn't let me in without an appointment, so I tried to see if I could make some headway with the cops."

"No luck?"

"None. I was told to get my butt off the property before they had me arrested. How did you know I was here?"

"I spotted your car. When Sarah, the receptionist, said that she hadn't seen you, I played a hunch that you might have come around the back."

"That car has been more trouble than it's worth. I need to trade it for a black Dodge. I'm not getting the complete story, Fiona, that's why I wanted to talk to your sister again."

"My sister is not a well woman, Sydney. There's no telling what will come out of her mouth. She becomes paranoid and imagines someone is trying to do her harm. I've spent most of my life dealing with this."

"Yet you're convinced she didn't kill Leland."

"I am."

Officer Crowley poked her head out of the door and gave me a stern look. Bless that woman. "Listen, I got to go before I'm arrested. I'll consider what you told me."

Chapter Twenty

I WENT BACK TO THE HOTEL and was happy to see that it was still standing in all its glory and not smoldering from a bad kitchen fire. The lobby was quiet, the dining room free of bodies doubled over from food poisoning, and the aroma wafting through was that of grilled steak. I used the lobby phone and called Ruth's room. No answer. She must still be on the job, but for some reason, that didn't give me much comfort.

When I got to the agency, we had a full house: Billy, Dixon, Jones Digmire, and Victor Nolan. Digmire and Nolan looked as nervous as two students called in before their principal.

"That was quick," I said to Dixon. "How did you manage to get these two gentlemen here in the middle of a workday?"

"The mention of murder gets people hopping," Dixon said.

"But we didn't kill Leland," Victor Nolan pleaded. "You gotta believe us."

Dixon ignored Nolan's whining and set his stare on Digmire. He squirmed in his chair and finally said, "I thought you were going to help us," Digmire said.

"I thought we were too, Mr. Digmire. Your visit yesterday gave us a lot to go on, but I have a hunch you know more than you told us. Leland asked you two to meet him at the hotel for moral support, but things obviously didn't go as planned. He came back angry and said he wanted to speak to his wife in private. So you left and went to The Blue Mist."

"That's what I told you last time I was here," Digmire said.

"You never showed back up at the hotel," Dixon said. "I didn't see you at the party."

"We didn't go," Nolan finally spoke up. "We couldn't watch Leland make that announcement, so we stayed at the bar all afternoon."

"Jones, we gotta tell them the truth. We gotta. Where's Serge anyway? Why isn't he here?" Nolan asked.

"We were hoping you could tell us," Dixon said. "Seems he skipped town yesterday."

"Blasted!" Digmire stood up, knocking his chair to the floor. "That stupid ass son-of-a-bitch." He looked as if he were ready to bolt. "Got any more of that bourbon?"

"Sit down, Mr. Digmire," Billy said. "I'll get it."

"Tell him," Nolan said.

Digmire shook his head.

"We stayed at The Blue Mist like I said," Nolan said. "When we left, we saw Serge running from the hotel."

"What time was this?" Dixon asked.

"A little before five," Nolan said.

"You think Serge killed Leland?" I asked.

"Oh, God. I don't know," Digmire looked over at Nolan whose head was in his hands. "He looked so spitting mad when we saw him leave the hotel."

"He couldn't have done it," Nolan said. "He and Leland were good friends. He had no reason to kill the guy."

"None that you know of," I said. "Did Leland ever confide in you about supporting the Austin Art and Cultural Center financially?"

"Except for the ranch, we didn't talk money," Digmire snapped.

"But Leland confided in you as a friend, telling you he was planning to sever things with Stringer, yet he never mentioned details about how he was going to support the Art Center?"

"That was Leland." Digmire was almost pleading now. "Catch him in the right mood and he could talk your ear off, other times, he was closed mouth. He was my friend, but also my employer, so I never asked him any nosy questions. I just did the listening."

"And you never heard anything about Leland financing La Beau's project?" Dixon said.

"No," Digmire said.

"And now Serge's left town, and you can't tell us anything about that, either?" I said.

"I told you everything I know," Digmire cried. "I know it looks bad for Serge."

"It certainly does." Dixon said.

"Listen, Serge's not the type who'd steal and murder," Nolan said.

"Those sentiments won't hold much water with a jury," Dixon said, "especially now that he's left town after the cops told him not to."

"I know that! But it wasn't him," Nolan said.

Digmire was almost beside himself. Sweat formed on his brow, and he kept wiping his hands on his trousers.

"Yeah, yeah, we know," Dixon said. "It wasn't Serge, it wasn't Eleanor, it wasn't either of you two. Did Leland own a gun?"

"Sure, he did. Who doesn't?" Nolan piped up. "He's got a collection at his house."

"You think Leland was killed with his own gun?" Digmire asked.

"Cops are still tracing it," Dixon said. "Did Leland carry a gun with him?"

"Not that I know of," Digmire said, "except for a shotgun in his truck. And what fool rancher wouldn't have one ready when he's driving around his property? You never know when you'll run up against rattlers or coyotes."

I looked at Dixon to see if he was finished with that line of questioning and he nodded, so I jumped in. "How did Stringer and Edwin get along?"

"I worked the ranch with Leland," Digmire said. "I didn't have much dealings with the business side of things."

"I understand, but you were around these people a lot, surely you got a feel for how they felt about one another."

"It always seemed kind of odd to me," Nolan commented. "The wife and I were often over at the Tatums for barbeques and cookouts, things like that. Edwin never seemed to be around much, and when he was, it was with Stringer. I never noticed any problems between them. It was like two business men discussing their business."

"What's odd about that?" I asked.

"What's odd is that Edwin was Leland's son, but they didn't have much in common. Edwin was more like Stringer, all business," Nolan said.

"Victor's right," Digmire said. "We always figured it was because of Eleanor's illness that Edwin spent much of his time with the Maynards. Why are you asking?"

"Just curious," I said. "The day before the murder, the day you went into Leland's office to talk to him about cattle, you said something had happened, but you can't give us a clue to what that might have been?"

"Like I said before, when Leland didn't want to talk, nothing or nobody could make him say a word."

The two men left the office in such a nervous state, I was afraid they wouldn't be able to drive.

"We have to locate Serge and find out what happened that day," Dixon said. "Any luck at the theatre, Billy?"

"The backdoor was opened and I walked in. A few lights were on, but otherwise, it was deserted. I went through the theatre and backstage, and then around to the office when I heard someone crying. I pushed open a door to what looked like a storeroom, and this girl was having a good cry."

"Auburn hair, green eyes? Looked sort of like Audrey Meadows with darker hair?" Dixon asked.

"That's her. Her name is Phoebe Sullivan. I told her I was looking for Serge LaBeau and this sent her into another wave of tears. I pulled up a chair and handed her my handkerchief. She said she didn't know where he was and couldn't believe he left without saying a word. I got the feeling she was sweet on him, so I played that card. I told her that if LaBeau was stupid enough to treat her that way he didn't deserve her."

"You're such a charmer, Billy," Dixon said.

"I wasn't blowing smoke, Boss. The nice young woman was upset."

I turned toward the window so Billy wouldn't see me smile. He was such a softhearted boy; I couldn't believe he hadn't been snatched up.

"Sorry, son," Dixon said. "Go on."

"Anyway, I leveled with her and told her who I was and why we needed to find him. I said that when people usually leave town quickly, they end up going someplace familiar. I told her to think."

"She said she'd only been with the theatre a couple of months and didn't know all that much about Serge's personal life. I asked if there had ever been a Mrs. LaBeau? She said she thought she'd died years ago when she and Serge lived in Bastrop where they operated a small theatre owned by his parents."

Before he could get the last words out of his mouth, Dixon had the phone in his hand. "Operator. Bastrop information. Yes, do you have a listing for a LaBeau; L-a B-e-a-u?" He picked up a pencil and I shoved a scrap of paper under it. "Thank you." He hung up. "Only one LaBeau in Bastrop, a René LaBeau, most likely the father."

"I don't think we should call," Billy said. "If LaBeau is there and he suspects we're on to him, he might bolt again. Bastrop's only about thirty miles from here. I'll drive out there and see if I can ferret him out of his hiding place."

"Makes sense," Dixon said. "It'll be late by the time you get there, so prepare to find a place to stay for the night if you have to. We'll see you tomorrow." Dixon unlocked the cash box and handed Billy a few extra bucks.

Billy left and Dixon and I decided to walk over to The Driskill. On our way out, I grabbed a stack of index cards. Neither of us had taken the time to grab lunch, and the club at The Driskill was a nice place to wind down our day and enjoy a meal; that is, when we weren't dealing with dead bodies.

Joey was on duty, so rather than get a table, we took our usual seats at the bar. The first thing I noticed when I sat down, was a card announcing the bar's drink special, a Gin Rickey. That brought my cousin to mind, and I wondered if she was still plying her talents in the kitchen. Ruth had never worked a day in her life, not unless you called spending an exhausting day in her apartment rearranging her shoes and handbags.

We ordered two BLTs, a glass of wine for me, and a bottle of beer for Dixon. The bar and restaurant were busy, and by the time we took our first bite, it was almost seven-thirty. "Surely, Ruth can't still be at work," I said. Dixon reached over the bar and helped himself to the phone.

"I'll call and see if she's in. Invite her down." After eight rings, he hung up.

"Maybe she got off work, discarded her disguise, and went out," I said.

"We'll hear from her soon enough. What do you think about Digmire and Nolan's story?"

"If what they said is true, it makes Serge a believable suspect, and he had a five hundred thousand dollar motive."

"After we finish eating, I'll call the station and see if Detective Bremmer's there and find out if he's got a lead on the gun. I also want to get his take on the position of the body."

I'd learned that, although being nosy was a necessary qualification for being a detective, connections with the local law enforcement were paramount. A few weeks before Dixon left his job with the Hot Springs Police Department, he asked around about detectives on the Austin police force. That's how Dixon became acquainted with Detective Bremmer. Having worked for a police department gave Dixon the advantage in knowing how to handle cops. Sharing information and being willing to allow them to take credit for solving crimes went a long way in gaining their trust. Dixon, having done his homework, resulted in Dixon, Lockhart, and Ludlow's having a connection to the Austin Police Department.

I pulled out my cards. "Let's talk suspects," I said. "Digmire, Nolan, Eleanor, and Serge. They were all at the hotel before the party. Right now, my money is on Serge. Let's hope Billy can root Serge out of his hiding place and haul him back here. Otherwise, the cops will find him, if they haven't already. Look how easy it was for us to get a lead on where he might be."

Dixon finished his sandwich and pushed his plate away. "Sit tight. I'll make that call to Bremmer."

I studied the index cards and couldn't help but feel we were missing something. The suspect list was long enough, but it was time to add a few artists to our inquiry.

"He's not in," Dixon said, signaling Joey to bring our bill. "I left a message for him to call me at the office as soon as he could. Your place or mine? I've always wanted to say that, now I can."

"Mine. Give me an hour. I'll run up to Ruth's room and check on things. If you get to my apartment before me, let yourself in and do the daddy-thing with my pets."

"That doesn't come free." He grinned.

"I'll pay. Whatever the price," I said and gave him an installment kiss.

Chapter Twenty-One

I LEFT DIXON WITH A HUGE GRIN on his face and flew up to Ruth's room, keeping my fingers crossed she would not be there. I knocked twice, feeling elated over my good luck until the elevator dinged and Betty Crocker wearing a mink rushed out.

"I told you to leave the mink here."

"Out of my way." She opened her door and rushed in. "I'm working a double. I came to get my cookbooks. And, Miss Know-It-All, they love the mink." Suddenly she stopped. "Someone's been in my room?"

"How can you tell?"

"Look, the bedspread's crinkled and twisted, and look, my bathroom towels have been used!"

"Are you sure you didn't do this? Maybe the housekeeper forgot to finish up."

"Of course I am sure! She cleaned it and brought fresh towels before I left." She ran over to her luggage and pulled out her jewelry box. "Thank goodness nothing's been stolen. You're responsible for this, Sydney Jean."

"Me?"

"I'm needed back at work. Find out what's going on. I'll see you in the morning."

I watched my cousin disappear down the hall and wondered who had slipped a work-ethic potion into her martini. I didn't give much thought to Ruth's suspicions. The bedspread was hardly wrinkled, no more than the result of tossing a few outfits across it, and only one bath towel was slightly damp.

WHEN I GOT TO MY APARTMENT, my three favorite people where sacked out on my sofa. Dixon, minus his fedora, jacket, and shoes was asleep sitting up. Monroe was snuggled up with her head in his lap. Mealworm had deposited a sufficient quantity of orange cat hair on his jacket turned cat nest. What did I do to deserve such a guy?

THE RISING SUN and my alarm clock played a dirty trick on me, arranging for Thursday morning to arrive way too early. Dixon thought so too and merely groaned when I knocked the alarm clock from the bedside table onto the floor. He rose up on his elbow and looked around. "The last thing I remember was being a pet sandwich on your sofa. Can you explain to me, in as few words as possible, how I ended up here with my clothes nowhere in sight?" I answered his question using not one single word. We must have eventually fallen back to sleep. Two hours later, we were awakened by what sounded like a battering ram trying to make its way through my bedroom wall.

"What the hell?" Dixon said.

I peeked through the blinds. "My neighbor/gardener Mr. Grimwall. Looks like his going after spiders with a hammer."

"Damn," Dixon said. "I'll make coffee, you walk the dog."

AT 9:15, DIXON AND I stepped onto the elevator right behind a familiar figure dressed in a rumpled gabardine dress the color of her bloodshot eyes. She held a Mason jar of milk and smiled shyly.

"Miss Sullivan," I said.

"I was just on the way to your office," she responded.

"I think it's going to be an interesting morning," Dixon said. "All you brought was milk? We could use some breakfast."

Phoebe Sullivan giggled.

Serge, and to my sheer delight, Lydia LaBeau were seated at our conference table. I wanted to run up and hug the girl around her scrawny neck, but Lydia was obviously in business mode.

"We didn't get very far," Lydia said. "It took me all night to talk him into coming here."

"You've a smart daughter, Serge." I said.

"Serge didn't plug Leland Tatum," Lydia said.

I glanced at Dixon who hid his smile behind his hand.

"Shut your mouth, Florence," Serge said. "I should have never agreed to let you play Sherlock Holmes. It went to your head."

Lydia shuddered at Serge's use of her real name."At least I

have a level head on which things can go, which is more than I can say for you. You can't even hide effectively. And it's Lydia!" She then directed her next comments to us as if her father was too insignificant to bother with. "It appears as if Serge here is in deep trouble, having been one of the last people to see Mr. Tatum alive. I'm not too good either, seeing as how we left Bastrop before I had breakfast." She shot Phoebe an impatient look and arranged the plate of Mrs. Granger's cookies in front of her while Billy rinsed out a coffee cup.

"Sorry, it took so long," Phoebe said. "Zeke's Grill was busy. I had to wait before they sold me the milk." She took the cup Billy had given her and sat it and the jar down in front of Lydia who filled it. She dunked the first of what would be many cookies to follow and said, "Mr. Dixon, you can take over from here."

"Are you sure, darling? You were doing such a good job," Dixon said.

"It's your show," she said.

"You go first, Billy," Dixon said.

"Sure thing. I decided to take Miss Sullivan along with me when I went to Bastrop."

Serge shots daggers at Phoebe who responded with a lip snarl.

"We arrived in Bastrop around ten and went straight for the theatre," Billy said.

"They found us in the aisle seats of the fourth and fifth rows," Lydia said. "The movie was *Streets of Laredo* with William Holden and Macdonald Carey. Holden looked dashing with those six guns strapped to his hips."

Serge picked up a cookie and shoved it in his daughter's mouth.

"What do you have to say for yourself, LaBeau?" Dixon said.

"Not a damn thing."

"He's pleading the fifth," Lydia said, spitting cookies crumbs over the table.

"I want my lawyer here," Serge said.

"We're not the cops, Serge," I said. "We're here to help you out of this mess and find out who killed Leland Tatum and why."

"But I don't know that," Serge said.

"Oh, come on, Serge, you're such a smart guy," Phoebe Sullivan said as she nuzzled Billy's arm.

"Mr. LaBeau, tell us everything you know. Start with the day Mr. Tatum was killed." Dixon said.

"I already told everything I know to your girlfriend."

"Tell it again," Dixon said.

"Why should I?"

"Because you were lying about the time you were at the hotel," I said. "There were witnesses who saw you were there much later than you said; much closer to the time of the murder."

"Go back over that day," Dixon said.

"Do it, Serge. I don't want to be forced to live with the grandparents and have to go to school with a bunch of kids from Bastrop while you're serving time," Lydia said.

"What did I ever do to deserve all this," Serge moaned. "Okay. Leland came to see me at the theater after he checked into the hotel. He'd just had the meeting with Stringer. Things didn't go as planned. Truthfully, I don't know what Leland expected. He could be naïve at times. I think he seriously thought Stringer would accept his decision about dissolving the partnership and not running for governor."

"So, Leland backed down?" Dixon asked.

"Not at all. He said he was going through with everything, but things were going to get really ugly for both him and Eleanor. Stringer told Leland that he'd ruin them, and by the time he got finished, they'd come crawling back. Leland also said the jerk was going to hire a PI and have him investigated." Serge paused and took a breath.

"How could Stringer do that to his family?" Billy asked.

"Easy," Serge said. "The man has no heart. He has no soul."

"Like a vampire," Lydia said. "Sucking people dry." She used her two index fingers and raised her upper lip, exposing her canines.

"How long was Leland at the theatre with you?" Dixon asked.

"Not long, less than an hour. He left and said he was going for a walk to think things over and that he'd see me at the party. I told him I wasn't going. He smiled and left."

"How about you?" I asked.

"I couldn't sit around either. The tension was killing me. I decided to go over to the post office and check my box. On the way, I saw Stringer Maynard going into the Scarborough Building. I decided to follow. The elevator door had just closed and I saw it go up to the eighth floor. He went up to your office. That's how I knew he'd hired you; Dixon, Lockhart, and Ludlow."

"But how did you know I was the Lockhart in the agency?" I said.

"Easy. I asked the elevator operator when he came down. I told him I needed a detective and asked if he knew anything about your agency."

"And he told you my name and where I lived?" I said.

"He told me your names and I looked you up in the phone book. Ralph Dixon and Billy Ludlow weren't listed. You were." Serge chuckled.

"What's so funny?" I said.

"He also said the two guys, Dixon and Ludlow, were top notch fellows, but Lockhart was a dame and probably couldn't find a lost cat if it was mewing in a tree right above her."

Lydia came to my defense. "I wouldn't put much stock in what that idiot says. I noticed on the way up here his fly was open."

"Back to the murder," Dixon said. "What made you decide to go to the hotel?"

"I knew something else was troubling Leland. I don't know what. Leland needed me, and I felt like a heel for refusing to go to the party. I went to his suite. I knocked, but there was no answer. I waited in that alcove, and when he didn't return, and I left and went back to the theatre."

"You didn't see or hear anything?" Billy asked.

"I noticed a couple of hotel guys getting ready for the party. They wheeled a bunch of liquor bottles off the elevator."

"So, you waited and left?" I asked.

"I just told you that! Are you deaf?"

"You lied about the time you were at the hotel," I said. "And you're lying now."

"You saw something, Serge," Lydia said. "You came back to the theatre and closed yourself in the office, and—"

"So, you're the one who squealed. My own flesh and blood."

"Mr. LaBeau," Dixon said, "if you know something, you need to talk."

"I didn't kill anyone. You have to believe me."

"Start talking," Dixon said, "or we're turning you over to the cops."

Serge sat back in his chair and did his best to look defiant.

"Billy," Dixon said. Billy picked up the receiver and dialed O.

"No, wait," Serge cried. "It's obvious why I lied about the time I was at the hotel. I was there right after it happened. I knew if anyone found out, it would look bad for me. You gotta believe me. I didn't kill Leland Tatum."

"How did you get the blood on your clothes?" I asked.

"Damn!" Serge slammed his fist on the table. "Florence!"

"Stop giving your daughter a hard time. She's trying to help you," Dixon said.

Serge pulled his handkerchief from his pocket and mopped his forehead. "I was on the fifth floor, like I said, waiting by the door for Leland to return. I finally gave up and decided to leave. On the way out, I passed the room next to the Yellow Rose Suite and saw the door was open a crack. I went in. At first, I didn't see him. Oh, God, I must have walked in right after Leland was shot. There was so much blood. I got it on my pants and shirtsleeve and realized how incriminating it looked. I heard someone coming down the hall and I panicked. There was a door, which I found out led to Leland's bedroom suite. I waited in there, and when no one came into the room, I climbed out the window and down the fire escape. You don't think...the gunshot could have been...self-inflicted, do you?"

Lydia blew air out her cheeks, but held her tongue. "The man was shot in the back, Serge."

Serge looked at his daughter, studying her face as if he'd seen her for the first time. "You obviously didn't get your smarts from me. Maybe you can work here part-time. Collect your pay in milk and cookies."

"What happened then?" I asked.

"Like I told you before. I left and went to the apartment where I changed my clothes and then went back to the theatre."

Dixon tapped his pencil on the desk. "Anything else you want to tell us?"

"You know it all," Serge said. "At least everything I know."

"Except for the money," I said.

"Money?" Serge squeaked.

"More than a half a mil that Leland gave to you." Dixon said. "Why?"

"It was for the Art Center. I was funneling it from his bank in Austin to one in Midland," Serge said. "Since he was planning on dissolving the partnership, he felt it best to get his money out of Austin before Stringer could figure out how to freeze his accounts."

"What bank in Midland?" I asked.

"Midland-Odessa Trust. Don't bother looking. It's not there."

"Oh, brother." Lydia sighed.

"We're listening," Dixon said.

"Because I haven't transferred it yet. It's in my account." He took his bankbook from his jacket pocket and handed it to Dixon. "It's all there."

Dixon flipped through it. "Mind if I keep this? I'll put it in the safe."

"Go ahead," Serge said.

"Anyone else know about the money?" I asked.

"As far as I know, only Eleanor knows about Leland writing me the checks."

"How about Leland funding the Art Center? Anyone else know about that," Dixon asked.

"That was no secret."

"I want to talk to some of your friends who were at the party that night," I said.

"I'm telling you the truth," Serge shouted.

I chose not to remind the guy that he'd lied to me a couple of times. "Get a grip, Serge. Your friends may have seen or heard something. The rather large, flamboyant woman, the one who'd used an eyebrow pencil to draw a veil on her face and a flashy guy who looked so slick, you could use him as a polishing rag."

"Savannah Swift and Cameron Ferguson. She's an artist and the owner of Swift's Gallery, and he's an artist too. Her gallery is a couple of doors down from the theatre. Cameron hangs out there most of the time."

"That's it for now," Dixon said. "I suggest Billy take you back to Bastrop. Try to keep from getting arrested until we can figure this out."

Serge glanced at Phoebe with a questioning look.

"Forget it, Serge" Lydia said. "She's too young for you. Can I go by the theatre and pick up my shoes on the way?" Lydia asked me.

"Look who's not very smart?" Serge said. "The place is probably swarming with cops."

"I'm not going back to Bastrop." Lydia folded her arms across her chest. "Grandma makes me go to bed at eight. She's a horrible cook. She puts sugar in everything, corn, beans, even mashed potatoes. I'm surprised she and Grandpa don't have sugar diabetes. I'm staying with Sydney."

Dixon glanced at me. I suspected the disappointed look on his face might be attributed to thoughts of not being able to repeat last night. Then he smiled. "Lydia's right. You're on the lam, Serge, and Lydia could be in danger. But I know where she'll be safe and we can keep an eye on her. I need to make a call to see if it's okay. Excuse me." Dixon walked into the outside office.

"I know I'm a horrible father. You're right. She shouldn't be with me."

"Do you know what he's got up his sleeve?" Lydia asked me.

"I think so. And don't worry. The food is excellent and you'll have the run of the property."

Dixon popped back in. "It's settled," he said. "My landlords, Les and Caroline Granger, great people, are delighted to have Lydia as a guest. Mrs. Granger's the one who baked those cookies, by the way."

"Okay," Lydia said. "I was hoping for the poodle and cat, but the Grangers will have to do."

Chapter Twenty-Two

I POURED OUT THE COLD COFFEE and made a fresh pot. Dixon and I attempted to make sense over these latest developments.

"What do you think about Serge's story; finding Leland dead an hour earlier?" I asked. "You have more experience with this sort of thing, and you had a closer look at the body."

"It is possible he'd been shot earlier, but not much earlier. If he didn't die right away, that would explain why the blood still looked fresh. I didn't get a chance to feel the body. But Serge's story doesn't explain why we heard the shot, followed by Eleanor's scream when she found her husband."

"And it doesn't explain why Eleanor confessed if her husband had been shot by someone else earlier."

The phone rang. It was Bremmer. I poured our coffee and listened to the one-sided conversation, trying to read from Dixon's deadpan face if the police detective was parting with any juicy info. Finally, he hung up.

"The gun was not Leland's. It was part of the loot stolen from a pawnshop on Red River a few weeks ago."

"So, that story Eleanor told about finding it in Leland's suitcase is a boldface lie."

"No surprise." Dixon sipped his coffee and rubbed his right earlobe. I don't remember when I first noticed him doing that, but it seemed as familiar to me as if I'd watched it my entire life. I also knew it meant that his brain was sorting.

"What is it?" I asked.

"Bremmer said the gun had been fired twice."

"We only heard one shot. If Leland *was* shot earlier, as Serge claimed, then Eleanor could have fired the second shot. The one we heard." I studied the notes on our corkboard board. "She walks in, finds her husband dead, picks up the gun and shoots it to make it look like she killed him because she's covering for someone."

"She must have had a damn good reason to suspect the person she was covering for."

"I doubt she'd cover for Digmire or Nolan. If she's really such good friends with LaBeau, she might cover for him. She might even cover for Fiona. No doubt she'd cover for Edwin. What did Bremmer think about the gun being fired twice or the position of the body?"

"He didn't sound concerned on either issue. He's playing his cards close to his chest. We need to find out if Nolan and Digmire were actually boozing it up at The Blue Mist when they said they were, and where Edwin and Fiona were around 4:30." He walked to the board and placed a big red circle around Edwin's name. "LaBeau didn't say anything about seeing a gun at the murder scene."

"If there was an earlier shot, wouldn't the hotel staff have heard it?"

"Let's pay a little visit to the hotel."

DIXON AND I MANAGED to get into the office suite where Leland was killed with no problem. After an hour of searching every space of wall and floor, every inch of ceiling, and every piece of furniture, we came up dry. No second bullet lodged anywhere.

"Could she have shot out the window?"

Dixon went to unlock the window and had to tug several times to raise it. When it finally gave, we heard a mild crack of dry paint snapping. "This window hasn't been opened in years. We need to start from the beginning; talk to every person who was on the fifth floor that day—hotel employees and guests who attended the party, anyone else who stayed on that floor—and see if they heard a shot before the party started. At this point, talking to Digmire and Nolan again is futile. What's the name of that guy who was checking invitations at the party?"

"Jasper Noells."

"Talk to him again. Think you can get a list of names of everyone who worked the party?"

"I will. I'll also see if the artists know anything."

"Good idea. If you need to, slip Jasper some cash to get him talking. I'll see if I can get a list of guests staying on the fifth floor. I'll talk with Bremmer again. See you later. Maybe by the end of the day, we'll have shaken something loose."

Dixon's last comment turned out to be the understatement of the year.

THE VICTORIAN WAS BUSY, but I managed to secure my usual seat at the bar. Right away I noticed a card announcing a new drink special; today it was a Margarita. Yesterday, it was a Gin Rickey. Shivers went up my spine.

Joey walked up looking a bit harried. "Hey, Miss Lockhart." He picked up the martini shaker and pointed it at me.

I laughed. "Too early, even for me. Coffee and some of your time, if you can spare it."

"Coffee's no problem. I'm yours if you don't mind me disappearing every once in a while. There's been a last-minute meeting called for all restaurant, bar, and catering staff in a few minutes."

The spine shivers of a moment ago had reached my scalp. I didn't want to, but I had to ask. "What's going on?"

"Chef and the restaurant manager have been sequestered behind closed doors all morning. I was off last night, so I'm not sure what happened."

I feared what happened last night was a petite, blonde, mink-wearing nightmare. Just then a deliveryman barged in pushing a clothes rack.

"Hey, buddy," he called to Joey. "My instructions say to take these to the kitchen, but I think that might be a mistake."

"Are you from Scarborough's Formal Wear?" Joey asked.

"Yep."

"Your instructions were correct." Joey came out from behind the bar. "Follow me."

As the guy pushed the rack around the bar, I noticed the logo on the garment bags as he walked by: Lowels Tuxedos. Suddenly, Ruth emerged from the kitchen wearing a short fur cape.

"It's about time you got here," she said to the deliveryman. "We were expecting you twenty minutes ago. Do you have the cummerbunds?"

"They're in a box on the truck," the guy said.

"Well, hurry then," Ruth chided him.

I tried to hide behind a hefty guy sitting a couple of stools down, but Ruth spotted me and marched over.

"While I'm hard at work, you're boozing it up at the bar," she said.

I held up my coffee cup. "Speaking of working, you're supposed to be on the case. What's going on in the kitchen?"

"I've been promoted to restaurant concierge. Helen loves my ideas. The waiter's uniforms were so common. Tonight, they'll wear purple satin tuxedo jackets, black pants, and guess what else?"

"Fur boxer shorts?"

"But how would that do any good? No one would see them. No, they are wearing fur cummerbunds to match my and Rosemary's capes. And you thought that furs in the kitchen were a bad idea!"

"Who's Rosemary?"

"She was the salad prep girl, but I promoted her to my assistant."

I picked up the cocktail card. "Is this your idea too?"

She wiggled her tiny body. "Of course."

"Nice job, Ruth, but what about the case?"

"Before I get information, I have to earn people's trust. Now I've got a new waiter to train and a big party's coming in for a private luncheon. And I shouldn't be seen talking to you. I'm undercover." She turned to go back to her reorganization of The Driskill's food staff and then turned back around. "I'll have something for you by the end of my shift. In the meantime, you might be interested to know that Mr. Stringer Maynard is holding court up in the Citadel Club." She snickered and disappeared into her lair.

Joey came back wearing the new getup and looking slightly embarrassed. "What do you think?" he asked me.

"The purple clashes with your green eyes, but don't worry, once you get busy mixing cocktails, no one will notice."

He ran his hands across the fur band surrounding his midsection. "I didn't even know they made these. Seems a waste of good animal fur. What did you want to talk to me about?"

"Actually, I wanted to see Jasper."

"He's serving in the Citadel. You'll have to come back tomorrow unless you want to hang around until he gets off work, but that won't be until around midnight." A waiter walked up and handed him a ticket order.

"Don't flip your wig, Joey," he said.

"Bummer. Excuse me, Miss Lockhart, I've got four of these new-fangled Margaritas to mix."

I wasn't going to wait until midnight, and with Stringer at the club, I'd just pop up there and kill two birds with one stone. On my way to the elevator, I passed the host stand where Ruth was running her jaws at whom I supposed was her new waiter-in-training. Then I stopped and did a double take. Hanging on to her every word, and decked out in the formal jacket and furry cummerbund and looking like a purple chipmunk, was Tweety Gilcrest. I waited until Ruth scurried back into the kitchen and walked over to have it out with my meddling colleague once and for all. Tweety saw me coming, and instantly his sallow complexion turned scarlet. I grabbed his jacket collar as he tried to duck into the restaurant. "Listen, either you tell me what you're up to, or I'm going straight to the lobby phone and ring Ernest."

"Don't have a cow, Sydney. I'm only moonlighting. I swear."

"Moonlighting on the newspaper's time? Cut the crap."

I saw Ruth, clipboard in hand, walking through the restaurant followed by a gaggle of waiters.

"I'm here for my training today. Ernest thinks I'm out on a job. Please don't tell him. I'll be working nights. I gotta be prepared for when Ernest gives me the chop. Now, I got work to do. Miss Adleburg, the person in charge, is depending on me. And one more thing, Sydney. I'm not the *only* one who's moonlighting."

So that's it. The little maggot found out about the detective agency. Although I hadn't kept my other profession a big secret, except for Ernest, I didn't want my newspaper colleagues to know, for obvious reasons. I didn't believe his moonlighting story, though. Tweety Gilcrest was up to something, but he slithered off before I could squeeze the truth out of him.

THE ELEVATOR OPERATOR haughtily informed me that the Citadel was a private club. He made no movement to close the gate and drive the elevator car up to the second floor. Finally, he said, "If there is someone visiting the club whom you wish to see, you are welcome to go to the front desk and they will page him."

"I'll ask at the door myself. Go ahead and take me up."

"I can't do that ma'am. It's against regulations."

Dixon didn't tell me how difficult it was to get into the damn club, but then Stringer had invited him. If it worked for Dixon, it should work for me. "Someone is expecting me."

"I doubt that, Miss. You'll have to go to the front desk. I'm sure you understand."

He won the staring contest so I left with the intention of taking the stairs, but the operator must have suspected my plan. He stepped out of the mechanical cage and watched me leave. I made as if to go to the front desk. When I reached the lobby bar, I ducked into the ladies' room to wait out the operator. I brushed my hair and applied a new layer of lipstick, all the while thinking of Tweety and how to handle him. Tattling to Ernest seemed petty, but Tweety was lying like a big dog. This was the third time I'd found him here at the hotel, not to mention the incident at my desk at the newspaper. I'd have to tell Ruth to be careful.

The coast was clear in the lobby and the elevator was on the way up. I took the stairs to the second floor, half expecting the National Guard to be on alert for a tall, redhead trying to get into the Citadel. The host at the stand greeted me with the same snobbish attitude as the elevator operator.

"May I help you, ma'am? Are you lost?"

"Yes, you may help me and no I am not lost. I'm here to see Stringer Maynard. I believe he's having drinks in one of the private rooms."

"You're meeting him here?"

"No, you jerk, we'd planned to meet in the alley by the

trashcans, but we figured the service might be better here." I bit back those words, and instead said, "Oh, I know I'm not properly dressed, but it won't take long. I need to speak to him for a moment. It's business."

"If you give me the message about this *business*, I'll be happy to deliver it to Mr. Maynard." A waiter came out of the club and handed the guy a note. He looked it over in frustration and said, "Thank you. I'll handle this." Then he turned back to me. "Wait here, Miss. I'll see what I can do," he said and followed the waiter into the club.

I'm sure the note contained the words "woman," "redhead," and "elevator operator," and since I didn't relish waiting here only to be escorted out, I walked in. The place was much smaller than I had expected. No more than a few tables and a bar that seated four. Several doors led to what must have been the private rooms. The lights were dim and a thick cloud of cigar smoke hung like a drape over the lounge. I let my eyes adjust, the quiet murmur of voices stopped as if someone had turned off a radio. I scanned the faces for Stringer's when I realized that mouths gaped and all eyes were on me. How rude! Then I noticed Stringer standing in the doorway leading into a private room, so I made my way over. "Excuse me, Stringer. I hope I'm not disturbing you, but we need to have a little talk."

"Sydney!"

Suddenly someone grabbed my arm. "Sorry, Mr. Maynard, she sneaked in when I wasn't looking." Private club or not, being drug through the Citadel by the hotel security guard was a bit extreme.

"Now listen here," I said. "I know this is a private club, but the last time I looked, this was a free country."

"Not here, Miss." the guard said.

"It's okay, Clyde," Stringer said. "There's been a misunderstanding. I'll escort Miss Lockhart to the downstairs bar."

Moments later, Stringer and I were in the lounge downstairs, the *public* lounge. "What the hell was that all about?"

"You didn't know?" Stringer asked. "The Citadel is a men's club. Women aren't allowed."

I thought about the suffragettes marching for women's right to vote a little over thirty years ago. Evidently, the news had not yet reached the Citadel. No wonder Dixon was evasive about the antiquated practices of the club. He knew better than to tell me and have me stage a protest in front of the hotel. However, there was no way I would do that. At least not until this case was solved.

"What did you want to see me about, Miss Sydney?"

"Actually, you weren't the only reason I wanted into the Citadel. I wanted to talk to one of the hotel's employees, Jasper Noells. He was the one checking invitations the night of your party."

"Yes, I know Jasper. I don't know how much good that would do. I'm sure it would be a waste of your time."

"I'll decide that. Seemed you'd be eager to have the charges against Eleanor dropped so they wouldn't affect your campaign."

"All I ask is for Richards to keep Eleanor out of jail. If she's institutionalized, I'm sure voters will understand."

"You don't consider an institute incarceration?"

"It's been her life, Sydney."

"But not the past few months. You know, Stringer, you're the most callous SOB I've ever met."

"I've been called worse. Okay, if you want to speak to Jasper, I'm sure you know what you're doing. I'm staying in the suite tonight. Here's the key. Go on up. I'll send him up to talk to you. Leave the key at the front desk when you're finished. I won't need it for a while." He had the gall to wink. "I have a few more important matters to attend to right now."

Chapter Twenty-Three

IF STRINGER THOUGHT I was going to wait in his hotel room, the man had a screw lose. But I took the key and agreed with the intention of meeting and questioning Jasper in the hall on the fifth floor.

I waited for Jasper outside Ruth's room. A discarded room service tray sat in front of the door of the room next to hers. It looked like things on the fifth floor were getting back to normal. Last week's murder was last week's news. I hadn't been there more than five minutes when I heard a door close. I looked around, but no one came out of any of the rooms. Then I realized that the noise came from inside Ruth's room. I put my ear to the door. All was quiet. I thought of The Driskill ghost. Damn Ruth and her stupid stories. Nevertheless, I needed to get into Ruth's room and check things out. Just as I inserted my trusty bobby pin into the lock, Jasper walked up.

"Miss Lockhart?"

I almost jumped out of my skin.

"Sorry I scared you. Mr. Maynard said you wanted to talk to me in his suite."

"Yes, but let's talk out here. I need a favor."

Apprehension settled upon his face. I was prepared for that. "I know this is highly irregular, but can you give me the names of the others who worked at the party that night?"

"I don't think I can do that."

I reached into my bag and pulled out a picture of Alexander Hamilton. Jasper leaned against the wall and stuck his hands in his pockets. He looked at the money, looked up and down the hall, but kept his mouth shut. The sight of a second bill loosened his tongue.

"After catering set everything up and left, there were three of us working the party."

I handed him the twenty bucks and pulled my notebook and a pencil from my bag. Jasper gave me the names of the two other people: Marvin, the bartender and Herby, the waiter. "Are they working tonight?"

"Yep. They're all working the club with me."

"Send them down one at a time."

"Miss Lockhart, you're going to get me fired."

"Go back to the club and tell Stringer Maynard what I want. Let him handle it. But I have another question for you. Did you hear anything strange while setting up?"

"Like what?"

"Like, say, a gunshot?"

"The only gunshot I heard was the one Mrs. Tatum fired when she killed her husband."

While I waited for my next guy to show up, I went into Ruth's room to check things out. My cousin was not the neatest person, but I knew she wouldn't leave her room in such a mess. I found food crumbs sprinkled across the bedspread; a used table napkin smeared with orange lipstick (not Ruth's color), lying on the floor next to the bed; the phone on the bedside table was knocked askew. I saw a sticky ring left by a wet glass. Except for a dash of vermouth and a couple of olives, Ruth, like me, drank her liquor straight. Now that my cousin had joined the working class, maybe this new prospective on life caused her to switched to Margaritas and live a more *laissez-faire* lifestyle. But the orange lipstick definitely did not belong to her. I called room service. "Excuse me, but I'm staying in room 534 and I placed an order earlier. I'm keeping to a rather strict expense account. Could you please tell me the charge for that order? Oh, yes, that's it. Two turkey clubs with extra mustard and onions, no tomatoes, an order of creamed spinach and a root beer. Three dollars and twenty-five cents. Thank you."

I didn't believe in ghosts with odd appetites, nor did I believe Ruth suddenly changed her usual breakfast of waffles, eggs, and bacon to turkey clubs and root beer.

"Excuse me. Are you Miss Lockhart?"

I didn't want to be seen in Ruth's room, but it was too late now. "Yes, come in. You're one of the staff who worked the Maynard party last Friday night?"

"I'm Marv Luca. I was bartending. You're that lady PI. Mr. Maynard said I should talk to you. You don't think the wife did it?"

"We're not sure. Notice anything unusual at the party?"

"I've waited a few of Stringer Maynard's parties. I've learned to expect the unusual."

"Like?"

"I'm not saying anything against Mr. Maynard. He's an important fellow around here, but there always seems to be some chaos going on."

"What was going on that afternoon?"

"A lot of fighting. Mrs. Maynard with Mrs. Tatum hissing at each other like two wildcats. To tell the truth, Mrs. Tatum was on her way to tying one on."

"What were they fighting about?"

"I couldn't hear. They got all hush-hush whenever one of us walked by. I mean, it was supposed to be a party. And then those beatniks arrived and I thought Mrs. Maynard would blow a gasket."

"Had you ever seen those people here before?"

"Never. It was like they showed up to watch the family brawl."

"How so?"

"Well, this woman, the one with the spider-web face and the guy in the beret came up to the bar to order drinks. The woman said something like she wouldn't miss this for the world."

"Mr. Tatum's announcement about running for governor?"

"I don't think so. She said she'd always wanted to see someone wipe Stringer Maynard's smile off his ugly face. She said that, not me. Then Mr. Maynard came in with this other guy and introduced him to Edwin Tatum. They went into the back room. Not two seconds later, Mr. Maynard comes out and has words with his wife about the beatniks being there. Then you showed up. Herby might be able to tell you more. He was waiting on everyone so he had a chance to get closer to the action."

"Okay, thanks, Marvin. Can you send Herby up?"

"Sure thing."

Herby must have been waiting in the stairwell. As soon as Marvin pushed open the service entrance door, Herby popped out.

"You're the PI lady. Everyone's been talking about this case. But everyone's got it all wrong. I figured it out that night it happened. Want to hear what I think?"

Herby reminded me of a Labrador puppy. He bounced around from one foot to another and even hopped when he wanted to make a point. I expected his tongue to loll from his mouth at any moment. I fought the urge to say, "down boy."

"I'm all ears."

"You see, it's never the most likely suspect, which in this case was Mrs. Tatum because she was the wife. She was framed, though."

"By whom?"

"The sister."

"Fiona Maynard? Why would she frame her sister?"

"Jealously. You see, this sister had this wonderful husband everyone liked and Mrs. Maynard married that oaf. This is off the record, understand. Anyway, if Mrs. Maynard couldn't have her sister's husband, she didn't want her sister to have him either. So, she bumped him off and made it look like her sister did it."

"It's a good theory. I'll keep it in mind."

"You think so? I might be able to use it. See, I'm writing this mystery...about a murder."

"Most mysteries are about murders. Now, let's get back to the real murder. You had the chance to mingle with the guests. Did you hear anything that might cause you to suspect one of them?"

Herby squinted his eyes, pursed his lips, stuck his little finger in his ear and wiggled it around. "That guy in the diamond patterned shirt said something like if Stringer Maynard screwed things up, he'd killed the asshole."

"Screwed what up?"

"Don't know. Think he's the guilty one?"

"Except Leland Tatum was murdered, not Stringer Maynard."

"Oh, right."

Interviewing Herby further was a waste of time. He wouldn't recognize anything of importance if it came riding naked down the hall on horseback. The threatening comments overheard during the party might be something to go on, but what I wanted to hear, I didn't. Neither Herby nor Marvin heard a gunshot before the party started.

After Herby left, I inspected the food tray sitting on the floor in the hall. Under the silver lids were two empty plates scrapped clean, a bowl containing a few dry spinach leaves, and sitting on a small dish, were a pile of sliced tomatoes, untouched. Suddenly, I heard another door slam and ran back into Ruth's room. Empty. This was too weird, even for me. I left making sure Ruth's door was locked. I was on my way to the elevator when Ruth stepped into the hall from the stairwell.

"Aren't you supposed to be in the restaurant?"

"I'm the boss now and I can take a break when I need it."

"Did anyone see you come up here?"

She rolled her eyes. "Give me some credit. No one saw me." She opened the door and went inside her room. "What the hell has been going on in here?" she shouted. She jerked off her wig and threw it across the room.

"I was about to ask you the same question."

"It looks as if someone's had a picnic in the middle of my bed!"

"I know. I picked your lock and came in to have a look. Weird things have been happening. Slamming doors, opening windows, closing windows. Using your name, someone ordered room service and enjoyed two turkey clubs, a bowl of spinach, and a root beer."

"Gag," she said. She removed her mink to hang it in the closet and let out a scream. "I feel like the three bears! Someone's been eating in my room, lounging on my bed, and rummaging through my closet. My shoes have been trampled on and my new Dior suit is on the floor. Oh, just look; my new handbag looks as if a stampede of yaks stomped it to pieces. You don't think it's The Driskill bride ghost, do you? The story goes her fiancée left her at the altar. They were to honeymoon in the hotel. She checked in alone and then threw herself out the window."

"They all do that. Every hotel has the same bride-ghost story. Where did you hear such rubbish?"

"Rosemary told me. That's why she won't come up to the fifth floor. Oh God!" She grabbed her throat with both hands. "What if it's Tatum's ghost?"

"Get a grip. I can't see Leland Tatum's ghost rummaging through your closet and drinking root beer. I'm sure there's a good explanation for this."

"I'm listening."

"Later. What's going on downstairs? Learn anything?"

"I certainly did. I have a knack for organizing people. I don't know why I hadn't realized it before. I should have majored in business instead of fashion design. But I don't know how much longer I can do this. That damn wig itches like hell. Why are you so red in the face? You look like you're about to have a stroke."

"Murder. Investigation. Have you forgotten? Did you have a chance to bring up the subject while you were bossing around the entire kitchen staff?"

"You're so impatient. That's all everyone talked about. Stringer Maynard spends a lot of time here at the hotel."

"We know this, Ruth. Tell me about your new hire, the waiter, Tweety Gilcrest."

"You mean Twellen? How do you know him?"

"The slimy maggot is not really a waiter. He's a mole; a reporter for the *American* and he claims he's moonlighting, but I don't buy that crap."

"But he's been a great help to me and he's so sweet. You sure you're not overreacting again? This detective stuff has gone to your head."

"Tweety's been hanging around this hotel ever since the murder, and now he's pretending to be a waiter. At first I thought he was trying to scoop my story. He knows I'm investigating Tatum's death, not only as a reporter, but as a detective. I want you to find out what he's up to. He seems to think you're swell. When are you working again?"

"Tonight."

"How about Tweety?"

"Tonight too."

"Great. Watch him. Try and get him talking. He's not too smart."

"But what about the ghost in my room?"

"Take care of Tweety. I'll take care of the ghost. Finding out how it gets in shouldn't be too hard."

"Unless it walks through walls."

I helped Ruth don her wig and sent her on her way.

Chapter Twenty-Four

ON MY WAY TO THE FRONT DESK to return Stringer's key, I thought about how to handle the Goldilocks who'd invaded Ruth's hotel room. If I complained to the manager, he'd probably insist I'd been imagining things, and if I persisted, he'd probably suggest another room. I'd just reached the lobby when the hotel's front door bound open and a flurry of people ran in: five cops, two ambulance attendants, and a few curious gawkers. The manager rushed up and said something about the Citadel. The mob headed for the elevator and I dashed for the stairs. We emerged outside the private club at the same time. This time, when the host tried to stop me from entering, I pulled out my press card and followed the cops. The hotel staff stood huddled near the bar, pale and speechless. The club members did the same near the fireplace.

"In here," the manager said.

Two cops stayed behind and attempted to block my way. I was close enough to the private room to see that a coffee table had been upturned and the corner of the area rug was flipped over.

"Is he dead?" the manager cried.

"Just look at the guy," one of the attendants replied. "Man, oh, man. Once these investigators are finished, this guy's going straight to the morgue."

I edged closer. I didn't have to be told who the guy was. The gleaming snakeskin boots splayed across the rumpled rug told me that another gubernatorial candidate had bitten the dust.

I did the best I could do to make myself invisible while taking in as much of the murder scene from the hallway as possible. The cops began to cordon off the area and move the rest of us back into the main room of the club. I ducked around for a quick look. Whoever shot Stringer in the face did so at close range. I joined the group of hotel employees to keep from being told to leave the scene.

"Right under our noses. Like last week's murder."

I turned and saw Herby bouncing around like a drop of water splattering on a hot griddle. Next to him was Marvin.

"Too close if you ask me," Marvin whispered. "I'd just brought him a bottle of champagne. Next thing I know, he's dead. This hotel's spooking me. Maybe the Stephen F. Austin is hiring."

"Who was with him?" I asked.

"No one," Marvin said. "He told me to set down the bucket and he'd open the bottle later."

"You didn't notice if anyone else went into that room, Marvin?"

"I wouldn't have noticed. We were so busy. We had to call down to the restaurant for extra help. They sent up some new guy."

"New guy! What new guy?"

Marvin looked around. "I saw him right after I delivered the champagne. He seems to have disappeared."

"Miss Lockhart," Herby cried. "Want to hear my theory on what happened?"

"Get lost, Herby!"

"Where's the body?" a gruff voice hushed all the mumbling. I turned to see two men walk into the room: one ignored me, the other didn't.

"Were you here when it happened?" Dixon asked.

"Me? Here? This is a men's club, didn't you know?" I snapped. "You could have told me."

"I planned to."

"When?"

"Soon."

"Someone told me I should ask you if I feel you're keeping things from me."

"Your dad? He's right. You can admonish me later. Back to the case. Why are you so edgy?"

"I had spoken to Stringer in the lobby not half an hour ago."

"You couldn't have prevented his murder."

"Maybe I could have."

"What do you know?"

"Evidently there was a new waiter here who seems to have

disappeared in the last few minutes. I think I know who that waiter is and I hope to God he's not the killer." I told Dixon about Tweety and his moonlighting gig.

"Hmmm," Dixon said. "Get whatever information you can from the staff before the cops tell you to butt out. It might not have been Tweety. We'll find out. Oh, I found out that there were no other guests around on the day of Tatum's murder. Stringer had reserved the entire fifth floor. Also, Digmire and Nolan's alibi checked out with Jelly Bluesteen."

"We're not getting very far. No one working the party heard an earlier gunshot."

"We'll keep digging. Right now, I'm sticking close to Bremmer." He started to leave toward the murder room, but turned back. "Oh, I think you should know. Eleanor Tatum is missing."

"How?"

"This morning around ten she had a seizure and they rushed her to the hospital. She was unconscious, or so everyone believed. By the time Dr. Richards arrived, she was gone. Slipped out the window."

THE CASE WAS TURNING into a tangled mess. Dixon, Billy, and I were back at the office by mid-afternoon, adding more information to our collection. Whoever shot Stringer stood no more than five feet away and had enough guts to do it with a lot of people around. It couldn't have been Tweety. He doesn't even have the nerve to ask to borrow my office supplies. We were getting to the subject of Eleanor's disappearance when the door flew open and Ruth walked in.

"What a day! How am I supposed to attend to a luncheon when people are getting murdered?"

"That person was Stringer Maynard," I said.

"Yeah, I heard."

"Was Tweety with you in the dining room the entire time?"

"Before I could talk to him, he was called up to help serve in the Citadel. Seems they were shorthanded, as if we weren't."

"Damn!" I shouted. I picked up the phone to call Ernest. As

soon as he answered, he peppered me with questions about the murder. I answered as patiently as possible. Yes, I was there. Yes, Stringer was shot. Yes, I'll have a story for the morning paper. "But that's not why I called. I think you should know Tweety might be involved." I told him about Tweety's appearances at the hotel; about his taking a job as a waiter; and about what happened in the Citadel Club. "I need his phone number and address." I wrote down the information then had to listen to a five-minute lecture about being careful and letting the cops handle Tweety. Yeah, right. I hung up before he finished. I dialed Tweety's number and was shocked when he answered.

"Tweety?"

"Sydney? Is that you? Hey, you never call me. What's up?"

"Hold on a sec." I placed my hand over the mouthpiece. "He doesn't sound guilty," I whispered.

"See if you can get him here," Dixon said.

"Tweety, since you've figured out what I do in my spare time, I—we—need some information from you."

"I didn't mean to sound threatening today. It's that you were kind of nosy."

"Bad habit. Listen, think you can come by the agency?"

"You mean your detective office?"

"That's the one."

"Sure, I'll be there. I know where it is. See you in a few minutes."

I hung up. "I've underestimated the twerp."

"I'm not changing back into Betty Crocker," Ruth said.

"I don't think that's necessary, honey," Dixon said.

"What if he's the guy who killed Stringer?" Billy said. "He could be dangerous."

"What does Tweety look like?" Dixon said.

"Early thirties, short, pudgy, balding," I said.

"Billy, wait for him in the lobby, then follow him up in the elevator," Dixon said. "See if he's packing. If he looks dangerous, escort him in with your .38"

"But Tweety is so sweet," Ruth said.

AN HOUR WENT BY and Twellen Theodore Gilcrest had not arrived. We'd polished off sandwiches from Zeke's and emptied a pot of coffee; Billy ate his on his feet in the lobby. The clock on the wall seemed to tick louder with every second. Finally, the phone rang, causing the three of us to jump. Dixon snatched up the receiver. "Dixon here." He listened for what seemed like eternity. "Sure, I'll put her on. Ernest," he said to me.

"I gave the scoop to your boyfriend. Tweety's been picked up for questioning for the murder of Stringer Maynard."

"Good God," I said.

"I'll meet you down at the police station."

We dropped Ruth off at the hotel so she could prepare for her next shift and drove to the station.

When we got there, Ernest was pacing in front of the desk sergeant. "Hear anything yet?" I asked.

"Not a damn thing," Ernest spat. "Are you here as a reporter or a detective?"

"Whatever works out best," I said. I looked around and Dixon and Billy were headed down the hall with Detective Bremmer. Dixon motioned for me to join them. "Looks like I'm a PI right now."

"Call me later," Ernest said and turned back to the sergeant.

"What's his story?" Dixon asked once we were seated in Bremmer's office.

"Gilcrest claims he was waiting tables in the main dining room when the restaurant manager told him to report to the maître' d at the Citadel to help out with a party. When he got there, he was assigned to take care of Stringer Maynard. He went in to check to see if Stringer needed anything and he told Gilcrest to run down to the lobby and buy him a pack of cigarettes. On his way to get the cigarettes, Gilcrest ran into some guy who said there was a mix up and Gilcrest was to go on home, they didn't need him after all. Gilcrest told him about the cigarettes and the guy said he'd take care of it. When Gilcrest didn't return, the maître' d got concerned. Seems he did not send anyone home."

"But why would Tweety kill Stringer Maynard?" I asked.

"Tweety?" Bremmer said.

"Twellen Theodore "Tweety" Gilcrest," I said.

"That's what we want to know," Bremmer said. "We got work to do. You guys need to beat it."

"I understand, "Dixon said. On the way out, he paused. "Bremmer, I've been thinking. Is there any possibility Leland Tatum could have been shot earlier?"

"How much earlier?" Bremmer said.

"About an hour," Dixon replied.

"Why do you ask?" Bremmer picked up another file and looked down at his notes.

"The gun being fired twice."

The tips of Bremmer's ears began to redden. Dixon must have noticed it too. "I could be wrong," he said, hoping, I'm sure, to put the police detective at ease.

"We're looking into every aspect of the case."

"Any word on Eleanor Tatum?" Dixon asked.

"Nope. Listen, Dixon. I know Maynard hired you, but now that he's dead, you no longer have a case. It's police business and time for you to butt out, which I know you won't do. That said, I want to know immediately if you turn up anything."

"Got it," Dixon said.

Once out on the street, Dixon, Billy, and I divvied up the work. Dixon's plan was to head out to the Maynard/Tatum ranch, while Billy checked on Serge in Bastrop. I'd return to The Driskill to talk to the waiters again. I bid my two partners farewell and decided to walk back to the office to get my thoughts in order. When I turned the corner, a four-and-a-half-foot Sherlock Holmes crossed the street.

"How did you get here?" I asked.

"How do I get anywhere? If I can't walk, I take an omnibus or a hansom."

"Neither of which we have in Austin, Lydia. It's time to return to the twentieth century."

"I talked Caroline into bringing me." Lydia nodded to the Plymouth parked across the street.

I waved at Caroline Granger.

"I had to promise to help her with her damn scrapbook project so she'd bring me here. If they've arrested someone for killing Maynard, are they thinking he might have killed Tatum too? If so, then Serge's off the hook?"

"How did you find out so quickly?"

"Radio news. Can I tell him to come home?"

"It's too early. I wouldn't get my hopes up. The guy hasn't been arrested, either. He's only in for questioning. Billy's on his way to Bastrop to check on your dad."

Lydia stuck her hands deep into her trouser pockets; a frown that should have only appeared on the mug of a strung-out adult spread across her twelve-year-old face.

"I know you're worried about him and miss him, but it's best if you stay with the Grangers for the time being."

"It's not that. It's the theatre. We need to get it up and running before our cast and crew find other jobs. It's not easy running a live venue. Also, I'm used to doing things on my own. Caroline is a sweet old lady, but she won't let me out of her sight. It's stifling." She stuck a pipe between her teeth.

I bit my tongue before I could extend an invitation to Lydia to stay the night with me. With Eleanor on the lamb and a killer loose, things could get nasty. "Be patient. Give it a day or two. If we don't get this situation sorted out by the end of the weekend, I promise I'll spring you from your scrapbook prison."

Caroline blew the horn. Lydia shook her head, started across the street, and called over her shoulder. "Thirty-six hours! No more."

"You're heavy into the drama, aren't you?"

"It's what I do."

I watched the pint-size Holmes crawl into the Grangers' car and drive away.

Chapter Twenty-five

THE GIGGLING I HEARD when I walked in was not the type you'd expect from someone reading the funnies. It was a lusty, naughty giggle that would cause most eavesdroppers to turn tail and run. Fortunately, that was not me. I cleared my throat and the giggle stopped, followed by the sound of rustling fabric and zippers being zipped.

"Be right there," a hurried voice called from a back room.

Savannah Swift lived up to her name. In less than a minute, she entered the main room of her gallery looking only slightly disheveled. Her temporary spider-web tattoo was gone as well as the fur. Instead, she was decked out in a flowing magenta shift accentuated with a long strand of pearls around her neck. Despite her size, she glided over and extended a hand bedazzled with jewels. "Savannah Swift. Welcome to my gallery. First time here?"

I decided to play the part of a potential customer and scanned the room looking interested. Watercolors depicting the lower halves of oddly shaped legs, each donning decorative shoes, covered two walls. "I've walked by your gallery many times, but never seemed to have the time to stop in. You have quite a collection."

"You will not see this type of artwork anywhere else in Austin. Let me give you a tour." When she turned to lead me to the front of the gallery, I noticed her dress gapped open at the top. I resisted the urge to zip it up.

"The shoes are mine," she said. "I have a fetish for footwear. The artists I represent are the most innovative, not to mention the most talented. This is Cameron Ferguson's work. Cam is a master at using subtle shades of light and shadow when painting his sensual characters."

The so-called sensual characters looked more like two-dimensional stick figures whose oversized heads lolled to the side as if their necks had been broken. I tilted my head to study the tears streaming down the face of a bug-eyed woman. The tears turned from a light pink to a blood red as they traveled down the painting. Sort of like Picasso meets Dali.

"Amazing," was all I could come up with at the moment.

"Are you into modern art?" she asked.

Evidently not, but my answer dredged up from the scant memories of my art appreciation class in college. "I've always had an interest in surrealism."

"Passé. It's abstract expressionism now. I was in New York for Willem de Kooning's first solo show in 1948 at Egan's Gallery. Stunning. Cam was with me in the city at the time, and he was influenced by de Kooning's black and white enamels."

"Yes, I can see that now," I lied.

"And over here," she directed me to a set of shockingly colorful paintings that filled the entire back wall. "These are by another young artist, Lisa Lenning. So vivid and alive. She studied in Chicago, but left her mentors not long ago. That atmosphere in Chi Town was too restricting. About a year ago, I met her and her husband, Howie, he's an actor, and encouraged them to come to Austin. She hasn't even reached her potential yet. I see great things for Lisa."

As I leaned closer to study a piece splashed intricately with various shades of pink, a shape took form, and suddenly I was looking into a female orifice, and it wasn't any of those located on a person's head. I realized Savannah was studying me.

"You look familiar," she said. She bit the tip of her red, thickly lacquered fingernail, as a dawn of recognition spread across her face.

"Last Friday night; The Driskill Hotel. That crazy party. When I saw you come in, I was sure you were one of us. Your hair, your clothes, that gorgeous man you were with and the cute, young Sinatra-looking boy. I was a bit flummoxed when you walked into the back room with that horrible man Stringer Maynard. You didn't seem like the type to socialize with him and his crowd."

"Savannah notices everything, don't you, dear?" This from the slick guy who wore the beret and the black and white diamond-patterned-shirt the night of the party. "I'm Cam

Ferguson." He reached over and zipped up Savannah's dress. "You're not really here to look at art, are you?"

"No, I'm not, Mr. Ferguson. My partners and I are investigating Leland Tatum's murder."

Savannah stiffened and folded her arms tightly across her ample bosom.

"I figured you'd be in here sooner or later," Cam said. He pulled a pack of cigarettes from his pocket and lit up. "You know, asking questions."

"Lydia?" I asked.

"Lydia," Cam responded. "And Howie Lenning. He said you came around to the theatre this morning looking for Serge. Relax, Savannah. Miss Lockhart doesn't believe Eleanor killed Leland any more than we do, and as far as Serge's involvement, she'll soon figure out our dear Serge was at the wrong place at the wrong time."

"Looks like I'm going to have to have a talk with Lydia about holding her tongue."

"Don't worry," Cam said. "We're a close-knit group. I just heard. Another murder; your favorite person, Savannah. Stringer Maynard."

"Oh, my God," Savannah said. "Cam, why didn't you tell me earlier?"

Cam shrugged his shoulders and took another puff. His evasive body language seemed like a good enough answer for Savannah.

"Mind answering some questions about that night?" I asked.

Savannah bit her lower lip and wound the strand of pearls tightly around her fingers. I was afraid the thread would snap and pearls would go flying. Cam draped his arm around her shoulder. I took that for a no they didn't mind.

"What time did you get to the party?"

"The four of us walked in around five," Cam answered.

"One being the woman with the bird headdress and the fellow you call Howie?"

"Howie and Lisa Lenning," Savannah said. "Even though we had invitations, we almost didn't get in because of the hoity-toity woman Fiona Maynard, but Eleanor Tatum told her to butt out. I can't believe those two are sisters."

"What happened next?"

"We went to the bar for drinks," Cam said. "Other guests started coming in."

"I was about to go over and talk to Eleanor, but I could see that she was upset," Savannah said. "She sat down by the fireplace, and she and Fiona got into a heated discussion."

"About what?"

"I couldn't hear much. Mrs. Maynard said something about being 'foolish, biggest mistake you'll ever make; you'll regret it.' Eleanor told her to shut up, that 'what was done was done.' Mrs. Maynard responded with 'that's what you think.' That's about all I heard. More people began pouring in, and Mrs. Maynard went to greet them."

"Why did you go to the party?"

"Why did we go?" Savannah asked. "We were invited."

"Is that the only reason?"

"What do you mean?"

"The bartender overheard you saying that you wouldn't miss the party for the world because you wanted to see Leland wipe the smile off of Stringer Maynard's ugly face."

"It was Howie," Cam said. "He was in the theatre when Leland came in and told Serge he was not going to run for governor. Howie ran over here and told us. You see, we all have a stake in this. The art center is something we've wanted for a long time. When Serge told us that he'd finally found someone to bankroll the project, we were elated. Savannah and I, and a few other artists met with Serge and Leland a few weeks ago. We'd plan to turn this entire block of old buildings into the Austin Art and Cultural Center with art studios, galleries, and stages. Even the Next to Nothing was to be remodeled, and thankfully, renamed. And Savannah was right. We wouldn't miss that announcement for the world. We were worried that Leland might back out with all this governor stuff. We thought maybe our presence would prevent him from doing that. We all liked Leland a lot, but the man didn't always show a lot of backbone. If he'd planned to stand up to that pushy partner of his, we wanted to be there to see it."

I thanked Savannah and Cam for their time. I knew where to find Howie, so I asked about Lisa Lenning, even though I didn't expect to get much more from them.

LISA LENNING'S STUDIO was on the second floor in the same building as The Next to Nothing. It was accessible through a door in the alley. The strong scent of turpentine stung my eyes as I stepped inside. The paint on the walls had pealed from the dampness, most likely caused by the leaky roof. Several buckets, situated in strategic places, contained a few inches of water. One window, clouded with soot, provided the only means of natural lighting. To augment that, Lisa had placed lamps in all four corners. "Knock, knock," I called.

"Bring the boxes back here," a female voice called from inside.

"Mrs. Lenning?" I said.

"Oh, I thought you were the delivery guy from the art store. I was expecting some supplies."

I maneuvered my way around several easels, drop-cloths draped over frames, and tall canvases, and found Lisa Lenning pouring turpentine from a jug into a small bucket. Except for her paint-splattered smock, she looked homely compared to the other night when I first saw her at the party. Her hair was brushed back into a ponytail. She wore no makeup. Underneath her smock, which hung down to her knees, I saw she was wearing dungarees and sneakers.

"Savannah Swift and Cam Ferguson told me where to find you. My name is Sydney Lockhart," I said. "I have a few questions concerning the party at The Driskill last Friday night. I won't take up too much of your time."

"Come in. Have a seat. I was about to clean my brushes."

"I saw your art at Savannah's gallery. Impressive."

"'Impressive.' I'll accept that. I usually get 'unique,' or 'different,' or 'loud,' which translates to, 'I don't like it.' I'm learning to develop a thick skin. Why are you asking questions?"

"My partners and I are investigating Leland Tatum's death. Did you know the Tatums well?"

"Howie knew them better than me. I'd spoken to Mr. Tatum at a few art gatherings, but I'd never met his wife. You don't think she did it?"

"There's that possibility. It was obvious that Mrs. Tatum and Mrs. Maynard were arguing at the party. Did you happen to hear anything that was said between them?"

"No. I was uncomfortable being there. It's not exactly my idea of a fun evening. I'm not into mingling and was looking forward to when we could leave. Mr. Tatum was such a nice man. I really hope it wasn't his wife who killed him. I wish I could help you, but I'm afraid I can't."

"Is your husband around?"

"You can find him at the theatre. He's trying to run things until Serge gets back. Go down the back stairs and take the first door on the right. It will take you down a hallway and to the theatre office. Howie should be there."

"Thanks," I said. "And I wasn't blowing smoke. I really do like your art."

Lisa Lenning handed me a flyer. "I'm having my own show at Savannah's gallery next month."

"I'll be there," I said.

I ENTERED THROUGH the back of the theatre and was surprised to hear a familiar voice.

"Once the children left home, life became so boring. But now we have a new tenant in our guest cottage and I have this cute little thing to attend to." Caroline Granger had Howie's attention, having probably earned it with the cookie he was munching.

I entered the theatre office in time to see Lydia stick out her tongue at Caroline who was seated with her back to the brazen young girl.

"Well, look who's here," Caroline said.

"I thought you two were on your way home," I said.

"Lydia wanted to show me her theatre." Caroline turned around and patted Lydia on her knee.

"Her theatre?" I asked.

"I inherit," Lydia said, "and the way things are going, it might be sooner than later."

"Now, now, dear," Caroline said. "Things will work out fine. You'll see."

"Your wife told me where to find you."

"This is the detective I told you about," Lydia offered.

"I know," said Howie. "She was in here before looking for Serge. Any word on where he is?" he asked me.

"Not yet," I said. I wanted to speak to Lenning without an audience, especially a too-curious audience. However, getting Lydia to go home with Caroline would be like prying a nail out of a two-by-four with my bare fingers.

"What can you tell me about the night Leland was killed?"

Howie told the same story I'd heard from Cameron and Savannah. He couldn't or wouldn't offer anything more. I've quickly learned that this detecting stuff was all about getting people to trust you, letting them know you were on their side and had their interest at heart. I tried another tactic. "Cameron said once the Art and Cultural Center is up and running, Serge planned to remodel the theatre. I'm sure you are looking forward to that."

"Were." He stood up and brushed cookie crumbs from his pants. "We were almost ready to sign the papers and get the ball rolling. When word got out that Leland had planned to run for governor, we became concerned that the art center might not happen."

"Why? How would that change anything?"

"Are you kidding? We all know Stringer Maynard. We all knew what we were up against. This governor thing was his ploy to manipulate Leland into dropping the entire project."

"What do you think will happen now? Maybe Mrs. Tatum will go ahead with Leland's plans."

"When pigs fly. If Leland had trouble standing his ground, how do you think his mentally unstable wife will? Excuse me, Miss Lockhart. I have to get back to work."

I thanked Howie for his time. Lydia had lost interest in our conversation and was negotiating with Caroline about staying at the theatre to make sure tonight's reopening went off as planned. On my way out the door, I assured Caroline that I would check in on her young ward later in the evening and make sure she arrived safely at Caroline and Lester's doorstep by midnight. Caroline hesitated, but finally agreed. I left as Lydia began bossing Howie around.

Chapter Twenty-Six

WHEN I GOT BACK TO THE AGENCY, I had a visitor waiting in the hall. Tweety looked as if he'd spent the night under the Congress Avenue Bridge with the pigeons and bats. His purple satin jacket had so many wrinkles it looked as if it had been pulled out of the bottom of a clothes hamper. The furry cummerbund was stained and matted. His hair was plastered against his skull and his face had broken out.

"Looks like a few hours in the police station didn't suit you," I said.

"Sydney, please, I need your help," he whimpered.

"Why should I help you? You've lied to me." I opened the door and he followed me in. His usual aroma of Old Spice had given in to pungent body odor. I opened the window. He sat down and dropped his head into his hands.

"Talk," I said, "fast. What's your connection to these two murders?"

"There is no connection!"

"Get out, Tweety. I've got more important things to do than watch you decompose here in my office."

"No, wait. Listen. I went to the hotel to nose around that first time after Leland Tatum was murdered. I wanted a scoop on the story. I needed something big so Ernest wouldn't boot me out."

"The story was assigned to me, Tweety. What did you expect to do?"

"I don't know. You always get the hot stories. I was desperate. I wasn't going to give up. I went back. I was hanging out at the bar when I saw you that day in the lounge. And it just happened." He tugged at what little hair sprouted on the sides of his head. "It just happened."

"What happened? Spit it out."

"It was your partner, your detective partner. At first, I thought she was a friend. She was with you in the lounge. But then I saw her again at the restaurant when she was disguised as Adele. I knew from the moment I saw her, I couldn't live without her. But I was afraid she was married. How could a woman that gorgeous not be married?" He looked at me as if I was to supply him with an answer. I simply stood there with my mouth opened.

"I'm not as stupid as you think. I figured out she was working undercover, and I applied for a job as a waiter to have an excuse to meet her. She's the most wonderful woman I've ever known. We were hitting it off. I had a hunch she was interested in me...me, fat, short Tweety Gilcrest. And now, she's lost to me forever. I'm a criminal. I'll lose my job, both jobs. I might as well throw myself into the river."

Toss in a bar of soap and the idea wasn't half bad.

"Forget Adele for the moment. You got bigger problems. Tell me what happened at the hotel."

"I was working in the restaurant when the lady manager, Miss Corbitt, told me to go up to the Citadel because they were shorthanded. When I got there, the guy out front—"

"The maître' d."

"Yeah, that guy. He told me that I was assigned to wait on Mr. Maynard. I went down to get him a pack of cigarettes when I ran into a guy who told me to go home. They didn't need me anymore. He sounded annoyed."

"Didn't you think it was odd to be called to help out at the Citadel Club and then immediately sent home?"

"Not really, once they found out it was me who was to help. See, I'm having a hard time with this waiter thing. Word must have gotten around that I'd dumped a pitcher of ice tea in a woman's lap. I'm not that clumsy, but I couldn't keep my eyes off Adele and I tripped."

"The guy who sent you home, describe him."

Tweety shrugged. "I didn't pay much attention. He was tall, slim, tanned."

If he couldn't notice details, no wonder Tweety was a failure at reporting the news.

"Age?"

"Thirty-one last month. My mom threw me a party."

"No, Tweety, *you moron*. The guy's age."

"Oh. Middle-aged."

"Have you ever seen him before?"

"No! I told you I just started working there!"

Tweety's voice turned high-pitched and squeaky. I thought he was about to cry.

"Take it easy. You asked me to help. If you didn't kill Stringer, someone else did. What else do you remember about this guy? How he spoke? Walked? Carried himself?"

"He looked important, like he knew what he was doing. Kind of like Ernest. You know, one of those guys you don't question."

"You said he was annoyed. Annoyed how? Tell me exactly what he said."

"I'd left the room and was headed down the service stairs when I almost ran into him. He made as if to shove me aside, but then sort of got a hold of himself. He asked me if Stringer Maynard was in the club. I told him Mr. Maynard was there and I was assigned to wait on him. That's when he told me he'd take care of everything and that I could go home. I said okay and told him which meeting room Maynard was in and that he needed cigarettes. He headed upstairs. I turned back and said, 'Camels.' He stared at me as if I were an idiot. I said, 'Camels. He wants a pack of Camels.' The guy said, 'Sure, sure, I'll get them.'"

"Did he follow you down to get the cigarettes?"

"Uh. No."

"So, some annoyed guy who you ran into in the stairwell, someone you've never seen before, finds out you're waiting on Maynard. He tells you he'll handle things and sends you home. Does that about sum it up?"

"Yeah, I'd say so."

"And right after you left, Stringer Maynard was murdered." I picked up a pencil and tapped it against my forehead, rolled my eyes, and waited for the reality to dawn on this lovesick, not-so-smart reporter/waiter. I was about to prod him with the window pole when Tweety's expression turned from confusion to enlightenment.

"It was him! He was the killer!"

"Well done, Tweety. Considering the ice-tea incident, my advice is to concentrate on your day job. At least you know the people who work at the newspaper, and Adele isn't there to distract you."

"I am an idiot. I should go back to the police station and tell them about this guy."

"That's not a good idea. Do you have a lawyer?"

"Not yet."

"Get one, now. Tell him what you told me and let him handle it."

"You're so smart, Sydney. When this is all over, do you think you could give me some pointers on how to get a date with Adele?"

"Sure, Tweety. I'd be glad to. I think she kind of likes you."

"I knew it!"

Tweety left in a much happier mood than when he arrived.

I RAN BY THE HOTEL to check on my undercover connection. She was getting off work when I walked in.

"I don't know what we'd do without you, Adele. I wasn't sure about your idea to change the waiters' uniforms, but you were right, they're a hit, and your menu suggestions are working out fine. Have a nice evening and I'll see you tomorrow." Helen Corbitt gave Ruth (or Adele) a hug and left.

I caught Ruth's eye and nodded her over to the fireplace. Lola Love was the entertainment again for the night, and her melancholy musical selection reflected my mood.

"You and Helen seem to have hit it off."

"She's a talented chef, but she can't run the kitchen without me. What a day! This double life is killing me."

"It won't be for much longer."

"I'm going up to my room to change out of these dreadful clothes. I'm sick of changing in the stall of that public restroom. Don't worry; no one will see me. There's hardly anyone around on the fifth floor. That reminds me—did you find the ghost? There's more than one hanging around on that floor, you know."

"Honestly, Ruth, I've been concerned with catching a killer or two rather than wrangling up a few ghosts. I suggest you do the same. You're always getting sidetracked."

"And whose fault is that?"

"Forget the damn ghosts for a moment. You might be

interested to know that Tweety came to see me at the agency. I found out why he wanted a job here at the hotel."

"Tell me later. I'm exhausted. I'm going to call the club and order a set-up so I can make a pitcher of martinis, which I will enjoy while soaking my feet. I deserve it."

"I'd ride up with you and make sure no one is playing Goldilocks in your room, but I can't stay. I'm supposed to meet Dixon."

"Stop!" Ruth squeezed my arm hard enough to leave a bruise. "See that man slumped on the sofa by the fireplace?"

"The one in the rumpled suit?"

"Do you really see him?"

"Of course I do."

"I'm sure he's another fifth-floor ghost. He's been lurking around lately. Maybe he's the one who's been eating in my room, lying around on my bed, hiding in my closet."

"Let's see. Now, there are three possible spirits you have to contend with: the distraught bride, the four-year-old, and now a lurker." I took another look at the man. "I've seen him someplace before. Wait...it *was* on the fifth floor. He was wearing a scarlet dinner jacket and was so drunk he could hardly stand. He mumbled something about a lost love. I asked him which room he was in and he said, 'pick a room, any room.'"

"That sounds like something a ghost would say. Do you think we're the only ones who can see him?"

"Let's find out." I walked over to the bar where Joey was mixing up a batch of Bloody Marys. "Hey, Joey, see that guy on the sofa?"

"Yeah, he's been hanging round lately. He never orders anything. He sets there and sulks. We don't think he's staying at the hotel and thought about throwing him out, but he never bothers anyone. Has he been causing trouble?"

"No, curious, that's all. Thanks." I broke the news to Ruth. "He's not a ghost. Joey's seen a lot of him recently."

"That means nothing. Some ghosts like to be seen," Ruth said.

"When did you first see him?"

"Shortly after I checked in. I've probably seen him at least four times since. Walk up to the fifth floor with me. Dixon won't mind if you're a few minutes late. No telling what's there to greet me."

I pushed opened the stairwell door to the fifth floor and Ruth looked both ways before stepping out. "All clear. I'll call you later, once I've recuperated."

"Are you sure you don't want me to check your room?"

"I'm so tired. If anyone's been in my room, I'll just pour them a drink."

Nevertheless, I watched as Ruth opened her door. She poked her head in and gave me the okay sign. I was about to step back into the elevator when I heard her scream. She ran out of the room holding a wadded up towel.

"Oh my God. Call the police. Call the hospital. Hurry!"

I ran back as another scream split the air. It wasn't Ruth this time. It was the towel she was holding.

"A baby! A baby! What do I do?"

Sure enough, squirming and squealing in the crock of Ruth's arm was a newborn wrapped in a hotel towel.

"It was lying in the middle of the bed," she cried. "I thought it was a napkin left by whoever's been in my room. I almost flung it across the room when it moved and a tiny arm came up from the towel like a periscope. What do we do?"

"You're first suggestion was the best. We call the police."

"But it's crying."

"Babies do that. Sit down on the bed and rock it back and forth." I had my hand on the receiver when the phone rang.

"Hello?"

"I'm at the office," Dixon said. "What's going on? We were supposed to meet here."

"I was on my way, but I'm afraid I'll be delayed."

"What's happened? Are you okay?"

"Yes, I'm okay. Your first question is not so easy to answer. Maybe you should come to the hotel and see for yourself."

"Not another murder."

"No. The world has gained another soul, not lost one."

"I'm on my way over."

Chapter Twenty-Seven

THE BABY HAD QUIETED DOWN and was sucking on the corner of the towel. Ruth stared at it as if it were a scorpion about ready to strike. We had the door open in anticipation of the cops' arrival when we heard, "Sydney?"

Ruth and I turned to see Tweety peering into the room. "I followed you up here. Adele, is that you? A baby," he said. "You had a baby since I left? You weren't even showing. Tiny women usually show. Don't worry about a thing. I love babies. I know it's premature; not the baby, but us. Sydney told me you were interested in me and I always say there's no time like the present." The stupid guy paused from his chattering and got down on one knee. "Will you marry me? Say, yes. I'll adopt your baby. I've always wanted to be a father."

"This is not my baby, you imbecile." Ruth cried and pulled off her wig. "And my name is not Adele."

The elevator dinged, and a few moments later, the ghost in the scarlet dinner jacket barged into the room, grabbed Tweety by the shoulder, spun him around, and knocked him out cold. He looked around and ran out. I've never seen Ruth speechless, but then I'd never seen her dressed as Betty Crocker, holding a baby, with an unconscious admirer lying at her feet. We stood there, staring at one another, staring at Tweety on the floor, staring at the baby who now had the hiccups.

My cousin and I have been through a lot of bizarre situations. We sat in a mineral pool as blood bubbled up from the spout, stood in a salt marsh as a drunken surveyor held us at gunpoint, tumbled out of a car into a cornfield after Ruth swerved to keep from hitting a pig, but this situation took the cake.

Five minutes later the room was crowded with, thankfully alive, adult flesh-and-blood bodies.

"Is this your baby?" one cop asked Ruth.

"I told her I'd marry her," Tweety whined as he held the ice pack over his eye.

Ruth kicked him in the shin and stomped her foot. "I already told you, this is not my baby. I found her when I came into the room."

A nurse from the child welfare office now held the little girl while the cops took down our statements. Ruth rattled on about the crumbs in her bed, the mess in her closet, the damp towels left in the bathroom, and finally, the ghost who kept fleeing. Dixon walked in as I was explaining that the guy who had decked Tweety and ran out was not really a ghost as Ruth had claimed. Dixon smiled and shook his head.

It was almost eleven by the time everyone: the cops, the nurse, the baby, and Tweety, vacated Ruth's room. Dixon called room service to bring up a pitcher of martinis and a bottle of bourbon.

"This is all your fault, you know," I said to Ruth.

"What are you talking about?"

"Mary Thompson. That's what I'm talking about. Your friend who checked into the Echland-Wheatly Home and then left without telling anyone because you wouldn't call her."

"Oh, because I didn't call this ditsy woman, unwed mothers all over the planet are going to start dumping their babies on me, is that what you're saying? You're always trying to blame me for stuff that is not my fault. I spent my hard-earned money to open up a home for unwed, destitute mothers, and that makes me responsible for all their mistakes and bad judgments." Her face went from beet red to ghost white. "You mean...this baby is Mary's?"

"Well, it certainly doesn't belong to the ghost bride."

"Ladies," Dixon said. "Calm down. We can call the hospital tomorrow and see if they are missing a newborn and its mother."

"What if she didn't have it at the hospital?" I argued.

"Then there's not much we can do," Dixon said.

"Are you sure you want to stay in this room tonight?" I asked Ruth.

The stricken look on Ruth's face was intensified when a loud knock interrupted our bickering. Dixon went to the door. "Who is it?"

"Front desk. I have a message for Miss Echland."

Dixon opened the door, took the envelope, and thanked the bellhop. He handed the note to Ruth. She read it, wadded it up and threw it across the room. "I hate you," she yelled at me. A second knock announced room service, which was a good thing since we all needed a stiff drink. While Dixon poured, I uncrumpled the note and read it out loud.

"Dear Ruth,
I've made a mess of my life. Please take care of my little girl.
You'd make a much better mother than me.
Your best friend from high school,
Mary"

A third knock had Ruth opening the window and sticking out her leg as if she were getting ready to jump. Dixon didn't bother with polite questions; he threw open the door. The guy in the scarlet dinner jacket burst in. "I'm tired of playing games. Which one of you is Ruth?"

"The potential jumper," I said.

He rushed over to my cousin, and in a flash, I grabbed Ruth and Dixon grabbed our intruder.

"He was going to push me!" Ruth screamed.

"I want Mary! Where have you been hiding her?" He pushed Dixon aside and seized Ruth by the arms and shook. "And where's that bald guy?"

Ruth kneed him in the groin. He buckled like a stack of cards. Dixon lifted the guy off his feet and threw him in a chair.

I readied myself for another attack, but the guy buried his head in his hands and cried. When he came up for air, he pointed to Dixon's drink. "I could use one of those." He downed two quick shots before he spoke again. "I know Mary's been here. I know you've been hiding her, but I can't seem to catch up with her."

"You don't mean Mary Thompson do you?" I asked.

"Mary Thompson," Ruth yelled. "I haven't seen that girl since high school. I don't even like her. Why would I hide her from you? I don't even know who you are."

"How do you know Mary?" I asked the guy.

"I'm her husband. Where's the baby? I want the baby."

"Maybe you should explain, Mister...," Dixon said.

"Donovan. Carl." The guy rubbed the back of his neck and paced the room. "I'll give it to you straight. Last year me and Mary met in a bar in Dallas. We got hitched a week later and began our life of bickering. She moved in and out so many times, I threatened to put in swinging doors. I figured once the baby came, she'd sort of settle down. Two weeks ago, we had this big fight about me going out with the boys every Friday night and not taking her to the movies. Crazy broad. What's a man to do? One night a week with the boys, big damn deal. She moved out again. I expected her back the next morning. When she didn't show, I said good riddance. Three days later, no Mary. I began to sweat. By the end of the week, I was climbing the walls. Then a letter came. She said she'd found someone else and that she was giving up the baby. I went wild. I had to find her. Mary's one crazy broad, but I love her."

"Didn't I tell you she was wacko?" Ruth added.

"How did you trace her to Austin?" I asked.

"Wasn't hard. I went to every hospital, home, and orphanage in Dallas until I ended up at the Echland-Wheatly Home. I remembered Mary talking about her friend named Ruth Echland. When I found out that Ruth was the founder of the Home, I knew this was where Mary had come. I asked to see her, but the receptionist told me she'd left and didn't say where she was going. Mary always said she could go to Ruth if she was in trouble, so I found out where Miss Echland lived. I called her house with a story about being a tax appraiser and needing to make an appointment about her property values. Her housekeeper said she'd gone to Austin. I asked for a number where she could be reached, and the woman told me she was staying at The Driskill, so I drove right down. I tried to check in, but I couldn't afford to stay here, so I checked into the Y and hung around The Driskill lobby, hoping to catch Mary. I mean, how hard can it be for a woman with an almost-baked bun in the oven to go around unnoticed? Tonight, I came back up to the fifth floor and heard all this commotion about a baby coming from this room...You know the rest."

"You're pretty slick, Mr. Donovan," Dixon said. "But we don't know where your wife is. Miss Echland found the baby when she came back to her room. Protective Services has her. The best thing you can do is go to the police."

"The best thing I can do is find that wife-stealing boyfriend of hers. I should have beat it out of him when I had the chance."

"Tweety's not her boyfriend," I said. "And we haven't laid eyes on Mary. All we have are traces of her sneaking into Ruth's room. We don't even know where she's staying or where she gave birth."

"Crazy broad," Donavan helped himself to another shot. "Man, I've been sleeping in my car for two days after the Y threw me out for being drunk."

Dixon reached in his wallet and pulled out a twenty. "The Alamo Hotel is down the street. Here's enough for a couple of nights and a meal. Sleep it off and go to the cops in the morning. We'll let you know if we hear from your wife."

Donovan left without so much as a word of thanks.

"Swell guy," Dixon said.

"He and Mary deserve one another," Ruth said. "And don't look at me like that, Miss Smarty Pants."

"All it would have taken was one little phone call, and this entire fiasco would never have happened."

"Well, as far as we're concerned, it's over," Dixon said.

Ruth filled her glass with the last of the martini. "Damn waiters. They never bring enough olives."

Chapter Twenty-Eight

YESTERDAY WENT FROM MY DISCOVERY of fur cummerbunds, to being thrown out of a private men's club, to having a newspaper colleague suspected of murder, to finding an abandoned newborn in Ruth's room. I was supposed to solve a murder and get a story. Instead, in only one afternoon, I've racked up enough wacky experiences to write my own O. Henry short stories. Before could I shut my eyes on another long day, I called Caroline Granger to check on little Sherlock. It wasn't necessary. Lester told me Caroline had stayed to watch the show and both she and Lydia were home at eleven-thirty.

The toast popped out of the toaster at the same time my phone rang. I knew it wasn't Dixon calling because I didn't have an extension in my bathroom. And since there was no one else I cared to talk to at seven-fifteen in the morning, I let it ring. I'd placed the plates on the table when Dixon walked in rubbing his wet hair with a towel.

"I know what to get you for Christmas," I said and handed him a cup of coffee.

"A clothes brush?"

"If you'd hang up your jacket and pants instead of throwing them on the floor, they wouldn't be covered in orange cat hair."

"I was sort of in a hurry last night," he smiled. "I give. What will I find under the tree?"

"Your own bathrobe. Mine's long enough for you, but it's a little snug across the shoulders."

He tossed the robe and wrapped the towel around his waist. "Who called?"

"I didn't answer. I have grape jelly or honey, what'll it be?"

"Jelly."

The phone rang again, and this time Dixon snatched up the receiver before I could grab it. I didn't care if the entire world knew he'd spent the night, except for one person, however. But unless the house was on fire, my mother should still be asleep.

"Yeah," he said and shrugged. "They hung up."

"No one I know would hang up on you. Ruth, Scott and Jeremiah (my brother and his roommate) would asked for details; Dad would stammer; Ernest and Marcella would think nothing of you being here, and Lydia would tell you to put your pants on. So it was probably the wrong number."

"I'm stopping by the cottage to get a clean shirt and then I'll be at the office. We should focus on the freshest murder and work backwards. Whoever killed Maynard most likely killed Tatum. We need to find that mysterious guy who sent Tweety home. Run by the hotel and see what you can find out. Can Ernest spare you today?"

"Are you kidding? He'd insist. Before I leave, I'm going to call Brackenridge Hospital to see if Mary delivered there."

"Good. I'll see you at the office as soon as you can get there. Think of something else to get me for Christmas. I plan to wear your robe as often as possible, since it results in you cooking breakfast in your nightie."

Dixon left, a bit later than he'd planned. I flipped open the phonebook to look up the number for Brackenridge Hospital when Monroe erupted and ran to the backdoor. I grabbed my gun and stepped out. A rustle from near the honeysuckle caused me to take aim.

"I come unarmed. Can we go inside?"

I motioned for Fiona to enter. "Why the backdoor?"

"Obvious. I don't want anyone to know I'm here. I did call first. I don't blame you for not answering the phone. If Ralph Dixon spent the night with me, I wouldn't leave the house for a week."

"You know, Fiona. I don't like your crude comments, and I'm beginning not to like you."

"I don't much care. Has my sister contacted you?"

"No."

Fiona sized up my apartment and scoffed at the dirty dishes in the sink. "She will. Call the ranch when she does. I'll be busy with the funeral this afternoon, but leave a message with my housekeeper."

"Fiona?" I hated it when annoying people tried to get the last word.

"What?"

"Where were you when you husband was killed?"

"Where was I?" She tapped her chin in that catty way I'd expect from an uppity, catty woman. "Oh, yes. I was at a meeting with the Junior League. Check it out if you want."

"No need. I trust you," I lied.

After Fiona disappeared through the secret portal of my honeysuckle, I called the hospital and learned that a woman who went by the name of Mary Echland (clever she is) had delivered a baby yesterday, but had disappeared, taking the baby with her.

I PARKED IN THE FREE LOT near the Scarborough Building and made my way toward The Driskill. I had gone a couple of blocks when it began to drizzle. I thought about going back to the car for my fedora. Instead, I turned up my collar and quickened my pace. Thunder rumbled overhead and lightening flashed bright enough to blind me. As I crossed Trinity Street, the drizzle morphed into a heavy rain. Most things in Texas seem to mosey along. Storms, however, rush in like an angry locomotive. The wind kicked up, and before I made it to the next corner, a horizontal deluge hit me in the face. I ducked into The Blue Mist to give the storm cloud a chance to pass. A couple of guys had the same idea. One who darted in behind me, called out his drink order before he made it to the bar. "Jack and Coke, double," he said, shaking out his suit coat and hanging it on the rack to dry. "No use standing at the bus stop and getting soaked. Damn number eleven's always late anyway."

A short guy stepped in next and stood next to me. "A drink sounds good. Care to join me?"

The voice sounded familiar, although I couldn't see the person's face since the overcoat collar was pulled up to the ears. I looked down and noticed the person's shoes. "Take that table in the corner," I said. "I'll get the drinks. How about brandy?"

"Brandy's fine."

"Your sister said you'd show up."

Eleanor kept her coat pulled up to cover her face and sat with her back to the door. "I hate my sister," she began when I sat down her drink. "She's the reason my husband is dead. I wish I could feel sorry that her husband is dead too, but I can't."

"Fiona killed Leland?"

"She didn't pull the trigger, but she's responsible."

"How?"

"She knew how unhappy I was. She knew that Leland and I wanted out of the partnership; wanted a different life for ourselves. Instead of supporting me and respecting my wishes, she went against everything, even to the point of trying to stick me back in the clinic."

"Then who pulled the trigger?"

She downed her drink. "I told you. I did."

I downed mine and motioned for the bartender to bring two more.

We sat in silence for a few minutes after our second round arrived. Finally, I said, "Why?"

"Long story."

"And you want me to know it?"

"I told you before about our plans to sever our ties with Stringer, but I didn't tell you the whole story. We'd made our decision, but the closer it came to the day to confront Stringer at The Driskill, the more depressed Leland became. The morning it happened, Leland disappeared from the house. I knew right where to find him. Whenever he was really upset, he'd go to the barn to see the horses. When I walked in, he turned and smiled, but I saw defeat written all over his face. I knew he'd back down again. I had an ace in the hole and I played it even though I feared it might destroy both of us. I couldn't live the lie any longer. You see, Edwin is really Stringer's son."

Her hands began to shake and she set down her glass and continued her story. "One afternoon after I returned home from a six-week stay in the hospital, Stringer came to see me. He was drunk. I won't describe what happened, but two weeks later I was pregnant. It wasn't Leland's because we hadn't had relations during those six weeks. Once I discovered I was pregnant, I resumed relations with my husband, so he would think the child was his. I was so young and naïve, and stupid."

"Leland must have been devastated when you told him."

"He was stunned. After a few minutes, it sank in, and I saw the look of hate spread across his face. I think my husband could have walked out of that barn, gone straight to Stringer's house and killed him. He blamed the worsening of my mental condition on what Stringer had done. Then he broke down and cried. I held him, and when he spoke again, I was the one who was stunned. He took my hands and said, 'This is what we needed, Eleanor. I've been such a fool, but no more. I'll tell Stringer the deal's off. And this time I mean it. Edwin is my son as far as I'm concerned.'"

I suggested we go together to break the news right then. But Leland still wanted to wait until the last minute so as not to give Stringer time to manipulate the situation. Reluctantly, I agreed, but I insisted that Leland do it before the party started. I wanted it over and done with before the guests arrived. What I told you before is true, except I didn't tell you what Stringer told Leland. Stringer said that if Leland went through with his plans, Stringer would tell Edwin who his real father is. Not only that, he'd tell Edwin that he and I were lovers all this time."

"Stringer knew about Edwin?"

"Of course he knew! You can just look at Edwin and tell, except for Leland. He often told me he saw my face in Edwin's. Besides, Leland and Stringer were often mistaken for brothers."

"How could you be around that guy all these years?"

"I wanted to tell Leland what had happened years ago, but Stringer threatened to take my son away. He'd manage to do it too. I wasn't mentally strong enough to deal with him, so I kept quiet."

"Does Fiona know what Stringer did to you?"

"I'm not sure. I don't really care, either."

"So your husband agreed, once again, to Stringer's demands, this time to protect Edwin."

"No, he didn't. When we made the decision the day before, we were firm about not backing down. When Leland came back to the room, he told me what had happened. He said he could play Stringer's game too."

"What did he mean?"

"I don't know, honestly. That's when he left and went to the theatre to find Serge."

"Where were you all afternoon? You weren't walking around downtown?"

"I was, for a while, then I called Edwin to meet me at a café. I told him everything that had happened in the last few weeks." She looked up, hesitated for a mere second, and continued. "I told him what had happened years ago. I told him who his real father was."

"How did he take it?"

"How do you expect? He was livid. It took a lot of talking to convince him not to go after Stringer and to let Leland handle things. I told him if he made a scene, everything Leland and I had planned would fall apart. I told him to go to the party and act like nothing had happened. I made him promise he'd hold it together. I knew it was a tall order, but I also knew that I could trust my son. After he left, I... went to the hotel and killed my husband."

"I don't' understand."

"It's simple, Miss Lockhart. I knew Stringer was about to make that announcement. I couldn't let that happen. I took Leland's gun from his suitcase and went into the room Stringer uses for an office next to the Yellow Rose. My intention was to kill Stringer. The door was opened. It was dark inside the room. I saw him pull something out of a desk drawer and move to the window to see it better. I shot my husband, thinking I was shooting Stringer. It wasn't until later after the party started when I went back to our suite to find out what was taking Leland so long that I realized what I'd done."

"But Stringer was in the back room of the Yellow Rose Suite."

"I didn't know that. When I couldn't find Leland, I had a bad feeling come over me. I went back into the office room, and there he was. I'd killed my own husband."

Eleanor was concocting such a good story, I didn't want to tell her that the gun used to kill her husband did not come from any suitcase.

"Why did you fake the seizure and disappear from the hospital?"

"I'd planned to take my own life. It was difficult to do at the clinic with so many people checking on me every five minutes. I had a purse full of pills. It would have been so easy. At the last minute, I realized that if I took my own life, then Stringer Maynard would have won again and my son would be left alone to deal with that vulture."

"So you killed Stringer instead."

"I'd planned to, but someone beat me to it."

"Edwin?"

"Would I be sitting here telling you all this if it was Edwin? Besides, Edwin was in Midland yesterday."

"Are you sure?"

The question stung, I could tell, but Eleanor chose not to answer. Instead she said, "It's funny, but for the first time since I met Stringer Maynard, I feel at peace. I'd like you to do me a favor."

"If I can."

"Walk me over to the police station. I'm turning myself in. Oh, and do not alert Dr. Richards or my sister. I don't think I can stomach either of them right now."

Chapter Twenty-Nine

BY THE TIME I WALKED INTO THE OFFICE, I was soaked to the bone. Another cloud had burst open and drenched me before I could take cover. I was beginning to wonder if that cloud had been waiting around the corner just to make my day a bit worse. Billy was staring at the corkboard and Dixon was staring out the window, his feet up on the desk and his chair leaning back. "Contemplating murder suspects?" I said.

"An umbrella might have been a good idea," Dixon said. "Squeeze yourself out and put this on." He reached in his drawer and tossed me one of his shirts. "I was about to go over this case from the beginning. Something's been nagging me. I know I'm missing something."

I went into the next room, stripped off my shirt and put on Dixon's spare.

"Did you find out anything at the hotel?" Dixon called.

"Never got there," I said rolling up my sleeves.

"The rain?" Billy asked.

"Not the rain. On my way to The Driskill, I ran into—" Before I could tell them about my surprise encounter with Eleanor, Jelly Bluesteen, wearing a white satin suit, pink shirt, yellow tie, and carrying an umbrella, waddled in without knocking.

"Hey, Bluesteen," Dixon said. "Easter come early this year?"

"What'd you talking about, man?" Jelly said. "You mean my duds? Hell, you white boys don't know how to dress. You look like a bunch of tree stumps: brown, brown, and brown." He opened his coat, pulled out an envelope and tossed it on the desk. "Thought I'd bring your check by since I was on my way to tote my mom to the church carnival. Though you didn't do much to get my money back from that thieving bartender."

"That wasn't part of the bargain," Dixon said. "You hired us to find out who had his hand in your till."

"I knew who had his hand in my till," Bluesteen said. "I only needed to be sure."

"You shouldn't have let Sydney run after that dirt bag," Dixon said.

"Hell knows I couldn't have stopped her. That gal's not afraid of nothing. She was lickety-split after him before I could do anything. I'm thinking about hiring you, Miss Sydney, as my bouncer."

"How did you know he was the one stealing from you?" I asked.

"'Cause I called a meeting a few days before and put the word out I knew someone was thieving me. I knew it was him when he showed up late and stood at the door as if he might need a quick getaway. You're a lifetime member at my club; no more membership fee. Anytime you want, you come on in, and the drinks are on the house, including today's." He handed me a five. "You paid before I could tear up your tab. Your two partners pay full price."

Jelly waddled back out. Dixon was right, the man looked like Humpty Dumpty decked out as the star of the Easter egg hunt. The door clicked shut.

"You were at The Blue Mist this morning?" Dixon asked. "Kind of early for a highball."

"I was about to tell you when Bluesteen interrupted."

"Wait." Dixon made as if to jump to his feet, almost tumbling backwards in his chair. "Damn! That's it. That's what's been bugging me. He stood by the door and didn't come in."

"Are you talking about Bluesteen's bartender?" Billy asked.

"Edwin Tatum," Dixon said. "We heard the shot and rushed down the hall. Stringer and Fiona were right behind me, and following them were half the guests, but not Edwin."

"But I saw him in the hall," I said.

"Dixon's right," Billy said. "I saw Edwin outside the door."

"Why didn't he come in?" Dixon asked. "His father was lying on the floor, and his mother was standing there with a gun in her hand. Wouldn't you be the first one in to see what had happened?"

"Not if you already knew your father was dead because you shot him an hour earlier," I said.

"The hotel staff didn't hear any gunshot around 4:30, though," Billy added.

"If they were making a racket setting up *and* if the killer muffled the shot," Dixon replied, "they might not have heard it. And if they did hear a popping sound, they probably wouldn't have associated it with the firing of a gun."

"We checked every inch of that room and didn't find another slug," I said.

"We could have missed it. It's worth another look."

"After what I'd heard, I can believe Edwin might very well have killed his father," I said. "This morning, Eleanor waylaid me in front of The Blue Mist and we had a cozy little visit over a couple of brandies before we strolled over to the police station so she could turn herself in." I relayed the details of Eleanor's new confession.

"Edwin Tatum was really Stringer's son," Dixon said. "Incredible. What a family. The boy had a strong motive for killing Stringer, but why would he kill his father?"

"Most of what Eleanor had told me was a pack of lies," I said. "She stuck to the story about finding the gun in Leland's suitcase. I didn't bother to tell her that the gun did not belonging to her husband and that Serge told us Leland had been shot earlier. But something she said made sense. She said she shot Leland thinking he was Stringer. Maybe Edwin did the same thing. He was angry after Eleanor told him what Stringer had done to her. So, he goes out and gets a gun from a pawnshop, walks into the office suite where Stringer usually conducts business. Edwin is in a blind rage. He grabs a pillow or something to muffle the sound, and he fires the gun. Only then does he realize he killed the wrong man."

"I think you're on to something," Dixon said. "Edwin goes to the party and starts slugging down scotch. Eleanor, also having drunk too much, leaves the Yellow Rose Suite to go find her husband, which she does. He's lying on the floor in the next room with a bullet hole in his back. She kneels down, turns him over, and realizes he's dead. She picks up the gun, fires it, and screams."

"Do you think the cops will believe Eleanor's cockamamie story?" I asked.

"They're not stupid. They'll see right through it," Dixon said.

"By lying about the gun being Leland's, the woman's plan to take the fall for her son will backfire. If I were still on the force, I'd put out warrant for Edwin Tatum's arrest for murder."

"And for Stringer Maynard's murder too. Edwin knows he botched it the first time, so he tries again, and this time, he succeeds," Billy said.

"And according to Tweety, the mystery guy who came up the service stairs and sent him home, was a tall, thin, tanned, middle-aged guy," I said. "That description fits half the men in Austin, including Edwin Tatum. Wait a minute... Edwin was in Midland when Stringer was shot."

"Was he? We need to find out exactly when Edwin returned from Midland," Dixon said.

"If it is Edwin, he's killing out of anger, and after finding out that Leland's Midland bank account is almost empty, he might go after Serge," I said. "He and Lydia might be in danger."

"Billy, can you find out what time Edwin returned from Midland?" Dixon asked.

"Will do," Billy said.

"And I'm going to see Caroline Granger," I said.

"To check on Lydia?" Billy asked.

"That and find out who's who in Junior League." I told them about Fiona's visit and about my call to Brackenridge Hospital. "I agree that Edwin looks guilty of killing Stringer, but I'm not ready to scratch Fiona off the list. I want to know if she was at a Junior League meeting when her husband was killed. She has a couple of zinger motives. Her husband raped her sister and got her pregnant."

"And the other?" Dixon asked.

"She didn't much like the guy."

Chapter Thirty

CAROLINE AND LESTER GRANGER were sitting on their back patio when I stepped out of my car. A pitcher of lemonade sat on the table between them.

"Can you believe this weather?" Caroline said. "This morning it was pouring, and now, the sun's out and it has gotten rather steamy. What brings you here, Miss Sydney? Lester, get another glass for our guest."

"Thanks, Caroline. Don't trouble yourself, Lester. I'm running down a story and don't have time to stay. I stopped by to asked you about the Junior League. I need to check out someone's alibi to make sure they attended a meeting when they said they did."

"I know who to talk to. Come on, I'll take you by her house. It's not far. Lester, there's leftover meatloaf in the ice box if I don't make it back in time to make supper."

I hadn't planned on having a partner this afternoon, but I should have known better. Caroline Granger would jump at any chance to add a little excitement to her life. She was in my car before I could object.

"How's Lydia today?"

"Oh, that girl is such a delight, but she does have a mind of her own. That show last night at the theatre was a bit too risqué. I worry about her not having a mother to guide her. She insisted I take her back to the theatre this morning. She said the stage blocking wasn't right and it needed to be fixed before tonight's performance. I'm not sure what she meant. Turn left at the next street. Stacy Pearson's house is down the block on Cherry Lane."

"Don't worry too much about Lydia. She can handle just about anything that comes her way."

"I don't like her being at the theatre so late every night."

"I'll go check on her right before the show starts and make sure she gets to your house safely. Listen, Caroline, since this interview is not about writing a piece on the Junior League, I have to be careful."

"Don't worry. I'll follow your lead however you handle it. Stacy is such a gossip, she won't care why you're asking questions."

We pulled in the driveway of a typical Tarrytown cottage-style home. A woman about Caroline's age was on her front porch cleaning out a birdfeeder. "Why, Caroline Granger, what brings you here?"

"I want you to meet my new friend, Sydney Lockhart, she's interested in the League."

Stacy Pearson eyed my unconventional attire and probably assumed that I would be the last woman the League would expect to see at their next meeting. I pulled out my notebook. "I'm a reporter at the *American*. Our society editor is planning on running a piece on the Junior League, but she's overbooked with interviews this week and asked me if I could step in. I knew my friend, Caroline, was a member, so I decided to give our editor a hand." Stacy's sigh of relief was all too evident when she realized I was not interested in becoming a member. "Can you tell me about some of the activities the League has planned for the upcoming year?" Twenty minutes later, I had enough information to write a book. When Stacy paused for air, I took over. "I met someone a couple of weeks ago who's active in the League. Perhaps you know Fiona Maynard? What a tragedy that woman's been through?"

Stacy's eyes lit up like the UT tower after the team wins a football game. "Oh, my word, we are all in shock over the murders of her husband and his partner."

"I understand she was at a meeting yesterday when her husband was killed."

"That's true. We were preparing for the Summer Style Show. Fiona is chairwoman of that committee. Life is so unfair. While that poor woman tirelessly was helping her community, her husband was murdered."

I wouldn't call preparing for a style show a tireless effort in community service, but what the hell do I know. I go around dressed as a man half the time. So, Fiona couldn't have killed her husband. Deep down inside, I was hoping to find a loophole in her story. She'd look great on the witness stand when the jury read their verdict of "guilty." I thanked Stacy for her time. As she walked us to the door, I thought of another question. "Was her sister Eleanor Tatum a member too?"

"Oh, my dear, no." She lowered her voice as if the neighborhood were listening. "She spent so much of her time at that Richards' sanitarium. Well, they call it a clinic, but we know what it really was. Frankly, I wouldn't send my cat there for help. Caroline, don't repeat a word of this."

Caroline made a locking gesture on her lips. Stacy looked satisfied and continued with her gossiping. "You see, Miss Lockhart, Julia Richards, Dr. Richards' wife, is a vital member of our League. But when the woman graces us with her presence at the few meetings she attends, all she does is brag about how much money they have, how she flies to Paris twice a year for new clothes, how her husband has his clothes specially made at Styman's Tailor and Men's Wear downtown. I mean, really. She acts like she's the only League member with money and a sense of style."

"The nerve," I said. Suddenly, I felt another lie bubble up in my brain and I grabbed it. "I wrote a story on his clinic here a while back. The place is pretty swanky."

"Oh, it is. I had a friend who went there; not that she was crazy, she just had a rough time after catching her husband with another woman. Anyway, she was hoping for some good old fashion advice. She should have saved her money. I could have told her all husbands cheat and she should look the other way. Dr. Richards gave her some pills and sent her home."

I could tell Caroline was dying to say something, but she waited until we were in the car. "Don't worry about what Stacy said, Sydney. You go ahead and marry that handsome young man of yours. Lester has never once cheated on me."

I was about to ask her where she got the idea that Dixon and I were getting married, but I knew that statement would fall on deaf ears. When we got back to the Granger home, it took some convincing to get Caroline out of the car. She was determined to accompany me for the rest of the day. I reminded her that Lydia might call and she needed to be available. I also suggested that the theatre crew could probably use a batch of cookies after their pint-size boss got through with them.

A LITTLE MORE THAN AN HOUR LATER, I was in the office analyzing the corkboard, trying to connect the facts in a way that would leave a clear trail from both bodies to the one person who had motive, means, and opportunity. It was still difficult for me to believe the mistaken identity story that Eleanor told. Could a mother, or son, not recognize their husband or father from behind, even if the room was dark? Besides the family, I couldn't ignore the artists. As far as I knew, none had a motive for wanting Leland dead, but Stringer was another story. He was a major roadblock in their plans for the art center. The phone rang, shaking me out of my squirrel cage. "Detective agency."

"Any luck?" Dixon asked.

"Fiona was definitely at the League all afternoon. How about you? Find out if Edwin was still in Midland when Stringer was killed?"

"Billy's still checking. I did check on Serge's back account. He was right. The money Leland gave him is still there. Do you think Edwin knows that his mother is sitting in jail right now?"

"Probably. Her one phone call would not have been to Dr. Richards or to Fiona."

"I'm going to hunt the young man down."

"I was thinking about calling Dr. Richards. I promised Eleanor I wouldn't call him about her turning herself in. I'll keep mute on that subject, instead I want to pick his brain about Eleanor's condition. She confesses, escapes from the hospital, and then turns herself in. Whenever I talk to that woman she seems like someone who has complete control of her senses, and then she turns around and does something insane."

"Sounds like a normal nut case to me," Dixon said. "Check with you later."

"Okay, I'll call you." I thought he'd hung up until I heard him clear his throat.

"What is it?"

"You're good at this, Sydney."

"Thanks, I . . ." This time, he did hang up.

DR. RICHARDS WAS IN, and to my surprise, agreed to see me. According to his receptionist, the cops had already been to see him about Eleanor's current stay in the city jail, so I didn't have to worry about keeping her secret. On my way down the hall to his office, I was trying to decide which hat I would wear: reporter or detective. I figured one was as bothersome as another. I introduced myself as a PI, working to try to clear Eleanor and asked if he could help.

"I know who you are, Miss Lockhart," he said. "Mrs. Maynard told me. Please sit down."

Dr. Richards' private office lacked the feel of intimacy one might expect to find in a room where secrets were spilled and emotions ran high. Two steel and chrome chairs were positioned side by side in front of a simple, but stylish, black lacquered desk. On the desk sat a calendar, phone, two file folders, a pen and ink set, and a framed photo of Dr. Richards and a woman whom I assumed was his wife. To the left of his desk, a putty gray chase lounge with a curved, tufted back, minus armrests and pillows, looked as comfortable as a slab of concrete.

"Thanks for seeing me, Dr. Richards."

"I'll be glad to help if I can. I just came from the jail. What a mess this is. I tried to see Mrs. Tatum, but she refused. She's dug herself a deep hole by disappearing from the hospital. They've charged her with Stringer Maynard's murder. I seriously doubt I'll be able to have her released into my care a second time, and I'm sure the police will not allow bail. Mrs. Maynard was waiting to see Eleanor too, and I hope she had better luck than me. From what I understand, Eleanor turned to you and you took her to the police station."

I thought I'd have to twist the guy's arm to get anything out of him. When he paused his nervous chatter, I jumped in. "That's right. She told me her story and asked me to escort her to the station. Can I be honest with you, Dr. Richards?"

"Please, by all means."

"I don't think she murdered either man."

"Well, she didn't mean to kill her husband, according to the statement she gave the police."

"I mean, I don't think she fired the gun that killed her

husband, and although her motive for killing Stringer is strong, I don't think she killed him either."

"Why do you believe that?"

"A hunch. She's protecting someone."

"Miss Lockhart, Mrs. Tatum is not a well woman. She's depressed, suicidal, often confused, and doesn't remember things. Having a mere hunch is not going to help you understand what's going on in that troubled mind."

"Couldn't those symptoms: depression, suicidal, confusion, be caused by the drugs she's been taking?"

"That's very possible, but without the drugs, she is violent. Before I released her about five months ago, I stressed to her husband that she must stay on the medication. I set up weekly appointments, which she never kept, so I'm assuming the warning about staying on her medication was ignored. And look what happened. She killed her husband and possibly her brother-in-law. The layperson doesn't understand mental illness. Science is only beginning to grasp the myriad complications involved. A few years ago, before these drugs were available, people like Eleanor Tatum spent their time in a sanitarium strapped to a bed. If she had stayed on the medication, none of this would have happened."

There was a soft knock on the door and Dr. Richards seemed to welcome the interruption. His secretary eased in. "Sorry, Doctor, but Mrs. Maynard is in the lobby insisting she see you immediately. I don't think I can keep her out much longer."

"That's okay, Sarah. Miss Lockhart was just leaving. Ah, I'll escort her out myself."

Sarah nodded her understanding, and two minutes later, I was leaving the clinic through the backdoor, Dr. Richards' apologizing for my secretive departure. "I hope you understand. I'm sure Mrs. Maynard is upset, and I don't want to make the situation worse."

"No problem. If she becomes too distraught, you can always slip her one of your pills."

The benevolent expression Dr. Richards had been wearing turned to a cold, hard stare. I smiled and left, knowing his attempt to hide my visit from Fiona would be futile. My flashy car was parked out front. I banked on her being in there for a while and went across the street to a phone booth and called Billy. Luckily, he was in the office and agreed to rush over and trade cars with me. By the time Fiona stormed out of the building twenty minutes later, I was across the street, sitting low in the front seat of Billy's black Plymouth. I don't know why I had the strong urge to follow her, except I had one of those *mere* hunches.

I expected her to go almost anywhere except where she ended up. Five miles outside of town on the interstate sat a Lodger's Motor Court. I pulled into the used car lot next door and watched as she walked into the office and then into a room on the first floor. Ten minutes later, Dr. Richards pulled up and went into the same room. I waited an hour. Finally, he stormed out, hopped in the car, and spun gravel on his way out of the motel's parking lot. Fiona emerged next, watched him disappear down the highway, and then calmly got into her car and left.

I followed Fiona back into town and to the Tarrytown Country Club. I parked down the street, waited five minutes, and went in. I asked to see Mrs. Maynard. The person in charge insisted I give my name. I pulled out a sheet of paper from my notebook and wrote down three words, folded it, and handed it to him. "This should do," I said.

I heard Fiona before I saw her. Her heels clicked so loudly, they sounded like jackhammers on concrete. She looked as if she were about to rip my head off, and at the last minute, changed her tactic. "It's not what you think."

"That's what they all say." I laughed.

"Well, it *was* what you think." She chuckled. "But no longer. I ended it, and it's not like Stringer didn't have his share of lady friends, although he met his at the fancy Driskill Hotel."

"Why did you end it?"

"I got tired of Andrew." She shrugged. "He was only a fling. Besides, his wife's getting suspicious."

"He's your sister's doctor. You weren't afraid that would cause problems?"

"Not in the least. He likes having notable cliental like my sister. And he's making a bundle off her. He'll get over the breakup, believe me."

"Were you able to talk to Eleanor?"

"She wouldn't see me or Andrew. After I left the jail, I went to see our lawyer. He's not too hopeful he can do much to help her situation. And I suspect you're not any closer to finding the real killer, otherwise Serge LaBeau would be sitting in jail rather than Eleanor."

Serge LaBeau was indeed on my mind, but I wasn't prepared to discuss the topic with Fiona, instead, I changed the subject. "What are your plans, Fiona?"

"You mean now that I'm a widow? Sell the ranch. Sell the house. Do what I can for Eleanor and Edwin. Then, when this is all over, I might leave on an extended trip to Europe—alone."

Chapter Thirty-One

THE AFTERNOON WAS FLYING BY and I had several things to do before I lay my head on the pillow. I left the country club, and I stopped by the apartment to check on the pets and give Monroe an early walk. When she saw me fill her food dish two hours earlier than usual, she cocked her head as if to say, "Another late night?" The cat, on the other hand, couldn't care less if I came back at all. I checked the milk in the icebox and decided it would last another day. As I puttered a while longer, giving Monroe a chance to feel like she really had a mother, my mind kept returning to the scene at the Lodger's Motor Court. I had no doubt Fiona Maynard had ice water in her veins, but Dr. Richards seemed pretty torn up about being dumped. On my way out, I left the kitchen light on. I stopped by the Texaco for a fill-up and drove back to the Richards' Clinic. I didn't know what I expected to find: Dr. Andrew Richards hanging by his neck from one of his pecan trees in his outdoor garden?

I noticed the parking lot was absent of Richards' car. Before I could figure out what I was going to say to get the tightlipped receptionist Sarah to spill forth some information, I was out of my car and standing in front of her. She tossed her fingernail file back in the desk drawer and smiled. "Yes?"

"I was here earlier," I said.

"Yes, Miss Lockhart, I know that."

"I was visiting with Dr. Richards about Eleanor Tatum's situation and . . ."

Sarah crossed her arms and cocked her head much the same manner as my poodle.

"And, well, we're both very concerned about Mrs. Tatum. I wondered if I could have another word with him. I'm afraid it's important."

"He's not here, Miss Lockhart. He came in about an hour ago. He said he wasn't feeling well and decided to go home."

"I see. You know, now that I think about it, he didn't look

well when I saw him before. Probably something he had for lunch."

"Sure." Sarah smirked.

"Or maybe he was coming down with something. The flu is going around again."

"I've worked here for seven years, and Dr. Richards has never left early because of illness."

"Poor man. He must really feel horrible."

"I'll say. His wife called four times while he was gone. I handed him the messages when he came back. He turned white, came up with the sick excuse, and fled."

"You don't think it was a family emergency?"

"When Mrs. Richards calls, it's always a family emergency."

"I'm afraid I don't understand."

Someone walked in and Sarah went back to her professional demeanor. "I'll tell Dr. Richards you stopped by again, Miss Lockhart. Have a good afternoon."

Having been clearly dismissed, I turned to leave. This case had me stymied. I need to push harder. After Sarah apologized to Dr. Richards' patient for having to reschedule her appointment, I went back to the reception desk. "Do you mind if I leave Dr. Richards a message? Like I said, it's important." Sarah huffed but presented me with a notepad and fountain pen. I wrote down the message, folded the note, and asked for an envelope. Reluctantly, she handed me one. I inserted the note, sealed the envelope, and wrote my name and phone number on the back.

I WENT BACK TO MY APARTMENT, feeling like I'd made an ass of myself. Either Dr. Richards would interpret the note as an invitation to continue where Fiona Maynard had left off or an audacious blackmail threat. Neither one would fare well. I left Dixon a message on my kitchen counter, saying I'd be at the theatre tonight, probably until the show's conclusion, and that I'd see him in the morning.

It was after six when I pushed through the backstage door. The first thing I heard was Lydia shouting to one of the actors. I took a seat in the back of the theatre to watch the performance.

"Johnny, if you stand with your back to half the audience, they will not hear a word you say. Why can't you get that through your thick head?"

Johnny turned and glared at little Sherlock, whose oversized deerstalker cap had slid down over her eyebrows. He opened his mouth to say something and apparently thought better of it. Rather than repeat her instructions, Lydia climbed up on stage, delivered his lines with perfect blocking, and turned to him. "See? That's what I mean." She climbed back down, grabbed a megaphone and shouted, "Take an early dinner break, everyone. Be back at seven and be ready to run through the entire production. I don't want tonight's show full of clumsy mistakes." A collective groan went through the theatre as the overworked crew turned to leave.

Howie Lenning was headed out the door when Lydia called him back. "Listen, Howie, you need to stop stealing my lines," Lydia chided.

"That's the only way anyone in this production can open his mouth and deliver anything worthwhile," Howie said. "We gotta adlib to bring the least bit of attention to the fact that other actors besides you are on stage."

"With these last minute changes, this was the best way to handle the script. Besides, Dr. Watson never says anything important anyway."

"Whatever you say, Lydia."

Howie slammed the stage door, causing the Texas flag to tumble from its bracket on the front of the Alamo.

"You're going to have a mutiny on your hands," I said when Lydia saw me coming down the aisle.

"I can handle it."

"Did I tell you my mother dabbles in community theatre?"

"Is she any good?"

"She thinks she is."

"Maybe I'll put her in a show. We're always short-handed."

"I shouldn't have brought it up. Your life is complicated enough. Come on. You need to get a bite to eat. Tip Top okay?"

"Sure."

WE TOOK A BOOTH BY THE WINDOW. I grabbed a menu and offered one to Lydia. "I know what I want," she said. "Are you buying?"

"I bought last time."

"Yeah, but I'm just a twelve-year-old kid."

"So you say. Can I have a ticket to the show tonight? You offered. Remember that first night we met under the Blue Moon?"

"I'll have a ticket for you at the box office."

"One for my cousin Ruth too."

"Is she still playing Betty Crocker?"

"Done with that."

"She needs to return the costume."

"We'll bring it tonight."

"Show starts at 9:00"

"Order anything you want, then."

The waitress came by and I ordered a tuna melt with fries. Lydia ordered a burger, onion rings, a chocolate milk shake, and a slice of cherry pie. "I have a long night ahead of me," she said. " So the Tatum woman's back in jail. Can Serge come home?"

"She didn't kill either man."

Lydia slapped her hand on the table, causing our water glasses to slosh. "Damn. Serge's an idiot, but he's the only father I have."

"I wish I could fix this for you, Lydia. The best I can do is take you home to my apartment after the show. I'll make up the sofa for you. You can have the poodle."

"And the cat?"

"Be my guest."

"'It has long been an axiom of mine that the little things are infinitely the most important.'"

Lydia surprised me. Not by the eloquence of her Holmes' quote, but by the large smile on her face.

I DROPPED LYDIA OFF AT THE THEATRE and told her I'd be there in time for the show. I headed over to the agency. Being Friday evening, our elevator in the building was closed. I made that breathless climb to the top floor. When I stepped into the dimly lit hallway, something hard crunched underfoot. The frosted glass that had once made up the panel of our office door was now busted and scattered over the floor. I pulled my gun from my holster and pushed open the door. The office was empty, very empty. Our notes had been ripped off the corkboard; file folders empty and scattered; drawers pulled out and tossed across the floor; even our telephone wire was ripped from the wall. All of Billy's hard work, down the drain.

All my hunches, bad feelings, frustrations were replaced by a small amount of encouragement. Sure, I was hacked someone ransacked our new agency. That would never have happened if we were moving in the wrong direction on this case. One of us hit pay dirt in the investigation. Billy was probably still in Bastrop keeping an eye on Serge. I'm sure it wasn't me, since all I managed to do was stir up a hornet's nest by leaving two people the same note with the words "Lodger's Motor Court" written on it, as if Fiona and Dr. Richards' affair were any of my business. My moment of encouragement disappeared as I thought of Dixon confronting Edwin. Surely, it wouldn't have taken this long.

I ran down to the fourth floor where accountant Bill Wooley usually worked all hours in his office. I was relieved to see his light still on. I used his phone to call the cops. I called Ruth and told her to meet me at the Next to Nothing Theatre at 9:00 and to bring her Crocker costume. Finally, I called Dixon at home. I got no answer.

By the time the cops took my statement and fingerprinted the office, it was almost eight thirty. I swept up the mess, stacked the files on the desk, checked to make sure the cash box was in the safe, and left, all the while hoping Dixon would walk in. The building security locked the building's outer doors at ten, so I felt okay about leaving the office. There was nothing of value anyone would want to steal except our second-hand furniture and a picture of a landscape no one could identify.

I had time before the show so I drove by the Granger cottage—no Dixon. I drove by my place—no Dixon. Since I'd already left him a note about being at the theatre, I wasn't all that worried. I'd probably find him at the stage door at the end of the show.

RUTH AND I WALKED UP to the box office at the same time. "Am I going to like this play? It better be good, or else." She handed me a paper bag with the Betty Crocker outfit inside.

"Or else what? You didn't have any plans for tonight anyway."

"Lucky for you, my plans were cancelled at the last minute. I was supposed to go have Mexican food with Edwin again, but he called a couple of hours ago and said something came up."

That brought me up short. "You had a date with Edwin?"

"Don't look so astonished? Because of your constant interference in my life, I do manage to socialize every now and then."

"No, I mean, when did you and Edwin make the date?"

"Why?"

"It's important, Ruth," I cried. "We have a murder investigation going on." The couple behind us gasped at the mention of murder.

I asked for our tickets and pulled Ruth over to the side. "Eleanor's in jail again. She turned herself in this morning. I haven't heard from Dixon all afternoon. He was supposed to try to locate Edwin today."

"Edwin called me last night and we made the date."

"That's odd. With his mother on the lam and his father and uncle murdered, seems like he'd have other things on his mind than dating."

"Oh, for heaven's sakes. It wasn't a date date. The man needed a friend to talk to."

"He must have cancelled the date because of Eleanor."

"He didn't say, but he sounded upset. I asked him if he was okay, and he said yes, but I know he wasn't. So much has happened to that poor guy."

"Did he say where he was when he called?'

"No. I told him I'd call him tomorrow."

"Let's go in and find our seats. I'm going to use the phone to see if I can contact Dixon again."

LYDIA HAD GIVEN US the two seats by the aisle in the second row. I sat down next to my cousin as the lights softened.

"Did you get him?"

"No. I hope everything's okay."

"Relax. Dixon's always okay."

The curtain rose and "Sherlock Holmes at the Alamo" began. Since the battle at the Alamo took place more than fifty years before Arthur Conan Doyle created the world's greatest detective, Holmes' presence was the result of time travel through a tunnel under Crockett Street behind the mission. The opening scene had Lydia, as Sherlock, crawling from a manhole as an enormous Mexican army, depicted by a famous painting made to shimmer behind a thin fabric, gathered in the distance. Following her was Howie as Dr. Watson.

"'What object is served by this circle of misery and violence and fear?'" Holmes said, looking over the future battle site. "'It must tend to some end, or else our universe is ruled by—'"

"Santa Anna, by the looks of it," Dr. Watson said in a Texas drawl that got a hardy chuckle out of the audience.

Holmes glared at her sidekick. Howie clearly stole the lead's first scene. The production continued in the same vein with Lydia and Howie trying to upstage one another. The audience probably thought it was part of the script, but I'd hate to be in Howie's shoes when the curtain fell.

When it was clear that Holmes would not be able to save the Texans, he offered to transport them into the future via the time-travel tunnel. Colonel Travis, Jim Bowie, Davy Crockett, and all the settlers who took refuge inside the mission, declined. They decided to stay and fight. When Holmes' final plea to the colonel to change the course of history fell on deaf ears, Holmes and Dr. Watson chose to join them in battle. In the final scene, as the great detective lay dying in a pool of blood, Dr. Watson (also with a bullet hole in his chest) chastised his friend and partner for getting them into a fatally impossible situation.

Seeing another line-steal coming, Holmes pulled his revolver and shot the good doctor. The audience gasped; the curtain fell.

"I don't get it," Ruth whispered.

"Just start clapping." I shouted "bravo" a few times. Everyone joined me, probably assuming they'd missed something.

Ruth and I made our way backstage in time to hear Lydia and Howie arguing about the ad-libbing. Howie was appalled over Holmes killing Dr. Watson. "You can't do that!" Howie yelled. "Everyone loves Dr. Watson. You can't kill him out of the blue."

"Conan Doyle did that to Holmes in 'The Final Problem,'" Lydia said.

"London went into mourning and Conan Doyle had to go into hiding," Howie said over his shoulder on the way to his dressing room. "I wouldn't leave this theatre wearing your costume, Lydia. You might get assassinated. On the other hand, that might not be a bad idea."

"I think Howie might have a good point," I said.

"He kept stealing my lines. I had to do something. Other than that, did you like the show?" Lydia asked.

"I didn't get it," Ruth said.

Lydia gave my cousin an I'm-not-surprised look. "Let's go over to my apartment. I need a change of clothes. My stuff is still at the Granger's, and I'm not about to go over there tonight."

Ruth and I followed Lydia up to her apartment and went to the kitchen to wait while Lydia gathered her things from her room.

"I can't believe she lives here," Ruth said. She opened the icebox. "Look, there's nothing in here but beer, and . . ." she unscrewed the cap on the milk bottle, ". . . sour milk."

"It hasn't been a normal week for the child," I said.

"Child? Are you sure you want her staying with you tonight?"

"She doesn't want to go back to the Granger's, and I can't very well let her stay here by herself. Besides, I enjoy her company."

"You would."

Lydia came out, still wearing the Holmes getup and carrying

a suitcase. In her other hand was, of all things, a Teddy Bear. "Don't look at me like that. I need to rewrite the damn script tonight and this ragged, smelly thing is my muse. Let's go down the back way through the prop room so I can put up the costume. I have to stay organized, otherwise the place is a nightmare."

We followed Lydia downstairs. "Why are we always following her?" Ruth said to me under her breath.

"Shut up," I said.

"I can't believe she's wearing that Holmes costume with purple patent leather shoes."

"You're jealous because you don't have the imagination to mix and match like I do," Lydia called over her shoulder. "And to set the record straight, the shoes are lavender."

"Watch your mouth, young lady. I can take you over my knee," Ruth said.

"I'd like to see you try," Lydia retorted.

I squeezed Ruth's arm. "Stop it. Both of you."

Lydia tossed me the wig. "Sydney, put this in that bottom drawer in that dresser to your right."

I bent down to pull open the drawer when a bullet shattered the ceramic urn, which sat where my head was a second ago.

Ruth screamed and Lydia let out an inappropriate expletive. I drew my gun. A small lamp by the door dimly lighted the prop room, causing most of the room to be cast in shadows. I saw Lydia had dived under an old desk and Ruth tucked herself in between two clothes racks, completely hidden from the ankles up. I crawled over to Lydia. "Is everyone okay?" I whispered. Lydia nodded and Ruth stuck out her hand and waved. Seasoned, she was.

Whoever had shot at us had not moved. I looked around, trying to determine exactly where the shot came from. Lydia nudged me and pointed up. I hadn't noticed it before. Above the room was a loft, similar to a gallery in a courthouse. A railing ran along the length of the loft, allowing whoever was up there a full view of the prop room below. All I could make out were more stacks of boxes and several trunks. "How do you get up there?" I asked.

"The backstairs," Lydia said.

"Stay here." Knowing she wouldn't, I added, "Watch Ruth for me."

Lydia grunted and I took that as an "okay." I left the safety of the desk and crouched among several stacks of chairs toward the door. The hall light illuminated the area, and as soon as I emerged from the shadows, another blast, shot from above, struck the wall a few feet to my right. I flattened myself on the floor, rolled over, and jerked the lamp cord from the wall, throwing the room into a deeper darkness. I aimed my gun toward the loft, fired off a couple of rounds, and then dashed into the hall and around to the stairs. I hit the light switch as I rounded the corner, darkening the hall too. The sound of running and stumbling echoed from above. If I remembered the building's design correctly, this was the staircase Lydia and I took to the roof that first night I ran in here chasing Bluesteen's bartender. If the shooter was trying to escape, he'd have to head to the roof and the fire escape or descend the stairs and run smack into me. I sincerely hoped he was smart enough to realize I'd be down here with my gun and decided to opt for the roof instead.

I listened for a moment. The sound of running faded into the distance, but I could tell he wasn't running up to the roof. Suddenly, I remembered the second floor hallway with the stairs leading down to the back door exit and the alley entrance to the prop room. I scrambled up the steps and followed, praying the guy was making his escape rather than heading down to where Ruth and Lydia were holed up. As I got to the back stairs, all was silent. No running; no opening or closing doors. Not a good sign. I crept downward. With each step, the old wood creaked in protest. When I reached the bottom, I noticed the exit door to the alley was still padlocked. The shooter was nowhere in sight. I scrambled toward the prop room door, flushing out my prey and sending him dashing into the room and slamming the door behind him. I pulled the handle. The door didn't budge. Inside I heard a struggle, followed by muddled voices. I blew the handle off the door and kicked it open. A small window emitted some light from the street. I saw Lydia was not in her hiding place. I also saw two sets of ankles from under the clothes hanging on the racks: Ruth's dainty ones in front and those of a man standing close behind her; very close. I'm sure the guy had one hand over her mouth and the other holding a gun to her temple. My only advantage was that he most likely couldn't see me, but if I made another move, he'd hear, and I didn't want his next shot to pierce Ruth's skull. She'd never forgive me.

I pretended I hadn't seen him and called out for Lydia, confident she'd catch on to my bluff. "Lydia, Ruth, where are you? The guy's gone. I'm pretty sure he left by the roof."

"Over here," Lydia called.

"Stay there until I get us some light." I maneuvered my way to the lamp and plugged it in. I joined Lydia where she was standing behind the guillotine and out of danger of getting shot. "Where's Ruth?" I motioned to the clothes rack indicating I knew where Ruth was and that the killer was standing behind her.

"I think she ran through the back door. I heard it slam."

"She must be okay too. If the guy went down the fire escape, he's probably long gone by now." I tiptoed toward the rack and motioned for Lydia to move toward the hallway door and slam the door when I gave the signal. "Come on. Let's get out of here." When I was directly behind the rack, I pantomimed to Lydia and she noisily walked over and slammed the door. Assuming we'd left, the clothes on the rack began to move. And Ruth and the guy, wearing a stocking over his face, stepped out. He jerked a belt from one of the dresses and tied Ruth's hands behind her. Out of the corner of my eye, I saw Lydia moving toward a box where she pulled something out. I motioned for her to stay still, but she ignored me and continued to move around toward the back of the room. Ruth now had a gag stuffed into her mouth.

I couldn't tell for sure who the guy was, since his face was covered and the collar of his overcoat pulled up. But judging by his build and height, it appeared that whatever caused Edwin to cancel his date with Ruth involved continuing his killing spree. He looked around, as if not sure what to do next. This momentary lapse of indecision ended with him dragging over a chair and tying Ruth to the seat. In order to do that, he laid he gun on the table next to him.

I glanced over at Lydia, who's small form seemed ghostly in the shadows. Before I could rush over and stop her, she raised what I thought was a gun and pointed it. Instead of a loud crack, a light shot from the end illuminating the headless man and the shiny blade of the guillotine. The guy jerked up, and in the blade's reflection, saw the Dracula image. He screamed and stumbled backwards. I realized at that moment Lydia must have positioned these props for that very effect, for that's what happened to me on that first night when I barged in here and found her dressed in organdy and lace. Wasting no time, I rushed him, but he was too quick in snatching his gun and running for the front door. On his way out, he turned, fired a couple of shots, and was gone.

"You shouldn't have done that, Lydia," I shouted. "You could have gotten someone killed! Lock all the doors in case he comes back." I pulled the gag from Ruth's mouth. "Was it Edwin?" I said to her.

"I couldn't tell," she spat. "That rag tastes like old socks. Untie me."

"How could you not tell? You had enchiladas with the guy just a few nights ago."

"It's not like we groped during dinner."

"Now that I gotta see," Lydia said.

"Let's get out of here," I said. At that moment, a loud pounding came from the alley door.

"Sydney! Are you in there?"

"Yeah, hold on."

Lydia unlocked the door and Dixon ran in.

"Where have you been?" I asked.

"Where have *I* been? Where have *you* been? I've been looking for you all evening."

"You didn't get my note? I left it on the kitchen counter."

"I came back into town to find the office in shambles. I called you at home, at the newspaper; no answer. I went by your apartment. There was no note. I called Mrs. Granger and she told me you were at the theatre, watching the show. I waited at your apartment until midnight. By that time, I knew something was wrong. I drove to the Next to Nothing. The door was closed and the place was dark. That's when I heard the shots. They weren't—"

"Coming from here?" I finished his question. "You're in the right place. Four from the attacker and three from me. You didn't see a harried guy running down the street did you?"

"I came down the alley," he said.

"We think it was Edwin," Ruth said.

"I think you're right," he said. "That's why I'm here. There are some new developments."

Chapter Thirty-Two

RUTH, LYDIA, AND I followed Dixon to the hotel in my car to drop Ruth off. Dixon walked her up to her room to make sure no killers were lurking. Lydia and I waited on the curb.

"Ruth doesn't like me," she said.

"Unless you're a man, handsome, and rich, she doesn't bother to turn on the charm, but that doesn't mean she doesn't like you. I wouldn't think you'd care what Ruth thought."

I studied Lydia's face and noticed the girl's skin had turned sallow. Dark rings had formed under her eyes. "You've had a heck of a day," I said. "And an even worse night. Are you okay?"

"I'm hungry," she responded, trying to hide the quiver in her voice.

"How about grilled cheese? I also can open up a can of tomato soup when we get to my apartment."

She nodded and I kept quiet.

DIXON FLIPPED THE SANDWICHES in the skillet while I made up the sofa for Lydia. Monroe was so excited to have an overnight guest that wasn't Ruth, she could hardly contain herself. Mealworm showed her pleasure, too, by curling up in Lydia's open suitcase and going to sleep.

At the sound of butter browning the bread in the skillet and the aroma of fresh coffee dripping in the percolator, I looked up to find Dixon with his sleeves rolled up past his elbows, exposing his muscular forearms, my apron tied neatly around his trim waist. The domestic scene left me breathless. Sure, we'd spent many evenings here: cooking, eating, drinking—among other things—but tonight it felt different. I wasn't sure why.

Dixon noticed me looking at him and grinned. He nodded toward Lydia who was asleep in the chair, Monroe squeezed in beside her. I went to the stove and put my arms around him. "Should we wake her?"

"I don't think so. She's exhausted. I'll put her sandwich in the oven and turn down the heat on the soup in case she wakes up. Sit down. I'll serve."

We ate in silence, both needing the food more than anything. When I cleared the empty plates and poured us a second cup, we shared the events of the day.

"Why do you think Edwin tried to kill us?" I asked. "Anything to do with those latest developments you spoke of?

"Afraid so."

We both turned to Lydia. "She's out for the night," Dixon said. "I never had a chance to talk to Edwin today. Billy brought Serge back from Bastrop, having convinced the guy to come clean."

"But I thought Edwin—"

"Hold on. That's what I'm trying to tell you. Serge finally fessed up. When he went to the hotel to check on Leland that fatal afternoon, he saw Edwin coming from the room where Leland was murdered about the time he was murdered. He said the guy was near panic. He pulled the door to and ran down the stairwell. Then he turned and came back to wipe his prints off the doorknob. Serge waited until Edwin was gone and went in. He found Leland on the floor, shot in the back."

"So we were right in suspecting Eleanor was covering for her son. Why didn't Serge say anything earlier?"

"He said at first he thought if he kept quiet, suspicion would fall on Stringer. That's how much Serge hated the guy. He didn't know Stringer was with me at the Citadel Club at the time Leland was killed. As more facts came out, Serge stuck with his story as not to throw suspicion on himself. He'd woven himself into the proverbial tangled web."

"I can't believe Edwin would let his mother take the rap for him."

"We don't know what's going on in Edwin's mind."

"Is Serge going to the police?"

"First thing in the morning. He's staying with Billy tonight. Find out anything?"

"I checked on Fiona's alibi. She was at the Junior League when Stringer was killed. But here's an interesting piece of information. Fiona and Dr. Richards are, or were, having an affair. When I left the clinic, I followed Fiona."

"Yeah, Billy told me you two switched cars."

"I waited outside the Lodger's Motor Court and watched the aftermath of Fiona dumping her boyfriend. I followed her to the Tarrytown Country Club and confronted her. She just laughed and said that she didn't care who knew and that she'd gotten tired of him and called it quits. Then I did something stupid. I went back to the clinic. The good doctor was suddenly too busy to see me so I left him a note."

"And?"

"Three words: Lodger's Motor Court."

Dixon let out a chortle. "You like to stir things up, don't you?"

"I couldn't help it. I don't like Fiona Maynard, and I think Dr. Richards is a quack."

"Those two aren't our problem now. We need to make sure Serge gets to the station tomorrow and tells his story." He looked over at Lydia and lowered his voice. "The guy's not the most trustworthy fellow. I'm going over to Billy's first thing in the morning to escort Serge myself. I'll also tell Bremmer about your shootout in the prop room. He'll want you and Ruth to come by and give your statements. Do you have an extra blanket and pillow? I'm staying here. I'm not leaving you and Lydia alone after what happened in the theatre."

I moved from my chair onto his lap. "You're a swell guy."

"You just now figured that out?"

"No, it was a few minutes ago when I saw you in that apron making grilled cheese sandwiches."

Lydia stirred. Dixon and I parted. He carried her to the sofa and tucked her in, placing the Teddy Bear next to her. I made Dixon a pallet on the living room rug. I checked both doors and every window to make sure they were locked while Dixon cleaned up the kitchen.

"Since I'm on watch tonight," he said. "I'm draining the coffee pot. Chances are I won't be able to sleep anyway."

"I'll find a couple more blankets to make your pallet a bit more comfortable."

"Sleeping on the floor is not the problem." He had me by my arms before I could say, "child on the sofa." I put the brakes on the kiss before things got out of control and wobbled to my bed—alone. Dixon wasn't the only one with a sleepless night ahead.

By NOON THE NEXT DAY, a warrant was issued for the arrest of one Edwin James Tatum for the murder of Leland Tatum and Stringer Maynard. Fiona and the family lawyer were in the cell, conferencing with Eleanor who still insisted she was guilty of her husband's murder and trying to act as an alibi for Edwin for Stringer's murder.

Serge took Lydia back to Bastrop with him until Edwin could be picked up. He decided not to close the theatre, since tickets were selling like hotcakes after last night's performance. He put Howie in charge, which delighted the actor to no end. Melvin was back from Mexico and would stand in as Sherlock during Lydia's absence, which caused her to pitch a royal fit. Lydia tried pleading her case to me, but after last night's close call, I sided with Serge.

Billy offered to head over to the office to meet the guy who was to replace our door window. I suggested Dixon and I accompany him and have a go with straightening out the files. Billy stammered and said he could handle it. I was about to object when Dixon suggested he and I go to Zeke's for breakfast.

We had our noses buried in the menu for several silent minutes. Finally, Dixon said, "I could use a greasy ham and cheese omelet." He wedged the menu back in the caddy. "How about you?" When I didn't respond, he said, "Something's on your brain."

"What's with Billy?"

"I'm surprised you haven't figured that out. But that's not what's bothering you. Spill."

"Why me?"

"That answer requires more than mere words, hon." He leaned over. "We could skip breakfast and go over to your place and I'll show you 'why you.'"

I knew I'd be a goner if I looked up into those deep, rich eyes, so I kept my focus on the menu until Dixon removed it from my hands and turned it right side up. "Well?" he said.

"I was thinking about last night. Why would Edwin want to kill me?"

"We were closing in on him."

"Right. *We* were closing in on him, but he chose to go after me—not you, not Billy."

The waitress came over and Dixon raised his brows expectantly at me.

"I think better with a little food in my stomach." I smiled. "I'll have the breakfast special; eggs scrambled soft, bacon crispy. And kept the coffee coming."

"Make that two," Dixon said.

The waitress left to turn in our order and we got back to business. "That thought crossed my mind too," Dixon said. "Who knows why Edwin went after you? He's killed two people. He's not thinking straight. There's not much we can do now, except watch our backs until the cops catch him."

"That's not very comforting. And another thing that has set my nerves on end. What happened to that note I left you on my kitchen counter? Could that have been Edwin too? He breaks in to my apartment, reads the note, and takes it? That's how he knew I'd be at the theatre. He must have been waiting and followed us to Serge's building after we left."

"We'll know soon enough."

"Yeah, that's what I'm afraid of."

We finished breakfast and got back to the office to find a repairman writing out our bill. Billy had the petty cash box out and was counting out enough to pay the guy.

"Billy, I think these current files should go in a different drawer. That way you can easily find them." Phoebe stood up from behind the new bookcase, which held an unusual collection of conversational items: a small globe, a miniature replica of an Egyptian pyramid, and a pair of antique field glasses. In her arms was a stack of files.

When he saw us, he blushed red.

"Oh, hello," Billy stammered. "Phoebe is helping out with

getting things back in order. She has great decorating skills." He pointed to the bookcase. "Classy, huh? We'll have some books evidently."

"I like it," I said. Looks like we have our new office helper and Billy has a new girlfriend.

"Gives the place some charm," Dixon added and went over to help Phoebe with the files. Since there was nothing for me to do, I called Ernest at home and told him the latest, and promised him my story first thing. Dixon was against me going back to the newspaper office. He didn't want Edwin to get another shot at me. Neither did I. I wheeled our typewriter into the back room, closed the door, and I began my story. An hour later, I was proofing my copy when Dixon walked in.

"We got a call."

"Yeah, I heard the phone."

"It was Victor Nolan. He said the police have picked up Edwin. I'm going down to the station. You should probably come too and tell Bremmer about last night."

"We should collect Ruth."

"Let's go."

WHILE RUTH AND I gave our statements to the sergeant, I noticed Bremmer doodling on his notepad. At first I thought he was merely drawing circles until I noticed the circles turned into little stick-figure flowers. When we signed the documents, Bremmer told the sergeant he could leave. He sat down and read through our statements. He lit a cigarette and doodled a bit more, filling in the flowers' centers with dark dots. Ruth and I looked at one another and shrugged. I looked at Dixon, who'd lit his own cigarette and appeared to study the cobwebs in the corner. Finally, Bremmer tossed his pencil down and he said, "I have two people in jail, both claiming to have killed the same two people."

"They are covering for one another," Dixon said.

"I know that." Bremmer stabbed his cigarette out in the ashtray. "The mother's protecting the son and the son's protecting the mother. Which one is lying?"

"Why ask us? That's your job to figure out who is lying," Ruth reminded the detective. "I have a brunch date at the hotel." Ruth stood to leave.

"Sit down, Miss Echland," Bremmer said. "Something's bothering me."

"But I—"

Dixon smiled at Ruth. She shut up and sat down. If the man could package that lopsided smile, he'd make millions.

"Are you sure about the time of the shooting last night?" Bremmer said.

Ruth and I looked at one another again. "No question," I said. "Why?"

"I can vouch for the time," Dixon said. "I heard the shots as I walked up."

"That's what I was afraid of. The Tatum boy said he didn't return from Midland until after one in the morning."

"There was a flight coming in that late?" Dixon asked.

"Yeah. He claims that the plane was delayed because of bad weather," Bremmer said. "I have someone checking on that now."

"Then if it wasn't Edwin who shot at us, who was it, Mr. Policeman?" Ruth demanded.

Bremmer looked at me, and then Dixon. There seemed to be more looking than talking; the old cops' intimidation tactic. "Is she always like this?" he asked.

"Yes, but we don't pay much attention anymore," I said.

"I'll send my boys over to the LaBeau's place to see what I can find out."

"Maybe we should go back to square one," I offered. "If Eleanor and Edwin are both lying to cover for one another and Serge was in Bastrop last night, then we need to look at our other suspects."

"Who are?" Bremmer asked.

"Others who had a motive to kill Stringer," I said.

"What about the Tatum killing?" said Bremmer.

"We might have two different killers," Dixon said. "Maybe Eleanor did accidently kill her husband. And we've known all along that there are several people who could benefit from Stringer's death."

"Name one," Bremmer said. He picked up his pencil and returned to his artwork.

"Any of one the artists," I said. "They were all counting on Tatum bankrolling the Art and Cultural Center. And they all knew what kind of influence Stringer had over the Tatums. They were extremely concerned Stringer would prevent Eleanor from following through with Leland's plans, so they killed Stringer."

"We thought of that too, Bremmer. Checked 'em out. Couldn't find anything."

The door opened and the sergeant stuck his head in. "The flight out of Midland was scheduled to leave at eight-thirty. It was delayed two hours because of weather. It landed in Austin at five after one. Edwin Tatum was on that plane."

"Let the boy go," Bremmer said. "No way he could have killed Maynard and been the one who shot at you last night."

"What about the first murder?" I asked. "Serge saw Edwin leaving the office suite where Tatum was lying with a bullet in his back."

"At this point, it's LaBeau's word against Edwin Tatum's." Bremmer tore off the flower sheet, crumbled up the paper, and tossed it into the trashcan. "Release Edwin Tatum," he said to his sergeant again. "The evidence is too weak to hold him. Get LaBeau back here."

"What about the woman?" The sergeant asked. "That doctor of hers has been calling about taking her back to the clinic."

"No!" I said, "I think Eleanor is better off where she is."

Either Bremmer agreed with me, or he didn't think my objection worth noting. "How's she holding up?" he asked.

"She ain't cracked up, if that's what you mean."

"Good. Leave her there for now. She's lied to us more than once. Just make sure she gets whatever she needs."

When we left Bremmer's office, he resumed doodling on a clean sheet of paper, which caused me to feel good about our investigation. Seemed like Austin's finest were as confused as we were.

Chapter Thirty-Three

"SOME DETECTIVES YOU ARE," Ruth said as we drove her back to the hotel so she could have brunch with her new friend and fellow food connoisseur, Helen Corbitt. "I could have told you you were barking up the wrong tree. My money is on one of the artsy people. My mother told me to never trust artists and actors."

"Aunt Frances would never make such a ridiculous statement," I said. "Besides, her sister-in-law and best friend, my mother, is an occasional actress." We pulled up to the curb. Ruth leaned over the front seat and said, "My point exactly." She stepped out of the car and slammed the door.

"You fell right into that one, hon," Dixon laughed. "Where to?"

"Ever been to Barton Springs?" I asked Dixon.

"You want to take a dip?" he said. "It's a bit chilly out."

"They have a great ice cream shop, and I don't want to go back to the office yet."

"Point me in the right direction."

"Turn left on Lamar and right on Barton Springs. This damn case, where did we go wrong?"

"Don't despair. This is one of the screwiest cases I've ever had. We're invited to a highbrow party at a ritzy hotel at the last minute so we can investigate a gubernatorial candidate. The first time we lay eyes on him, he's dead. We find out the dead man is a wonderful guy; loved by all, and the one who hired us is hated by everyone, including his wife. A few days later, the hated-by-everyone guy is killed in the same hotel. Two people, mother and son, both claimed they killed the first guy, who happens to be their husband and father respectively. Several people are brought in for questioning for both murders and most of them are released. Before long, someone takes a pot shot at you." He took his eyes off the wheel and gave me that look. "That happens a lot, you know. I've been in this business for several years and I've only been shot at a few times. Come to think of it, most of those incidents happened after I met you."

"Are you having second thoughts about me being your partner?"

"Not in the least. Like I said, my life in Hot Springs was unexciting. I was beginning to feel old before my time. But we may have to invest in a suit of body armor and a steel helmet for you."

"Here we are. Turn left and drive down by the water and there's a parking lot behind the shop. Peach ice cream is my favorite. I'm buying."

"I'm a vanilla man."

"Hardly."

We took our cones back to the car and, for several minutes, watched a mother duck lead her brood into the springs.

"You think they'll release Eleanor?" I asked.

"Probably. Bremmer knows his case against her is weak and will probably not go to trial."

"I never really considered the artists as serious suspects, merely witnesses. Maybe we should interview them again."

"I have a better idea. It's time for a powwow. It might take some effort, but we're going to round up the key players: Serge, Nolan, Digmire, Tweety, Edwin, and your favorite person, Fiona."

"And afterward, you and I will share a bottle of gin for our troubles. I might even let you have your way with me."

"Let's not waste any more time then." Dixon tossed the remainder of his ice cream to the ants and we left.

BY FOUR O'CLOCK, our conference table in the office was surrounded by nine adults and a Lone Ranger, a small Lone Ranger. Fiona agreed to come out of curiosity, Nolan and Digmire out of fear, Edwin out of need to protect his mother, and Serge because the Lone Ranger demanded it. But the one person, Tweety Gilcrest, who I wanted most to be here, I was not able to locate. I left a message with Ernest at the newspaper, telling him that if Tweety showed up to send him over to the office. Phoebe had made a pot of coffee and settled herself next to Billy, notepad at the ready. She glared at Serge, causing a sweat to break out on his brow. Lydia had informed me as soon as she walked in that Melvin refused to fork over the Holmes cape and deerstalker, so she was forced to come as a different agent of law enforcement, the masked Lone Ranger.

"Since you have a sold out theatre tonight, you couldn't deny Melvin his complete costume," I said. "Unless you wanted to rewrite the script at the last minute and call it "The Lone Ranger at the Alamo."

Lydia harrumphed. "This better be over by curtain time, or I'm walking out."

Dixon cleared his throat and the room got quiet, but before he could begin, Lydia took the floor.

"I want to know if these people were frisked before they sat down," Lydia said. "Because if the killer is in this room, I don't plan on getting shot at again."

Dixon opened his jacket and pulled out his revolver. He laid it on the table in front of him.

"Okay," Lydia said. "That will do."

"Who's the child in the Halloween costume with the smart mouth?" Fiona said. "And why is she here?"

"You must be the wife of the second victim. I heard about you," Lydia responded.

Dixon shot me a glance that said, "Do something."

"Everyone except Lydia and Phoebe knows one another," I said. "Since Phoebe is taking notes, and Lydia will continue to interrupt with questions, I'll introduce you. Fiona Maynard, Stringer Maynard's wife."

"Widow," she corrected me.

"Widow. Edwin Tatum, Eleanor and Leland's son, Jones Digmire, the ranch manager, Victor Nolan, ranch neighbor and family friend of the Tatums, and Serge LaBeau, Leland's friend and Lydia's father."

"We're going to start with Serge," Dixon said.

"Goddamn thief," Edwin spat.

"Wait," Lydia said, "Isn't that the guy who we suspected of shooting at us last night?"

"Shot at you?" Edwin said.

Instead of the coffee, I longed for the aforementioned gin bottle. It was going to be a long, long, meeting. "He had an alibi," I explained. "Go ahead, Serge."

"You got some nerve calling me a thief," Serge said. "Your father's money is safe. Mr. Dixon can vouch for me. Don't you think it's kind of odd that Leland trusted me with it rather than you? What I want to know is how you can sit here while your mother's in jail for a murder you committed? Since we're all here, tell us, Edwin why you killed your father."

"I did no such thing, you son-of-bitch," Edwin said.

"I saw you come out of that room where Leland was killed. I saw you go back in, and when you came out again, you wiped your fingerprints off the doorknob."

"Listen to this fool," Edwin said. "You saw me coming out of that room. What in the hell were *you* doing there?"

"Edwin?" Fiona whispered.

"Okay, I was there, but I didn't kill him. I didn't say anything because I realized how bad it looked."

"You think your mother killed him?" I asked.

"At first I did, but now I'm not so sure, and you must not be either or we wouldn't all be sitting here."

"So, let me get this straight," Serge said. "You find your father lying on the floor with a bullet in his back, and a short time later, you're attending a party like nothing happened?"

"Is that why you were drinking so much, Edwin?" Fiona asked.

"Who can believe anything this family says?" Serge said. "You're all a bunch of cutthroats. Leland wanted out in a bad way. Who can blame him?"

"You seem to forget, Mr. LaBeau, my husband was murdered too," Fiona said.

"Convenient for you," Serge said.

Fiona picked up her, now thankfully, lukewarm coffee and flung it in Serge's face.

A knock on the door kept the room from breaking out into a brawl. Tweety walked in. "Ernest told me to get over here. What's going on?"

"Tweety," I pointed to Edwin. "Do you recognize this guy?"

"Never seen him before."

THE POWWOW BROKE UP around six. We had another piece of evidence that made it impossible for Edwin to have killed his uncle. Whomever Tweety saw posing as a hotel employee in order to murder Maynard was still a mystery. Dixon and Billy stayed at the office. I needed to make a quick trip home to take care of the girls. I told Dixon I'd call him as soon as I got to my apartment, so he wouldn't worry. As I left the front door of the building, Officer Madge Crowley walked up.

"Just the person I wanted to see," she said. "I've been calling your apartment for the last two days. Are you *ever* there?"

"Not much lately. What's up?"

"I thought you'd like to know. The morning Eleanor Tatum faked her fit and got sent to the hospital, I found something interesting in her room at the clinic."

"Go ahead."

"A wadded up tissue in her waste basket. Inside were a few pills. The tissue had stuck to them. It was obvious they had been in Eleanor's mouth before she spit them out. The coating had bled into the tissue. Very clever she is. Whenever the nurse came in to give her her medication, she must have pretended to swallow the pills."

"How many were there?"

Madge held up four fingers. "I've been at the clinic long enough to know they empty the trash every day. It's my guess that she had been spitting them out the entire time she was there, at least after that first day. When I first saw her, she could hardy hold her head up. After that, she was fairly alert. At first, I laughed it off."

"Or she could have been saving the pills until she had enough. She told me she had intended to kill herself before she realized she couldn't do that to her son."

"Those pills would have done it too. I did a little research and found out they were Thorazine." Madge opened her notebook. "It's a new, controversial drug used to treat schizophrenia."

"Schizophrenia? I thought she was hospitalized for depression."

"That's what I thought too. I've been keeping up with the case. Anyway, the side effects of this drug are severe. It's only been on the market a year or so."

"And from what I understand, Eleanor has had these emotional problems her entire life. So, did Dr. Richards recently switch his diagnosis from depression to schizophrenia?"

"Seems odd, doesn't it? I told Detective Bremmer about the pills, but he didn't think they were significant. You didn't hear this from me, Sydney. You know what I think?"

"What?"

"The woman's pretty damn normal without any drugs, but who am I to say?"

"Too observant to be a beat cop. Thanks, Madge. I owe you again."

Officer Crowley tipped her cap and turned to leave.

"You'd make a crackerjack detective," I added. "Don't give up."

"I won't," she called over her shoulder.

ON MY WAY TO MY CAR, I noticed Backyard Benny digging cigarette butts out of the gutter. I felt sorry for the guy. I stopped at the newsstand and bought a pack of Viceroys.

"Benny," I called.

He stumbled around and squinted. "Who are you?" he grunted. The scent of cheap wine hit me in the face.

"It's me, Sydney." I handed him the pack. "A thank you gift."

"A what?"

"A few nights ago, I was chasing this thief down the alley behind The Driskill. You pointed me in the right direction."

"Whatever you say." He turned around to leave when I noticed it.

"Benny, wait. Where did you get that coat?"

"None of your goddamn business."

I caught up to him. "I'll give you five bucks for it."

"Make it ten."

"It's warm outside. You don't need it. Five bucks or nothing."

I sent Benny on his way in his shirtsleeves and quickly I turned the collar of the coat over and looked at the label. Five minutes later, I left Styman's Tailor and Men's Wear after having had a nice conversation with Eli Styman. I rushed back to the office. Dixon and Billy had left, probably to get a head start on the martinis. Who could blame them after that crazy meeting we'd had? I thought about hanging the coat on the peg, so it would be in full view when they returned, but I remembered our recent break-in and decided to tuck it away on Dixon's desk chair instead. I didn't want this valuable piece of evidence disappearing. I grabbed the field glasses Phoebe had placed on the new bookcase and left.

On my way down, I asked my favorite elevator operator if he knew where my partners had gone. Mr. Jorgenson's sarcastic response was typical: "Out doing something important, I suspect."

"Like plucking someone's cat from a tree? If they return, tell them I'm at The Driskill doing something *really* important."

"Not my job to take messages."

I thought of a million rude comebacks, but held my tongue.

Chapter Thirty-Four

ALL WAS QUIET ON THE FIFTH FLOOR. It only took a few seconds to pick the lock of the room where Leland Tatum was murdered. Once inside, I turned on a table lamp. The room was unoccupied, so I wouldn't have to hurry. A new rug had been placed over the area where Leland's body had lain several days ago, but otherwise, the place looked the same. I polished the lens of the field glasses and began my search of the twelve-foot-high ceiling. The naked eye could easily see the cracks, and even the cobwebs in the corner, but it would take a magnifying glass to detect something as small as a slug wedged in the crown modeling.

"What did you find?"

Some clever detective I was; I never heard him come in. I turned around to see Andrew Richards smiling and pointing a gun at my chest. I stood to meet him face to face.

"You fired the first shot and Eleanor fired the second."

"I was wondering about that," Richards said. "I read in the papers that those at the party heard a shot. And I couldn't figure out why Eleanor would claim she shot her husband when I did. But with all the drugs she was on, what did it matter? And it made things a whole lot easier for me."

"Actually, she was thinking clearly. She assumed Edwin had killed Leland, and by firing the gun at the ceiling, she tried to make it look like she was the killer. Mothers do that, you know, protect their young. Most competent psychiatrists know that." He merely scoffed, but his smile was gone. "You followed me here?"

"I've been following you ever since you left me that note. I knew you were on to me."

"Since we're clearing the air, tell me why you killed Leland Tatum."

"Leland, that bastard, found out about my affair with Fiona Maynard."

"How did he find out?"

"Fiona must have let something slip. He barged to my office that Friday morning, accused me of trying to poison Eleanor and threatened to tell my wife about the affair."

"Thorazine is a pretty powerful, addictive drug. I thought you were treating Eleanor for depression. You weren't trying to get the woman dependent on drugs so you could keep her in your clinic, were you?"

"I don't know and I don't care how you found out about the drug, but I'm not here to discuss her case with you. You finding out about Fiona and me means you can link me to Leland's murder. Once I get you and that tubby waiter out of the picture, everything will be fine. The cops will never figure it out. It's too bad if they can't make a case against Eleanor and her son, but they'll never connect me to the murders."

"You killed Stringer too. Why?"

"Eleanor gave me that idea. Since the stupid woman claimed she killed her husband by accident, and her escaping from the hospital right before Stringer was killed makes her the mostly likely suspect in his murder too. Having him out of the way was convenient and would put another nail in Eleanor's coffin."

I'd been in this situation before and discovered that killers love to talk about their dirty deeds. Unfortunately, they choose to spill their guts to someone who they are sure will not live to tell, but keeping him talking was my only hope.

"What did you hope to find when you broke into our office?"

"Anything with my name on it, of course. After my receptionist called me and told me about the mysterious note you left, I drove back to the clinic and read it. I wasn't sure how much you knew, but I knew you were getting too close. I found out where you lived and went by your apartment."

"The note. That's how you found out I was going to the theatre."

"You left an easy trail, Miss Lockhart. After I left your office, all I had to do was be at the theatre when the show was over and follow you."

"Too bad you're a bad shot. You could have finished me off in the prop room."

"It's much better here at the hotel. Think of the great press your newspaper will generate: 'Another Murder at The Driskill!'"

He took a few steps toward me and took direct aim.

"You can kill me, but I assure you that the cops will have you in jail within the hour. You see, I found a curious piece of evidence today. That one-of-a-kind tan cashmere coat you're wearing. I noticed it on you at Leland Tatum's funeral. But this is a different one, a newer one, isn't it?"

His mouth fell open and the cocky looked on his faced disappeared.

"The tailors at Styman's must work quickly, or did you pay them extra to make you a new coat as soon as possible? The original one, the one you used to muffle the sound of the gunshot when you killed Tatum, has just been turned over to the cops," I lied. "I found it today. A bum who hangs around the downtown area was wearing it. His favorite sleeping place is in the alley behind The Driskill. My guess is he pulled it out of the dumpster after you deposited it there the night you committed the murder."

"Who's in here?" a timid voice called.

Richards jerked around and I dove. He swung back in my direction and fired a couple of shots. I pulled my gun from its holster. Just as I was about to return fire, I noticed the housemaid had come into the room. She screamed. He took aim. Our shots went off at the same time. His bullet struck the wall inches from the housemaid's head. Mine struck his back inches from his spine.

Fifteen minutes later, two stretchers were carried from the room: one holding the housemaid who'd passed out and was knocked unconscious, and the other holding Richards, who was still breathing. Dixon arrived first and Bremmer soon after. I told my story. Afterwards, Dixon and I were free to go. Once back at my apartment, he mixed a pitcher of martinis, and half way through the first one, my color returned to normal.

"How are you feeling?" Dixon asked.

"Stupid. I haven't learned to watch my back."

"Yeah, that wasn't too smart. You should have waited for me. You shouldn't have gone over to the hotel by yourself. I know you're used to operating alone when you're investigating a story. That's not the way we operate at the agency when we're closing in on a murder investigation. Your hunch about following Richards and Fiona to the Lodger's Motor Court put you on the right track. It almost got you killed too."

"Being on the right track and not knowing I'm on the right track isn't good detective work, either."

"Don't be so hard on yourself. We all make mistakes. I've been a bit distracted lately too."

"By what?"

"I'll show you."

WHILE WE WERE ON OUR WAY to fully understanding the severity of our distractions, the ice in the martini pitcher melted, and Mealworm deposited another, rather large quantity of cat hair on Dixon's jacket when a low rumble traveled through the room, interrupting any further distractions.

"Is that your dog snoring or your stomach growling?" Dixon asked.

"It's me. Most men take their dates out to dinner first," I said.

"I didn't hear you complaining." He smiled. "Let's go. Steaks at the Nighthawk?"

"Perfect."

Suddenly, my backdoor burst open. Mr. Grimwall walked in carrying my large pot of dahlias. "You've got earwigs, Miss Sydney. I told you you needed to let me spray. These guy will eat every plant on your patio." He looked up just as I grabbed Dixon's jacket to cover myself. The pot of dahlias landed on the floor.

"Maybe you should hand over that key, Mr. Grimwall," Dixon said, buttoning his shirt. My neighbor threw the key on the kitchen counter and fled.

While Dixon cleaned up the mess, I combed my hair and touched up my lipstick. When I came out of the bathroom, Mealworm was licking up the remnants of milk Dixon had poured into her dish.

"I'm thinking of changing her name to Ava. Lydia said it would help Mealworm's disposition."

"What's wrong with her disposition?"

"Never mind. I'm the one who needs feeding. Remember?"

Chapter Thirty-five

IN THE COMFORT OF RUTH'S HOTEL ROOM, Dixon and I told her about last night's events. I thought for sure she'd be fuming, having missed out on all the fun.

"Well, I'm glad that mess is over. Sorry I couldn't be there to help, but I was busy."

"I thought you were through with the restaurant gig?"

"This had nothing to do with me working at the restaurant."

"You were having a séance with your ghost friends?"

She merely scoffed.

"Heading back to Dallas now?" Dixon said.

"Tomorrow's soon enough. I'm meeting with Helen today, and she's going to give me some recipes to take back to the Home. She's also going to show me how to make a pineapple cake upside down. Although, I'm not sure why anyone would or could do that."

"I think it's call a pineapple-up—"

I nudged Dixon in the ribs before he could clear up Ruth's confusion. This was one situation I wanted Ruth to clear up herself. "How did Helen take the news of your undercover operation?"

"Surprised, when I told her I was the key to solving the murders; sad, when I told her I was leaving. She said business in the restaurant has never been better."

"We are driving out to the lake today. Want to come along?"

"Can't. Edwin and I have a date tonight for enchiladas and Margaritas."

"Ruth, with all the trouble over Mary Thompson, you might want to listen to Marcella's idea about providing an adoption service at the Home."

"No way. I made my decision and that is final. If I give into every whim she has, she'll soon be running the place."

"Isn't that what you hired her for?"

"Besides, I've taken care of that stupid Mary Thom—"

Suddenly, the room door shot open, and a short, dark haired

woman, waving a gun, stormed in. "You horrible bitch! You said you were my friend!"

"I never said that," Ruth said calmly. "You always blow things out of proportion. Now throw that gun down before it goes off."

"Mary Thompson?" I asked.

"That's her. The woman who has been causing all the trouble."

"Since she's holding a gun on you, Ruth. I wouldn't make her angrier than she is already."

"Hey, that's my Derringer! You stole it from me!"

"I wanted you to help me," Mary cried. "I wanted you to take my baby and raise her."

"Me? I don't know beans about being a mother, and I'm not married!"

"I thought I could count on you." Mary steadied the gun with both hands.

"I didn't say I wouldn't help, you stupid little fool. Although I don't know why I bothered. Your baby is at the Home about to be adopted."

"But...who?" The gun in Mary's had begun to tremble so hard, I feared she would shake the bullet right out.

"You don't deserve to know. We don't divulge that information, but considering the circumstances, what choice did I have. The adoption agency found a nice couple eager to adopt her. All you have to do is sign the damn papers. They are missionaries and want to return to Coo Chi Cooa by the end of the week."

"Where?"

"Coo Chi Cooa. Don't you know anything? It's in the Amazon jungle near the border of Burundi."

"Brazil," I whispered to my cartographer cousin.

"Brazil. But don't worry, we checked with the state department—"

Wow! Ruth knew "state department." I'm impressed. The only two adjectives I'd ever heard her use before "department" were "lingerie" and "shoe."

"—and the incidents of cannibalism have gone from 'often'

to 'occasional.' It's been almost a year since one of the missionaries got thrown into the cooking pot. Esmeralda will have the time of her life growing up in the jungle with the hollow monkeys."

"That's howler monkeys," I said, but my words were lost in Mary's scream.

"Esmeralda!" Now it was Mary's lip that trembled.

"Oh, stop crying," Ruth chided. "You never were able to make a rational decision. Just look at that doofus you married. You should be happy he's gone, and giving up your baby was the only sensible thing you've ever done."

"Carl? Carl was here?"

This was so much fun. I wanted to join in and add my own tantalizing tidbits to the ingeniously insane story, but since Ruth was on a roll, so I kept my mouth shut. Dixon was trying hard not to laugh.

"In a couple of days, the baby will be gone too, and you'll be free to do whatever you want to continue screwing up your pathetic life."

Mary did exactly what Ruth told her to do. She threw the gun, but at Ruth's head. The three of us hit the floor at the same time, but the Derringer didn't discharge. Mary threw herself on the bed and began bawling. "I want my baby!"

The door flew open again, and Carl Donavon rushed in and gathered his wife into his arms. "Everything's gonna be okay, honey. No one is taking *our* kid. I've been to Protective Services and cleared up the matter. There is a bus leaving for Dallas in a couple of hours and I have two tickets. We'll pick up the baby on the way...Wanna go?

"Yes," Mary blubbered.

Carl ushered his wife out the room, and then turned and whispered a "thank you" to Ruth. And just like that, the happy couple was gone.

The three of us stood there in quietude for a couple of minutes. Ruth lit a cigarette, acting, for all the world, like the cleverest person this side of Burundi. I poured our drinks. Dixon opened the window. I'm not sure why, except maybe to allow some of the insanity to escape from the room.

"Maybe one day, you'll learn not to doubt my ability to solve problems." She blew smoke in my direction.

"Maybe one day, you'll learn not to create those problems." I handed her a martini. "One little phone call could have prevented all of this. You could have gotten you brains blown out."

"Well, I didn't."

"How did you manage this little drama?" Dixon asked.

"Mr. Donovan came to see me at the hotel last night. He had remembered that Mary had an aunt living in Austin. He found her staying there and tried to persuade Mary to give him a second chance. She refused and said she didn't want him and didn't want the baby. He knew Mary was speaking out of anger, and if she were faced with the reality of what she'd done, she'd change her mind. So, he came here and we cooked up this plan. And it worked."

"Like I said before, the plan almost got you killed."

"It's broken."

"What?"

"The Derringer. It's broken. It happened when Mary ransacked my closet and stomped on my handbag." Ruth picked up her gun. "See, this little trigger thing is jammed." Suddenly the gun discharged and a bullet shattered the table lamp. "Whoops."

Dixon and I left before Ruth could do any more damage to her hotel room. We had a few stops to make on the way out to the lake. The first was to our office to take a look at the improvements Billy and Phoebe had made. Our new door window had a mail slot (Billy's idea) and lying on the floor was an envelope with a check inside and a note from Eleanor Tatum, thanking us for the work we'd done. She was selling her ranch house and moving into an apartment in town. She will continue with Leland's plans to establish the art center, which will be named the Leland Tatum Art and Cultural Center. She hoped that Edwin and Serge would soon get over their animosity toward one another. Fiona left for Spain yesterday, and Eleanor hoped it would be a long while before she saw her sister again.

Our second stop was The Next to Nothing Theatre where we

were to collect Lydia. The child had never been to Lake Travis, and we felt she needed a drastic change of scenery. We found her waiting outside on the corner, holding an inner tube and wearing a bathing suit with a pair of swimming goggles around her neck. To ward off the slight chill in the air, she also had on an overcoat, and yes, her lavender shoes.

"Esther Williams?" I asked as she climbed into the backseat.

"I was trying for Johnny Weissmuller, but couldn't find a Tarzan outfit."

"The Olympic swimmer was a good choice," Dixon said. "Maybe you can work her into one of your future plays. We'll stop at the cottage where Mrs. Granger is preparing a picnic basket for us."

"She's not going too?" Lydia cried.

"Nope. Just the three of us, and the poodle," I assured her.

"Perfect," Lydia said.

By the time we reached the edge of town, Lydia was humming "Blue Moon," and Monroe was asleep with her head on the girl's lap.

Chapter Thirty-Six

ON MONDAY MORNING, I arrived at the newspaper office early and began my story of the two murders at The Driskill. I'd rolled the last page from my typewriter when Ernest stuck his head out his office door.

"Syd, get in here," he yelled loud enough to make every reporter look up. He opened his door wider and Tweety walked out, looking pale and sweaty.

I closed the door behind me. He handed me an envelope.

"What's this?"

"Your pink slip."

I tore it open. "You're not kidding."

"Nope. I'm afraid you're fired!"

"You don't have to shout. I'm right here holding the damn pink slip. I can't believe you actually fired me."

"Neither can I. Actually, you're not really fired."

Instead of sinking down into the cushion of his intimidating chair, I walked around and parked my tush on the corner of his desk. I figured, what did I have to lose. "I'm listening."

"You'll still be on the payroll. Get off my desk. I can't talk to you with those legs staring me in the face."

I stood up, straight and tall, hoping my posture would give me courage.

"You'll still be reporting, but you're doing it undercover."

"Isn't that unethical?"

"Probably, but it's the wave of the future. Herman loves the idea. Your salary won't change."

"Byline?"

"No."

"Health benefits?"

"Okay, I'll stick an extra ten bucks a month into your envelope."

"You're paying me cash?"

"It's the only way. What do you think? You going for it?"

"I don't have much choice." I thought for a minute, staring

out the window toward the river. "I might have an idea for my first story. It involves a certain church scam in town."

"Atta girl. We'll pick a place to meet."

I turned to leave. "Did you fire Tweety too?"

"I demoted him to obits. Now go clean out your desk. Here." He handed me his handkerchief. "Put on a good show. Spill tears, slam your things around, spit out a few cuss words. You might mumble something about what an asshole I am."

"Before I go, do you mind me asking how things are with your wife?"

"I took your advice and went to Waco to see her yesterday. I even brought flowers."

"Did she come home?

"Nah, she's getting an apartment and enrolling in college. Said she always wanted to be a teacher."

"So, it's over?"

"Separated. She said she needs time away from me. Said she needs to 'find herself.' Imagine that."

A sadness came over me, and for a moment, I thought about refusing his offer, but I trusted the guy. After all, this might be a good opportunity. "I just got used to you. I'm going to miss you."

"Yeah, well, you'll see me often enough. I'll be your only contact. There are big things ahead for you, Sydney Lockhart."

"Well, I see *good* things ahead for you, Ernest. Once your wife finds herself, you two will have something to talk about."

He pulled open his bottom drawer, brought out two shot glasses, and filled them with bourbon. "I'll be in touch soon with your first assignment." He handed me a glass. "Slug this down. This will help to bring on tears."

We clinked glasses. I emptied mine and left. The tears began to flow.

They had nothing to do with the bourbon.

~ THE END ~

Author's Note

Every historic hotel featured in my Sydney Lockhart mysteries is still in operation. And many of the businesses I write about actually existed in the early 1950s. In *Murder at The Driskill*, there's mention of a few places I frequented during my twenty-five years of living in Austin. My favorite Mexican restaurant, Matt's El Rancho, opened in 1952 and is still owned and operated by the Martinez family, although it has moved from the original location on 1st Street. Rarely a week would pass without my appearance at Barton Springs Park—still there, and the location of Austin's many outdoor festivals. The infamous Alamo Hotel and Zeke's Café are no longer standing, but you can see an actual hotel room and the café itself in Willie Nelson and Merle Haggards's "Pancho and Lefty" music video. The breathtakingly beautiful Driskill Hotel still holds forth at 6th and Brazos, looming elegantly over the nocturnal partygoers and daytime street-people on Austin's most famous thoroughfare. While living downtown, I often unwound after work with a cocktail at The Driskill Bar.

A clarification on liquor sales and service in Texas: liquor stores existed in the 1950s, but liquor-by-the-drink was not legalized until 1971. Bars and restaurants served beer, wine, and set-ups. Patrons could bring their own bottle and mix their drinks at the table. There were also "private" clubs, fairly numerous with admittance easily obtained by paying a token "membership" fee. So, I've taken some brief liberties here and there. After all, Sydney and martinis are inseparable.

Before Austin...Sydney took Galveston by storm

Murder at The Galvez
The Sydney Lockhart Mysteries: Book Three
By Kathleen Kaska
Published by LL-Publications
$13.99 (US) / £9.99 (UK/EU) /$5.99 (ebook)
ISBN   978-0-9574726-1-7   (print)   /   978-0-9574726-2-4
(ebook)
© Kathleen Kaska

Another hotel, another murder, another family crisis.

Eighteen years after discovering the murdered body of her grandfather in the foyer of the historic Galvez Hotel, reporter Sydney Lockhart reluctantly returns to Galveston, Texas to cover the controversial Pelican Island Development Project conference. Soon after her arrival, the conference is cancelled and the keynote speaker is missing. When his body turns up in the trunk of Sydney's car, she's hauled down to the police station for questioning.

The good news is Sydney has an alibi this time; the bad news is she finds another body—her father's new friend—he's floating face down in a fish tank with a bullet in his head. Her father's odd behavior and the threatening notes delivered to her hotel room leads Sydney to suspect that her grandfather's unsolved murder and the present murders are connected.

As if this wasn't bad enough, just a few blocks from the hotel at her parents' home, people are gathering, sparks are flying, another controversial event is in the planning, one that just might rival the Great Storm of 1900.

"Fast paced and great fun, Kathleen Kaska's Murder at The Galvez *takes readers on a breathless jaunt into the past. Sydney Lockhart is a strong, spirited protagonist, good company in this suspenseful and entertaining thriller."*
                    —**Kathryn Casey**, mystery and true crime author

Also by Kathleen Kaska

The Classic Mystery Triviography™ Series
Second Edition

These trivia books will appeal to Agatha Christie, Alfred Hitchcock, and Sherlock Holmes fans of all ages, as well as trivia enthusiasts, mystery buffs, and lovers of classic films.

 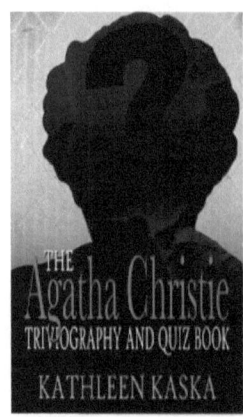 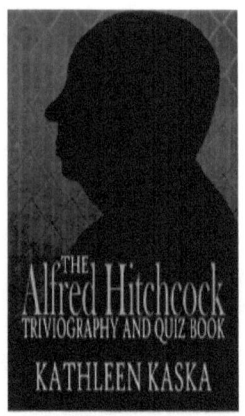

www.ll-publications.com/triviography.html

The Sherlock Holmes Triviography and Quiz Book

"Kathleen Kaska has put together a wonderful mind teaser for all Sherlock Holmes aficionados. She covers it all: stories, books, the media; with lots of questions, puzzles, and trivia facts. No true Sherlockian will want to miss this grand Triviography and Quiz Book."
—Michael R. Pitts,
author of *Famous Movie Detectives I, II,* and *III,* and co-author of *The Great Detective Pictures*

The Agatha Christie Triviography and Quiz Book

"As a lifelong Agatha Christie aficionado, I was treated to a true brain workout over the challenging trivia questions and crossword puzzles."
—Ralf M.M. Stultiëns,
Curator of *The Queen of Crime Library*
containing over 5,700 books by and about Agatha Christie

"This book, fiendishly clever and remarkably researched, is pure gold for fans of Agatha Christie."
—Kate Stine, *Mystery Scene* Magazine

The Alfred Hitchcock Triviography and Quiz Book

"A must for any fan of filmmaker Alfred Hitchcock and movie history. The quizzes are fun and challenging—and the surrounding text provides a wealth of information on the life/work of the revered filmmaker. A real treat for pop culture enthusiasts!"
—James Robert Parish, author of *The Hollywood Book of Scandals*

About the Author

Kathleen Kaska writes the award-winning Sydney Lockhart mystery series set in the 1950s when women were caught between the dichotomy of career and marriage; when fashion exploded with a never-before-seen flair; and movies and music had the country dancing with gusto. Her first mystery, Murder at the Arlington, won the 2008 Salvo Press Manuscript Contest. This book, along with her second mystery, Murder at the Luther, were selected as bonus-books for the Pulpwood Queens Book Group, the largest book group in the country. The third book in the series, Murder at the Galvez, published by LL-Publications, was released in 2012.

Before bringing Sydney into the world of murder and mayhem, Kathleen published three mystery-trivia books in the Classic Triviography Mystery Series: The Agatha Christie Triviography and Quiz Book, The Alfred Hitchcock Triviography and Quiz Book, and The Sherlock Holmes Triviography and Quiz Book. The Alfred Hitchcock and the Sherlock Holmes trivia books were finalists for the 2013 EPIC eBook Award in nonfiction.

Her nonfiction book, The Man Who Saved the Whooping Crane: The Robert Porter Allen Story, was released by University Press of Florida in 2012.

When she is not writing, Kathleen and her husband spend much of their time traveling the back roads and byways around the country, looking for new venues for her mysteries and bird watching along the Texas coast and beyond. It was her passion for birds that led to the publication The Man Who Saved the Whooping Crane.

http://www.kathleenkaska.com

www.ingramcontent.com/pod-product-compliance
Lightning Source LLC
Chambersburg PA
CBHW030246200626
46816CB00002BA/527